The Hand of Amun

The Hand of Amun

JULIET HASTINGS

BLACK
lace

Black Lace novels are sexual fantasies.
In real life, make sure you practise safe sex.

First published in 1997 by
Black Lace
Thames Wharf Studios,
Rainville Road, London W6 9HA

Reprinted 1999

Typeset by CentraCet, Cambridge
Printed and bound by Mackays of Chatham PLC

ISBN 0 352 33144 5

In the beginning there was chaos. Chaos was darkness, the waters of the abyss.

The first god, Amun, arose from the waters, using nothing but his own strength to give form to his body. Amun existed alone. All was his. Yesterday and tomorrow were his.

He took his penis in his hand. He made love to his fist. He took his exquisite joy with his fingers. From the flame of the fiery blast which he kindled with his hand, the universe was formed.

From the hieroglyphs of the Sacred Texts

Prologue

The Temple of Karnak, 1175 BC

*T*he River Nile flowed swift and silent under the fading stars. In the east the sky glowed the colour of molten copper over the bitter desert. Soon the sun would rise.

Within the temple of the god Amun, the great columned halls, the massive pylon gateways and the cool porticos were shrouded in darkness. Only in the furthest, most secret recesses of the temple was there movement, as the faithful servants of the god prepared for the rite which would re-enact the creation of the world.

Already the priests were moving in procession from the sacred lake towards the shrine of the god. They walked in silence, their white linen robes gleaming in the growing dawn light. The candles they bore illuminated fleeting glimpses of the magnificence through which they passed – columns made like lotus flowers or like bundles of papyrus reed, walls of smooth stone covered with delicate carvings, great doors of wood bound with bronze. They carried censers, and the smoke of the burning incense wreathed around them, filling the air with the exotic, heavy scent of frankincense and terebintha.

In a small room near to the god's shrine the women of

1

the temple were making ready the Lady Hunro, high priestess of Karnak, god's wife of Amun, Hand of God, for her part in the rite. She stood naked in the close scented air, her arms extended, as two of the young women who were her servants and the god's anointed her body with perfumed unguents to soften and beautify her golden skin. In one corner of the room another of the god's handmaidens plucked a little harp and sang softly of the power and strength of Amun, and it seemed that the music and the thought of the approaching rite had driven the Lady Hunro into a trance. Her eyes were fixed on nothingness and her breathing was slow and shallow. She did not respond as the young women who anointed her rubbed the tingling scented cream on to her nipples or slipped their hands between her thighs to moisten and prepare her to receive the embrace of the god.

The anointing completed, the young women guided the Lady Hunro to a stone chair. She sat with closed eyes as one of her servants painted her eyelids with powdered green malachite and then outlined her dark lashes with liquid kohl. Another girl brought powdered carmine to brighten the lips of the wife of god. Then the chief of the handmaidens, a small slender girl with startlingly pale eyes and hair the colour of copper, brushed back the Lady Hunro's glossy black locks. She placed on her mistress's head a wig of human hair braided and sheathed in gold, adorned and interwoven with beads of turquoise and jasper. Each plait was tipped with lapis lazuli and chinked softly as the braids settled upon the high priestess's naked shoulders. The copper-haired girl stooped slowly forward and kissed the Lady Hunro on her mouth. She put her tongue between the lips of her mistress and stroked her glistening breasts with slender fingers. The Lady Hunro drew a deep breath, as women do when they are lost in the erotic darkness of dreams, and her full firm legs moved slightly apart. In silence the copper-haired handmaiden dropped to her knees and pressed her open lips to the

2

gleaming rosy darkness between the Lady Hunro's spread thighs.

The high priestess did not move or open her eyes. Only the shuddering depth of her gasping breaths and the increasing stiffness of her darkening nipples betrayed her growing arousal. The other women leant over her, trailing their fingers down her shining limbs, caressing the curves of her heavy breasts, teasing the crinkled points with their long nails. The copper-haired girl continued to lap slowly and sweetly at the delicate whorls of her mistress's sex, and in the close warmth of the confined room glittering points of sweat began to appear on the Lady Hunro's throat, on her shoulders, and between her heaving breasts.

Then came the faint sound of a ram's horn trumpet, signalling the beginning of the rite. The servants of the god unhurriedly ceased their caressing of the priestess's body and one by one stood up. The copper-haired girl rose, her lips gleaming with the juice of desire, and once again kissed the Lady Hunro on the mouth.

The god's wife stood up, still enfolded in trance, and allowed her women to slip onto her shoulders a robe of the finest translucent linen, pure white, pleated and folded to adorn her fine body without concealing it. It fastened at the front over her navel, revealing her breasts above and the dense shadows of her loins below. Thus enrobed she left the tiring room, and her handmaidens walked before her and beside her and behind her, lighting her way with candles.

In silence they came to the great portals of Amun's shrine, the darkest and most secret place in the temple. The doorkeepers made obeisance and drew back the mighty bolts, that the wife of god might enter in to her husband.

The shrine was dark and enclosed, its shadows lit by flickering candles. Only the golden statue of the god gleamed like the sun, illuminated by two great torches. Taller than a man, perfect and mighty, the god Amun stood before his servants, shining with the scented oil with which his priests had anointed him. He was like a young man in the flower of his strength, broad shouldered and slender, with a face of serene, unearthly beauty. On his head he wore the diadem of Egypt, and in his raised right hand he held a flail – a symbol of his power. He was proudly naked as he emerged from the primal chaos, and from his slender muscled loins his penis thrust forward. It was as long as a man's arm from his elbow to the tip of his finger, massive as befitted the power of the greatest of the gods, and fiercely erect, turgid with the promise of creation. At the base of this splendid phallus was the god's left hand, clamped at the root of all things, preparing to pump his semen forth and engender the universe.

The chief priest of the god raised his hands as the god's wife entered the temple, and began the chant which would call the god from the darkness of night. 'Oh Lord Amun, greatest of the gods, father of all . . .'

The Lady Hunro stood before the statue, her glowing eyes fixed on the golden face of Amun. She lifted her hands and began to clap, a steady double rhythm like the beat of a human heart. Her handmaidens stood behind her and one by one they joined in the music, clapping their hands, shaking the sistra whose sound stimulates desire, plucking their sweet-toned harps and singing for the pleasure of the god. 'Awake, oh mighty Amun, awake and see the beauty that awaits you. Show us yourself in your godhead, let us be surrounded by the scent of God, enfold us with your divine strength.'

The music swelled like the dawn brightening towards sunrise, and the lady who was the Hand of God unfastened her linen robe. She let it fall behind her and was naked in the light of the torches. She danced to the rhythm of the music, her supple arms swaying like a field of barley in the breeze, her hips circling, her breasts lifting and swinging with her movements. The lapis and gems that tipped the plaits of her wig shifted and chinked, adding their own subtle counterpoint to the clapping and the shimmering of sound from sistra and cymbals. Her body twisted and heaved and her lips were parted and gleaming. She offered her breasts to the god, then she leant back and spread her thighs and showed him the secret heart of her body, for she danced to arouse his divine desire. As she danced she approached the statue and at last dropped to her knees before it and lifted her hands to touch the god; to caress his thighs and loins and stroke his belly and buttocks. Her body undulated and shuddered with pleasure, and when at last she opened her lips and drew the tip of the god's golden phallus into her mouth she moaned, a moan of lust and delight that could be clearly heard above the chanting of the chief priest and the music of her women.

'Accept our gift, Amun,' intoned the chief priest, and at his words the other priests moved forward from the shadows of the temple. They were clad in white and their bodies were shaved in case a single hair might sully the purity of the servants of the god. The dancing of the Hand of God had aroused them too, and their penises protruded from their robes, bouncing as they walked, stiff and eager. They surrounded the high priestess as she knelt at the feet of Amun, caressing his golden phallus with her tongue and lips. Stooping, they laid their hands on her and lifted her. She lay unprotesting in their grasp, her head hanging, the gold-sheathed braids of her wig sweeping the legs of the men who held her.

The priests lifted the Lady Hunro to the height of their shoulders. They parted her thighs. The copper-haired girl bowed to the statue of the god and stood between the knees of her mistress. With her fingers she parted the glistening lips of the Lady Hunro's sex, then slid her tongue into the velvet depths. As the high priestess sighed and heaved, the girl withdrew her probing tongue and caressed her mistress's clitoris, flickering her tongue against it; sucking and enfolding it with her full lips. At last the Lady Hunro began to moan and shift her hips rhythmically, wrapped in the sensation of approaching orgasm. The girl stood back, bowed again, and murmured, 'The Hand of God is prepared.'

The music swelled again, lifting towards an inexorable climax. The chief priest raised his hands to the god and prayed aloud. Before the golden statue the priests lifted the Lady Hunro and held her spreadeagled, arms and legs flung wide. They brought her closer, closer to the god, until her open thighs embraced his golden loins and his glittering phallus touched the lips of her sex. She cried out and arched her back, lifting her breasts towards the god's impassive face. Her bearers moved her still closer, and that massive shining penis slowly began to penetrate the moist folds of her sex, opening her gleaming vulva, sliding up into her until her body rested against the giant fist which clasped the god's erection.

The Lady Hunro cried out aloud and began to move, undulating her loins, rubbing her body against the body of the god, drawing herself to orgasm as the golden penis stirred and shifted deep, deep within her. Her breasts lifted and fell with her cries, and her hands opened and closed helplessly. The smell of the incense and the perfumed oil embraced her and she shuddered as she approached the final, ultimate moment.

At last she writhed against the hands that held her and her naked body stiffened all over. The pulsing waves of orgasm shimmered through her glistening flesh. The music fell silent as the watchers rejoiced in the sounds of the high priestess's climax. For long moments she was still and tense, pressed tight in the god's embrace.

'Our gift is accepted,' announced the chief priest. 'Behold, the god's seed has been called forth by the god's wife, the Hand of Amun. The Lord Amun appears on earth, he is present among us.'

And outside the darkness of the temple, the golden sun lifted above the desert and shimmered in the waters of the Nile.

Chapter One

The Village of the Tombmakers, Waset

Naunakhte lay awake beneath the warm stars, gazing upward into the velvet sky. A great glowing moon hung above her, casting brilliant silver light across the sleeping village. On each flat roof of the close-packed houses on either side of the main street people slept, naked for coolness in the waxing heat. A cat yowled in the graveyard and cicadas whirred from every stone in the desert.

A great moth fluttered past Naunakhte's face, grazing her with its spotted wings and making her jump. She brushed off the insect and turned over, stretching out her long limbs under the single linen sheet. Sleep was far away.

That morning Akhtay, wife of Djutmose, had given birth to her third child. She had given her husband a strong healthy boy, but afterwards the bleeding had not stopped but worsened, and before the sun had set Akhtay was dead. Naunakhte and Akhtay were the same age. They had played together when they were children, making dolls from straw and clay, and had gone hand in hand to the Valley of the Tombs to take food to Akhtay's father, who was a master-mason. Five years ago Akhtay had married Djutmose, and now she was dead.

'Great goddess Nut,' Naunakhte whispered, turning her face to the glittering sky. 'Lady of the sky, guide me. Send me a sign.'

She did not know what sign she sought. She only knew that she was strange; that no other girl in the village was like her. She was adopted. Her father Ammenakht and her mother Hatia had taken her into their house at the request of the high priest of Amun. Her mother and father loved her, but they seemed always to keep her at a distance, as if she were not quite real. And the high priest had said that the god Amun had ordained that Naunakhte should never marry. So one by one, at fourteen and fifteen years of age, her friends had married the young men of the village and gone to their husbands' houses to have children and grow old and die, while Naunakhte remained in the house of Ammenakht, puzzled and alone.

Until today Naunakhte had believed that she was accursed. Why should her friends have weddings, the status of married women, the love of their husbands, the sound of children in their houses, while she had nothing? She was nineteen years old now – almost too old for marriage in the village's way of things. Outcast; accursed.

But Akhtay was dead, and Naunakhte's other friends were growing old before her eyes, losing the youthful elasticity of their skin, spreading with childbirth and tiring with the cares of a household. Naunakhte was nineteen, but the men of the village still looked at her with admiration when they saw her dressed for work in a simple linen kilt. They admired her small, high breasts, round and firm as pomegranates, the suppleness of her narrow waist, the swell of her soft belly, the opulent fullness of her hips and thighs, the elegant slenderness of her calves, the high strong arches of her delicate feet. One or two of the bolder boys quoted love poems to her: *If only I were your laundryman, just for a single month, I would rejoice to wash out the perfume from your dress.*

They admired her. But none of them ever came near

her, or tried to kiss her, or offered to take her to his house as his wife. She was set apart, taboo, forbidden by the word of the god Amun. And the god had set his mark upon her, for on her left arm, just above the elbow, there was a little birthmark. It was dark red and as long as Naunakhte's little finger, and it was the exact shape of an erect phallus, thickening at the base as if it were clasped by a fist. Nobody doubted that it was the sign of Amun. Naunakhte wore an arm-ring of gilded copper and enamel to cover the birthmark, because when it was on view the people of the village would stare and whisper. She hid it as if she could hide herself from her fate. What did the god intend for her? Was she cursed or blessed?

'Lady of the sky,' Naunakhte whispered, 'send me a sign.'

As she lifted her hands to heaven in the attitude of prayer, a vivid white meteor flashed across the blue basin of the sky. Another brilliant flash followed it, then another. Then there was nothing, only the glowing of the stars and the creaking cries of the cicadas.

Naunakhte's eyes opened wide. They were beautiful eyes, the shape of almonds, with long dark lashes, pure smoky whites and irises darker than polished ebony. She lifted herself on one elbow, gazing upward with parted lips, wondering what this sign could mean. She pushed back the sheet and rose soundlessly to her knees, then crossed her hands on her bosom in respect for the goddess. She felt her pulse striking within her breast as hard as the mason's hammer.

She had thought herself the only person awake, but she was wrong. As she knelt looking up at the sky she realised that her father Ammenakht was waking too. He pushed himself up from his sleeping mat with many grunts and gasps, for he was corpulent, and stepped with absurd delicacy over the body of his sleeping wife.

Naunakhte was very pleased to be distracted from the uncomfortable thoughts which had filled her. She forgot her vigil and covered her mouth with her hands to keep in a giggle. She knew well what her father was about. Only three days ago he had got himself a new servant, a girl from Punt, the hot, strange land far to the south where incense grew. Pati was a pretty, round creature, with skin the colour of polished mahogany and woolly dark hair cropped close to her well-shaped head. Her bottom was large and succulent and moved most enticingly while she walked. According to Ammenakht she would help his wife around the house, but Hatia had not been convinced, and everyone in the family knew that the new servant was really intended as a concubine. Ammenakht had not succeeded in having her yet, but it looked as if he was going to put things to rights that night.

Moving slowly, so that her father might not notice her, Naunakhte leant across to the reed mat beside hers. Her brother Harshire slept there, Ammenakht's oldest son. Like his father, Harshire worked as one of the village scribes. He was twenty years old and ready for marriage, though he had not yet found the right girl. Naunakhte believed that Pati had caught her brother's eye too, and she did not want Harshire to miss the first encounter between the girl and her father.

'Mmph,' Harshire said as Naunakhte shook his naked shoulder. 'What – ' Then he saw Naunakhte leaning over him in the moonlight, one hand on her lips and the other pointing towards Pati's pallet, and he fell silent and pushed himself to a sitting position.

Ammenakht was intent on his task and had not noticed that his eldest children were awake. He tiptoed across the flat roof, like a hippopotamus manoeuvring its way through a papyrus field, until he reached the pallet where the new servant slept. His big belly swayed from side to side. Naunakhte saw with a quick thrill of excitement that beneath it his penis was erect, sticking up as stiff as the long thin palette in which he kept his pens and inks. Ammenakht looked down for a moment, rubbing his hands together. Then he lowered himself awkwardly to the ground beside Pati, who was asleep on her belly, and shook her shoulder. She came awake with a protesting little squeak and rolled over, then gasped as she saw her master above her.

'Hush,' said Ammenakht, and he put his hand on the girl's breast. She gave a single wriggle which might have been of protest and might have been of pleasure. Then she sat up and smiled. Her white teeth flashed in her dark face.

Ammenakht lay down on Pati's pallet and tugged at her until she was lying half across him. He caught hold of her by her woolly hair and pulled down her head to kiss her. The girl began to giggle – little breathless, soft giggles as if she didn't quite believe that this was really happening. Ammenakht arranged her astride him, plump thighs spread across his bulging belly. Her back was towards Naunakhte and the full glistening moons of her backside gleamed as she shifted up and down, rubbing herself against her master's body with lewd determination.

'Ah,' Ammenakht grunted in satisfaction. He put his hands on the girl's back and ran them down from her shoulders to her buttocks, then pulled roughly. Pati gave a gasp and leant forward as he dragged the cheeks of her arse wide apart and thrust his fingers between them, exploring the lush moist folds of flesh and the dark inviting cleft thus exposed to the warm night air.

'By Seth,' whispered Harshire. Naunakhte turned to look at him in shock and disapproval, for it was both blasphemous and dangerous to swear by Seth, god of darkness, of chaos, of war and disorder. But she said nothing, because in the silver moonlight she saw that Harshire was fully aroused, his member thick and erect, its bulbous tip glistening wetly. He was clasping the stiff shaft in his right fist, and as she watched he began to masturbate, rubbing his closed hand strongly up and down, up and down, the swollen rod. His breathing turned into regular gasps, their rhythm aligned with the movement of his gripping fingers.

He took his penis in his hand. He made love to his fist. At

11

once the words came back to Naunakhte, the story of how the god Amun had created the world with the spurting of his semen. She watched, entranced, as Harshire thrust harder into the clasp of his hand and breathed quickly through his gritted teeth. She had never seen a man do this before, and suddenly the story of the god came alive for her. She imagined Amun, great and mighty, beautiful and powerful beyond men. The delicate skin of her brother's penis slid up and down as he rubbed himself, and her mind pictured the god's penis, glowing with the life contained in it. Harshire gasped with pleasure, and she heard the god's sighs, strong as the winds over the desert.

A stifled squeal drew her wide eyes back to her father and the servant girl. They were in the same position – Pati straddling Ammenakht's belly and leaning forward to allow his mouth to suck at her dangling breasts – but now her father had three fingers thrust deep within the folds of the girl's sex, moving slowly, juicily in and out. Every time the fingers sank again into her moist opening she gave a long sigh, almost like a sob. Ammenakht's other hand was at the base of Pati's belly, rubbing and stroking.

Suddenly Pati twisted away, pulling herself upright. She reached behind her and found her master's penis with her hand, lying engorged against the folds of his stomach. Her fingers explored its length and then hoisted it upright, and without hesitation she guided its shining head between the lips of her sex, then sank down.

Harshire made a sound halfway between a gasp and a moan as Pati impaled herself upon Ammenakht's erect phallus. She twisted her head and leant back, tensing her belly and loins. Her hands clasped Ammenakht's spread thighs to give her purchase and she began to ride him, grunting as if she urged on a galloping horse. The soft dark flesh of her thighs and buttocks shook as she lifted and lowered herself upon her master's shining penis. For a moment Ammenakht held on to her hips, then he seemed to realise that she needed no guidance. His hands slid up her writhing body and found her heavy breasts. She moaned and flung her head from side to side as his fingers clasped her dark red nipples and tugged at them. Her body struck his with a soft, urgent sound, and she began to let out little shrill yelps in rhythm with her movements. Ammenakht squeezed and pinched her bouncing breasts, and the speed of her lunges increased to a desperate climax.

At last she let out an odd, strangled cry and arched backward, her mouth open, her eyelids fluttering. Ammenakht grunted and grasped her hips tightly and thrust his penis up into her with all the strength he could command; once, twice, and then he snarled and pulled her rigid body down on to him as if he wanted to split her in two.

Naunakhte was breathing quickly, as if someone were doing to her what her father had done to the servant. She licked her lips and looked at her brother just in time to see him bare his teeth in pleasure and clutch fervently at the jerking head of his phallus. White semen spurted from it, glistening in the moonlight.

For long moments there was silence, broken only by irregular gasps. Then Ammenakht gently rolled the girl off him, patted her flank and pushed himself to his feet to creep back to his own pallet.

If he believed that his adventure had gone unnoticed, he was mistaken. As he knelt down his wife Hatia's voice spoke, shockingly loud after the smothered silence of secret sex. 'Well, was she good?'

'Hatia!' exclaimed Ammenakht, his voice revealing his surprise. 'Whatever are you doing awake?'

'Listening to you copulating with Pati,' said Hatia acidly. 'What do you expect?'

Ammenakht lowered himself cautiously to the pallet and said in soothing tones, 'Don't be angry, my wife. Go to sleep.'

'Go to sleep? I shall not. If you had enough energy to

13

make Pati squeal, husband, you can do the same for me.'

'Oh,' said Ammenakht. 'Ah, I don't think I could quite manage that, wife. I'm not as young as I used to be.'

Hatia's voice dripped irony. 'Well, Ammenakht, if you don't want me to tell the women in the marketplace that your papyrus reed is too soft to write with, you'd better think of another way of satisfying me.' She shifted beneath the linen sheet. 'Try putting that slick tongue of yours to another use.'

Naunakhte knelt a little more upright on her pallet, trying to see what her father and mother were doing. She frowned in puzzlement as with many gasps and groans of discomfort Ammenakht positioned himself face down between his wife's legs, his head buried between her spread thighs. Hatia gave a long sigh and rested both hands on her husband's head, stroking her fingers lovingly across the bald patch which by day was covered by a smart wig.

Silence fell again, broken only by the sound of lapping and Hatia's liquid moans. Presently her hands moved from Ammenakht's head to her breasts and she began to caress and tease her erect nipples. It was not long before she gave a great cry of delight and wrapped her thighs so closely around her husband's ears that Naunakhte was afraid her father would be smothered.

After a few minutes Ammenakht crawled grumbling up the pallet and fell flat on his face with a sound like a water melon being dropped from a height. Hatia whispered in his ear and kissed his cheek, then sighed. Soon both of them were snoring.

Harshire and Naunakhte, on the other hand, were still wide awake. Harshire lifted himself half to his feet and hissed, 'Do you think they'll wake up?'

'Why should they?' Naunakhte whispered back.

Harshire grinned at her, a devilish grin. 'Because, sister, by Seth, I'm going to give that little witch Pati the screwing of her life. What's good enough for father is good enough for me.'

14

'But – ' Naunakhte began, but it was too late. Harshire was on his feet and moving silently across the roof to Pati's pallet. His sister pressed her hands to her mouth, astonished by his insolence. If her father awoke he would be furious. Such an insult!

Harshire had reached the servant girl's pallet. The girl's dark figure lay below him, sprawled in the abandon of sleep. Naunakhte expected Harshire to lie on Pati at once and thrust himself inside her, but he did not. He knelt beside her and then swung one leg over her, straddling her chest, his half-erect penis pointing towards her parted lips. Leaning a little forward, he caught hold of the girl's hair. She woke with a sleepy moan and without a word he pushed the head of his phallus into her open mouth.

Pati's eyes opened very wide. She made a smothered sound of protest, then suddenly seemed to realise what was happening to her. Protest turned to delighted acquiescence and she began to suck, her cheeks hollowing as she worked on Harshire's penis with tongue and lips.

No wonder she was delighted, because the phallus in her mouth was larger than her master's. Harshire was young and strong and his penis was splendid; thick and long and beautifully hard, like the penis of the ithyphallic god Min in the temple hieroglyphs. Pati sucked eagerly at the glistening shaft and lifted her dark hands to caress Harshire's sturdy thighs and muscular, taut buttocks. Naunakhte took a quick breath of shock, for she was sure that she saw one dusky finger wriggling its way deep between the cheeks of Harshire's backside, sliding into the little tight forbidden hole between them. Could that possibly be true? And if it was true, why was Harshire breathing hard and clenching his cheeks with what must be pleasure?

Pati had done well: Harshire's fine phallus was restored to full hardness. He kicked her feet apart, then caught her beneath her thighs and lifted her plump legs to wrap them around his waist. His lips sought hers and he pushed his tongue into her panting mouth to silence her, then without another word plunged into her to the hilt.

The servant girl had ridden her master vigorously enough, but all her efforts were as nothing compared to the shafting that Harshire gave her now. He had already spurted his seed once that evening and now he seemed tireless. Over and over again his thick rod drove into her and withdrew, glistening with her eager dampness, only to lunge again. Beneath him Pati gasped with helpless delight, arching her juicy hips up towards him to welcome his thrusts. He held her lush breasts in his hands and slid his full length into her with feverish strength, grunting as his hot swollen flesh was simultaneously soothed and maddened by her silky folds. Pati moaned and whimpered as her climax approached, but Harshire did not stop. He forced his mouth down on hers to smother her little quivering cries of orgasm and seemed to relish the sensation as her body tensed and shuddered beneath his and the velvety glove of her sex pulsed and tightened around his plunging penis. Then, when she was limp and helpless beneath him, he caught hold of her wrists and spread them wide apart so that her bouncing breasts were exposed to his gaze. He held her beneath him, pinned down like a slave, and worked his gleaming phallus to and fro, to and fro, until at last he gasped and drove himself into her and his fierce climax overwhelmed him.

Everything was very quiet as Harshire tottered back to his own reed mat and lay down again. The servant girl gave a little whimper of disbelief and delight, then subsided into slumber. Naunakhte slid down beneath her sheet and stared up at the hot stars, breathing fast.

Between her legs she ached; a dull, numb ache. She touched herself there, hesitantly, and felt that the tender petals of her secret flesh were moist and slippery and slightly swollen. They were so sensitive that even the lightest touch of her finger made her shiver.

She was ready for a man, ripe for love. She knew it was true. Whenever she heard or saw people in the act

16

of generation it had the same effect on her. Even thinking about it had the same effect.

Thinking about it ... There was a man in the village whom Naunakhte desired. He was one of the medjay, the state policemen, and his name was Psaro. Psaro was of Nubian extraction. His skin was as black as charcoal and as smooth as polished stone, and his lips were full and red. He was beautiful, and whenever Naunakhte saw him she wondered what it would be like to be kissed by those full lips, to be pressed against that strong burnished torso. She thought of him now as she touched herself, hoping to bring herself to some sort of release from her frustration and misery.

But she was taboo, the prisoner of Amun's word. Psaro would never hold her, would never press his lips to her flesh, would never penetrate her with the ebony staff that hung at his loins. The god had forbidden it.

For a moment she was angry. She wanted to deny the god's command and assert herself; to seize her freedom at all costs. Her fists clenched and her jaw set. She was ready to swear by Seth and invoke the forces of darkness, if only she could be free.

Then, above her, another meteor streaked over the sky. Another followed it, and another. Naunakhte's eyes filled with tears as she watched the tracks of burning brilliance. How much more clearly could the gods reveal themselves?

The meteors ceased. 'Oh lord Amun,' Naunakhte prayed, 'I beg you to release me from this life. If I am to be yours, mighty Amun, if you truly set your seal upon me when I was born, send another star. Let it fall from my right hand to my left, great god of life.'

And, in answer, a blue line of flame scored its way across the sky. It fell from right to left, and as it flamed and vanished the tears which stood in Naunakhte's eyes brimmed over and slid down her cheeks, brighter than the stars.

Chapter Two

'Nakhte!' Hatia's voice shrilled up the hole that led to the flat roof. 'Nakhte, come down here at once!'

'You're in trouble,' said one of Naunakhte's smaller sisters, with satisfaction.

Naunakhte frowned. Her mother's voice sounded to her not angry, but afraid. She pushed her bundle of clean white linen, the family's working clothes, into the hands of the next oldest girl. 'Fold it carefully,' she said, then smoothed down the tight knee-length kilt which was her only garment and ran to the stairs.

As she descended she closed her eyes, but even so when she opened them again she was quite blind for a few minutes. The reflection of the sun on the white linen shimmered before her, dancing like red motes. At last, though, her vision cleared. The dark room where the family lived swam into view before her, and she gasped.

Psaro the medjay was standing there beside her mother, his head brushing against the roof, he was so tall. Naunakhte's heart began to flutter and thump. Psaro looked nervous. Uncomfortable. Could this be the answer to her prayers? Had Psaro come for her?

'Naunakhte,' Hatia said. Naunakhte jumped, because her family hardly ever used her full name. She looked at her mother and saw with a shock that Hatia was

18

weeping. Tears left shining trails down her weather-beaten face. 'Naunakhte, Psaro has come to take you away.'

'To take me away?' Naunakhte repeated. She took a step towards Psaro, her face revealing her vivid eagerness.

'To the temple,' Psaro said, looking at the ground. His deep voice was like the rumble of thunder over the desert. 'I'm sorry, Naunakhte.'

Suddenly Naunakhte felt cold all over. 'To the temple?' She pushed her hand through her thick black hair, pulling her braids awry, and looked beseechingly at Hatia. 'Mother – '

The street door opened and Ammenakht entered, puffing like a bull. He must have walked all the way from the Valley of the Tombs in the morning heat, an unheard-of exertion for a respected scribe. Naunakhte began to tremble. 'What's this?' Ammenakht demanded, between gasps.

'The high priest of Amun has sent for Naunakhte,' said Hatia, and Psaro silently held out to Ammenakht a small papyrus scroll. Ammenakht unfolded it and quickly scanned the writing. As he read his face changed.

'Naunakhte,' he said at last, rolling up the papyrus, 'I am afraid it is true. The god Amun has summoned you at last. You must go to the temple at once.'

So this was the meaning of the omen. This was why the god had answered her prayer. Suddenly Naunakhte was terrified of leaving the cramped little house where she had spent all her life. 'No,' she said, putting her hands to her face. 'I don't want to go.'

Her mother hugged her. She was smaller than Naunakhte by a head, but her embrace was still as comforting as it had been when Naunakhte was a little child. 'Hush,' she said. 'There is no use fighting the gods. You were only ever lent to us, Naunakhte. You have always belonged to Amun.'

'We must not delay,' said Psaro, making patterns with his toe in the sand on the floor.

Naunakhte began to weep. Hatia pulled the girl's head down on to her shoulder and said past her ear to Ammenakht, 'Get some of the children to find Naunakhte's best things. She must go to the god looking her finest.'

The people of the village watched her go, standing in silence on either side of the dusty path that led down to the River Nile. Hatia stood at the village gate, holding the hands of her two youngest children and calling out messages of love and good fortune. Naunakhte hid her face as the village dwindled behind her.

Psaro walked with her as far as the river. He was courteous, carrying her bundle and holding a broad papyrus leaf to shade her from the fierce sun, but he said not a word. It was as if the summons of the god had made her almost a god herself – no longer the ordinary female mortal that had lived in the village of the tombmakers. They descended the slope of the hill in silence, and the white and red dust rose up from their sandalled feet and stained Naunakhte's best long dress and caught in the folds of the linen wrap over her shoulders.

Below them lay the bright stripe of the cultivated lands on either side of the Nile, green and golden now with ripe cereals ready for harvest. On the other side of the river sprawled the dusty tangle of the city of Waset, with the temples of Luxor rising out of it like elephants standing in scrub. And there on the left of the city, isolated from it by distance and holiness, the temple complex of Karnak, the most divine place in all Egypt. From his shrine within the huge labyrinth of stone, temples and halls, gateways and chapels, the god Amun had summoned her and now awaited her coming.

At the quay a boat was tied up and Psaro led her towards it. Naunakhte gasped, because it was one of the temple barges, a huge splendid construction of papyrus bundles, with a fine canopy of dyed linen to shield its passengers from heat. It dwarfed the little fishing vessels and the ferries that carried people to and fro to the city of Waset. At the gangplank Psaro waved to someone on board, then bowed low as another medjay, a senior officer by his headdress, came down towards them.

'Naunakhte,' Psaro said, 'farewell. Remember us all, when you are in the god's service.' And he bowed to her, too, as if she were a priest or a noblewoman.

'Goodbye, Psaro,' Naunakhte said. She was startled by how shaky and timid her voice sounded. Was she so afraid?

The boat soon pulled up to the temple quay. At a little distance the first pylon gateway of the temple loomed huge and awesome. Naunakhte walked between the medjay captain and another of the medjay until they reached the gateway. It stood open, guarded only by its holiness. No Egyptian would dare to trespass on such sacred ground. The captain led her through it and into the precinct of the temple.

A second gateway followed the first, and then Naunakhte stopped in her tracks and gazed about her, hardly able to believe her eyes. She stood in a massive hall, the largest enclosed space she had ever entered. The walls were decorated with painted sculptures of the gods and holy texts, and the roof was held up by a seemingly endless forest of columns, hundreds of them, some painted, some sheathed in gold. The columns were the shape of papyrus plants; smooth, thick stems capped with a bulbous tip. Naunakhte found her eye drawn to a representation of the god on one wall. He appeared as a handsome young man, naked and powerful, with a long, erect penis. The shape of his phallus irresistibly recalled the shape of the columns. Naunakhte stared at the image of the god, imagining her tender body ravished by his might, immolated by the flame of his ejaculation. She began to shiver uncontrollably.

'Is this the new girl?' A young woman's voice echoed

21

back from the myriad columns and the coffered roof. Naunakhte jumped and pulled herself back to reality with an effort. Approaching her was a girl of about her own age, petite and no taller than her shoulder, dressed in a splendid gown of folded and pleated linen, like a noble lady's best dinner dress. The girl wore no wig, which was hardly surprising, for her own hair was a bright copper-gold, an astonishing colour for Egpyt. As she drew closer, Naunakhte saw that her eyes, which were painted with green malachite and black antimony, were brilliant pale green.

'I am Tiy,' said the girl, stopping in front of Naunakhte and looking her up and down. 'I am the chief handmaiden to the Hand of God. She has sent me to fetch you.'

'I am Naunakhte,' Naunakhte whispered, thoroughly cowed by Tiy's striking appearance and cool confidence, 'daughter of the scribe Ammenakht.'

'Is that what they told you?' asked Tiy, with arch superiority. 'You do have a lot to learn. Follow me.'

She turned her back and began to walk away. 'But – ' Naunakhte protested feebly, 'my bundle.'

Tiy stopped and looked at the linen-wrapped bundle with distaste. 'What is in it?' she demanded.

'Another dress,' said Naunakhte timidly, 'and my kilt, and my eye paint.'

The pale green eyes examined Naunakhte again from head to heel. Naunakhte was a little irritated by Tiy's disdain, especially as she was wearing her best dress. It was made of fine pleated linen, closely fitted around her slender waist with two broad straps covering her breasts, and at her ankles it was embroidered. She had embroidered it herself.

'If it's no better than that one,' said Tiy at last, 'I would throw it in the Nile. But the servants will bring it, if you must. Now come with me. The Lady Hunro awaits you.'

Fighting down a surge of anger, Naunakhte hurried

after Tiy through the multitude of columns. 'Who is the Lady Hunro?'

'She is the god's wife of Amun,' said Tiy over her shoulder, 'the Hand of God. Her husband is the Lord Merybast, the high priest. Don't worry about him, you'll hardly ever see him; he delegates the temple services and keeps himself busy with administration.'

Naunakhte raised her eyebrows. How could anyone whose duty it was to serve the god prefer to undertake tasks that could be discharged by a scribe? But she did not dare say this aloud, and in any case Tiy was still speaking.

'The Lady Hunro,' Tiy went on, 'is well past her thirtieth year. She will soon choose another to take on her titles. It should be her daughter, but she and Merybast have no children. So she will probably adopt someone and make her the Hand of God.' Tiy glanced around and met Naunakhte's eyes. Her smile had a brittle edge. 'People say that she is likely to choose me. It would be suitable. I have served a long time in the temple and I understand the rite. Also, I am attached to the chief priest, who undertakes the temple duties in Merybast's stead. His name is Panhesi. It would be convenient for all if Panhesi became Merybast's successor as I am intended to be Hunro's.'

Tiy's pale eyes shone. Inexperienced as she was, Naunakhte understood the unspoken message. She was not to interfere with Tiy's plans. She was surprised to hear of Tiy's attachment to the priest Panhesi, which seemed a rather worldly thing for the servants of a god. But there again, the high priestess herself was a married woman. Naunakhte adopted an expression of suitable meekness and followed Tiy into the labyrinth of the temple without another word.

They went through gateways and passages and at some point seemed to turn away from the main processional route into the temple. Naunakhte gazed from side to side, lost and puzzled. Tiy did not attempt to enlighten her. At last they came to a small closed door. Tiy knocked and said loudly, 'It is I, Tiy.'

The door swung open and Tiy led Naunakhte through it. Beyond it was a big room, pillared like the hypostyle hall but on a much smaller, more intimate scale. The floor was paved with smooth glittering stone and at one side the room was open to admit the sunlight. Beyond the portico lay a broad shimmering lake, green with waterlilies and flanked by ornamental trees. A woman in a long white dress was walking around the pool, followed by a little black slave girl carrying a parasol made of palm leaves. The smell of costly perfumes caressed Naunakhte's nostrils.

The room was full of women, mostly young girls like Naunakhte, although some were older. Some were sleeping; others were playing games, making music, or attending to their clothes and hair. They looked up when Tiy entered and one of them called out, 'The new girl!' and another sprang to her feet and ran out through the portico to the pool.

'Welcome,' said one of the girls, running up with a smile. 'I am Neferure. Welcome to the temple.'

'Thank you,' said Naunakhte, reassured.

Then all the girls in the room drew back and made obeisance as the woman who had been walking by the pool entered, stepping soundlessly with bare feet. Naunakhte bowed too, for she had guessed that this was the Lady Hunro.

The Lady Hunro was not tall, but she carried herself like a queen. She was curved and rounded in shape, with full breasts and heavy thighs beneath her translucent linen garment. Her face was high boned and haughty and her eyes were very bright. She was clearly a woman of middle years, but she was still beautiful.

'Naunakhte,' said the Lady Hunro. 'You are welcome.'

'Thank you, lady,' Naunakhte murmured.

The Lady Hunro took hold of Naunakhte's hand and felt it. 'Ah,' she said, 'hard fingers. You have worked, Naunakhte, in the village of the tombmakers.'

'Yes, lady.' Naunakhte was astonished by the softness of Hunro's hand. It was as if she had never known toil. She was suddenly afraid that she had failed a test, that she would be turned away like a peasant girl turned out of the kitchens.

'It is nothing,' said Hunro, looking Naunakhte up and down. 'Nothing, when compared to your beauty, Naunakhte. By all the gods, you are the image of your mother, and I never saw a woman to rival her.' Naunakhte gasped with astonishment and Hunro smiled. 'I was going to ask you to show the mark on your arm, to ensure that the scribe Ammenakht and his wife had not substituted a daughter of their own for the god's servant. But you are so like your mother that there is no need.'

'I will show you, lady, if you wish,' said Naunakhte. Hastily she pulled the gilded bracelet from above her elbow, revealing the small dark image on her golden skin. The temple girls pressed close around her, sighing with amazement as they saw the sign of the god on Naunakhte's arm.

'There,' said Hunro. 'I said there was no doubt.'

'Lady,' Naunakhte asked timidly, 'will you tell me about my mother? I know nothing of her.'

Hunro nodded. 'Ammenakht was told to keep it secret. I am glad he obeyed. I will tell you, Naunakhte, it is right that you should know now. But it is not a pleasant tale. Come and sit with me under the portico. We will drink a little date wine.' Then Hunro frowned as she noticed the dust on Naunakhte's feet and clothing. 'But you are hot and tired,' she said. 'Let the girls wash you first. Then I will tell you everything.'

At once the girls descended on Naunakhte, unfastening the straps of her dress and peeling the linen from her so that she was quite naked. Like all Egyptians she was unselfconscious about her nude body, and she helped the girls to strip her. The sooner she was washed, the sooner Hunro would tell her about her mother. Her real mother, the woman that nobody in the village had ever mentioned.

'Oh,' said Neferure with a smile, 'you are lovely, Naunakhte. The god will be pleased to see you play for him.' She shook her head, making the tiny plaits of her long heavy wig bounce and sway.

Naunakhte smiled in return, but as she turned to walk to the pool she saw Tiy watching her with an expression of distaste and anger in her shining green eyes. It chilled her so that she shivered.

'Come,' said another of the girls, 'let us wash you. You'll enjoy it!' And they flung off their clothes and surrounded Naunakhte and guided her down into the cool water of the lake. Glittering red fish darted away from them to hide beneath the shadows of the waterlilies. Naunakhte shivered afresh at the chill kiss of the water, and her skin came out in goosepimples and the dark points of her nipples lengthened and hardened.

One of the girls cupped the shining water in her hands and splashed it over Naunakhte's body. Another brought a phial of scented soap to cleanse her. A third began to rub the soap into her skin, coaxing away the dust of the road. Naunakhte had never smelt a scent like the perfume of the soap, like tuberoses and lilies and lotus flowers mingled with the essence of nard. She sighed with pleasure as the girl's fingers rubbed up and down her back, then slipped to the front of her body to cup and caress her breasts.

'Such lovely breasts,' whispered Neferure. She stood in front of Naunakhte and placed her hands gently over her erect nipples, rubbing with her palms. A spear of sensation lanced from Naunakhte's breasts to her belly, wakening the hollow aching feeling that filled her when she saw men and women making love. She took a quick deep breath and Neferure reached up and kissed her on the mouth.

Nobody had ever kissed Naunakhte on the mouth. For a moment she tensed, almost frightened by the unfamiliar sensation of Neferure's hot tongue probing between her lips. Then she was filled with a sudden rush of immediate, uncomplicated desire, acceptance of the pleasure which the kiss gave her and eagerness to have more. She pressed her body against Neferure's and moaned.

'Ah,' murmured Neferure, smiling as she pulled away. 'More in a moment, little lotus flower. Come and let us anoint you.'

She took Naunakhte's hand and led her out of the pool and into the shade of the portico. There she laid her down on a linen couch and knelt beside her, a jar of scented unguent in her hand. She poured a little of the fragrant oil into her palms and then set her hands to Naunakhte's body and began to glide her fingers across her soft skin, soothing and moisturising it and at the same time stirring Naunakhte to almost unbearable arousal.

Naunakhte had forgotten how much she wanted to hear the Lady Hunro tell her of her mother. She was conscious only of Neferure's hands moving up and down her skin, kneading her breasts, flickering over her swollen nipples, teasing at the delicate flesh of her thighs until she sighed and flung her head helplessly from side to side, rejoicing at these unfamiliar, delicious sensations.

She opened her eyes and looked up at Neferure. The temple girl was leaning over her with the heavy locks of her wig falling on to her naked shoulders and her face set in an expression of deep concentration. A tiny smile touched the corners of her mouth. She was beautiful, and the delicate, refined detail of her highly dressed wig above her simple nakedness was infinitely attractive. Naunakhte remembered how the men of the village used to draw little pictures on the scraps of limestone left over from their building – pictures of girls stark naked except for their luxuriant wigs, and she understood why they found this combination so alluring.

'That's right,' Neferure whispered. She had her hands on Naunakhte's breasts and was gently fondling her nipples, making them longer, stiffer, more sensitive. 'Yes, Naunakhte, yes. How beautiful you look.' And over her shoulder she whispered, 'Touch her there.'

Naunakhte closed her eyes and whimpered. Another pair of hands was fondling her thighs, moving them apart gently but very firmly. A long, slender finger coiled in the nest of dark curls at the base of her belly, then slithered a little further down.

'Ah,' Naunakhte moaned, for the finger was caressing her in a way that gave her such exquisite pleasure that she could not keep silent. 'Oh, oh, please.'

'Such a sweet blossom,' murmured another voice. The finger between her legs stroked and stroked at one particular place, and whenever it touched her she was pierced by arrows of the purest bliss. 'Pretty as a desert rose and glistening with dew. Ah, sweet.'

And now another finger was on her, sliding its way into her secret places even as the first continued to touch and caress that magic spot. No perfumed unguent was needed to make her slippery and soft, for the delicate flesh between her legs was already soothed and lubricated by her own fragrant dew. The pleasure that filled Naunakhte changed, becoming more urgent. Tension increased within her, making her moan. Every time the finger rubbed against her she wanted it to touch her harder, to soothe the unbearable emptiness that grew even as her pleasure grew. Her round hips lifted upward, a motion like the waves on the surface of the Nile. As if in answer the finger slid inside her. Pleasure turned suddenly to pain and Naunakhte cried out.

At once all the hands that touched her withdrew. She opened her eyes to see Neferure leaning over her, frowning in astonishment. 'Naunakhte,' she said softly, 'are you a virgin?'

Unable to speak, Naunakhte nodded. Everything was so strange. Was it wrong to be a virgin? How could she help it? The men of the village had never wanted her. It was not her fault.

The Lady Hunro appeared above her, smiling, and

Naunakhte felt immediately reassured. 'Naunakhte,' she said, 'if this is true, it will be most pleasing to the god. But you are nineteen years old. None of us expected you still to be a virgin, when you have waited so long to enter your service, and you are so – ' She gestured with one soft hand at Naunakhte's still-quivering body ' – so easily aroused. But lie still, Naunakhte, until I discover whether this is true.'

'It is true,' Naunakhte whispered. But Hunro shook her head and held out her other hand. In it rested an object shaped like an egg, but made of sparkling white alabaster. 'Let us see,' said the Lady Hunro.

Naunakhte lay very still. Dragged from everything she knew into a strange and erotic place, she was uncertain of what she should say or do. She closed her eyes and tried to think herself away from where she was now. Her memory conjured up a festival at the village, when everyone took three days off work and spent the whole time feasting and drinking. They ate together under the stars, enjoying the good meat and fish which Pharaoh sent them, and drank the best beer and date wine in such quantity that most of them were paralytic. People played and sang and the villagers danced under the bright stars and laughed and went off into corners to make love to each other. All except Naunakhte, the strange one, the girl marked by Amun, who sat beside her little brothers and sisters, drunken and melancholy and alone.

Her mind shied away from the memory of her own strangeness. Now she was in Amun's own place, his temple, the seat of his power, and the lady who was the god's wife on earth was parting her thighs to make some arcane trial of her chastity. Naunakhte gave a little helpless moan as she felt Hunro's soft hands gently, delicately, exploring between her legs, fondling the place where she was liquid and melting with longing. The high priestess's touch reawakened all the hot desire that had filled her when Neferure had put her hands on her breasts and another girl had skilfully, dexterously fingered her vulva and clitoris. She bit her lip, trying to keep silent.

Then she felt something cool and hard pressing against her, pushing its way between the lips of her sex. It felt painful, wonderful. It was thick and it stretched her, making her want all sorts of contradictory things. She wanted to part her legs further, to close her thighs against the unexpected intrusion, to resist, to submit.

The pain grew and she let out a sharp cry. Then, as suddenly as it had come, the cool hard thing withdrew and the Lady Hunro's voice said, 'By Hathor, it is true.'

What could make the priestess of Amun swear by the goddess of love? Naunakhte opened her eyes and saw Hunro holding up the alabaster egg, examining its rounded tip. The smooth white stone gleamed with the slippery juices of Naunakhte's desire, and the pointed end was just stained with pink.

'Naunakhte,' said the Lady Hunro, 'you will be most acceptable to the god. And . . .' She opened her lips and delicately drew the tip of the alabaster egg between them, tasting it. 'And you will be most acceptable to me.'

Without another word the high priestess sank to her knees beside the couch on which Naunakhte lay. She kissed her soft rounded belly and the swell of her mound of love. Naunakhte made a sound of protest, sure that it was not her place to have the Hand of God thus worship her. But Hunro said, 'Naunakhte, the place of the women of the temple is to arouse the god, and to arouse me, the god's wife of Amun. Your beauty arouses me, Naunakhte. Be still.'

A soft hiss beside Naunakhte made her glance around. Tiy stood there, close to her, staring with malevolent anger in her pale eyes and repeating that cold vicious sound, a hiss like the hiss of a cobra as it prepares to strike. Clearly Tiy was most displeased that the high priestess found Naunakhte attractive. The hatred in her face struck Naunakhte with a chill of fear.

But then she forgot her fear, because the Lady Hunro's head had moved between her open thighs. For the first time in her life Naunakhte felt the warmth of a mouth caressing her sex, the softness of lips encircling her swollen clitoris, the warm prodding of a strong, hard tongue between the moist petals of her vulva. The pleasure was indescribable. She closed her eyes and leant back her head and let out a long, breathy sigh of ecstasy. The tension that had filled her earlier had quite vanished. She was immersed in sensual joy, lifted to higher and higher planes of bliss by the steady lapping of Hunro's tongue. The sensations swelled and grew and Naunakhte's soft cries became sharper. Her hands gripped helplessly at the linen of the couch. And then Hunro caught her engorged clitoris between her lips and drew the tender bud of flesh into her mouth and sucked at it gently, her tongue thrilling against the tiny shaft, and Naunakhte let out a long dying wail and arched her back as her first orgasm blazed through her, soaking her in sensual ecstasy and shaking her to the roots of her being.

Presently she opened her languid eyes and looked up at the Lady Hunro with an expression of stunned amazement. 'Lady, I am sorry,' she whispered. 'Did I cry out? I didn't realise – '

Hunro smiled kindly. 'Naunakhte, little golden flower,' she said, 'I took as much pleasure in your cries as you did. All is very well, little one. Think of it as your introduction to the service of the god. There is great pleasure in serving the temple, Naunakhte, as you will find.'

The Lady Hunro got up from the floor by the couch, where she had knelt to caress Naunakhte with her mouth, and stretched. 'Now,' she said, 'come and sit by me, and I shall tell you of your mother. Girls, help her.'

She turned and walked away and the temple hand-maidens hurried to help Naunakhte up from the couch. All except Tiy, who stood with her slender arms folded and her lips curling with disdain. 'Very clever,' she

31

hissed, in a voice just loud enough to carry to Naunakhte's ears. 'Very clever, village girl. Who told you that the Lady Hunro finds innocents amusing? Don't worry. She will soon find out that you are a whore, just as your mother was.'

Naunakhte was shocked and furious. She was about to make an angry retort when one of the girls caught her arm and whispered, 'Don't argue with Tiy if you can help it, Naunakhte. She knows people. She can make things very difficult if she doesn't like you.'

In a tense silence Naunakhte met Tiy's eyes. They were bright and hard as green stones, gleaming with spite. After a moment Tiy turned away without another word and Naunakhte prepared to follow the Lady Hunro to the shady spot under a date palm by the shimmering pool. As she went she noticed how the temple girls looked at her askance, as if she carried bad luck with her. It was clear that they feared Tiy's resentment more than they hoped to befriend their new colleague. Was she destined to be alone in the temple of Amun as she had been alone in the village of the tombmakers?

'Don't argue with Tiy if you can help it,' Naunakhte repeated sadly to herself. 'What was there for me to help?'

Chapter Three

'Come and sit by me, Naunakhte,' said the Lady Hunro, patting the cushioned seat beneath the spreading date palm. 'Bring us something to eat and drink,' she commanded one of the girls, who hurried to obey. The others settled down around them in the shade of the palm tree, excited at the prospect of a tale.

'Now,' said Hunro, looking at Naunakhte's face with a sober expression, 'where to begin? Naunakhte, do you know anything of your parentage?'

Naunakhte shook her head and regarded the Lady Hunro with all her attention. At last she would find out why all her life she had been different.

The girl brought a gilded dish laden with dainties, slivers of roasted meat, salted fish, honeyed dates and ripe figs. She set beside it a flagon of wine made from grapes and two cups. The cups were made of chased gold, with designs inlaid in blue enamel. Naunakhte had never seen so much luxury in one small space, but although the girl filled one of the golden cups and put it into her hand she could not drink. 'Please, lady,' she begged, as Hunro sipped her wine and enjoyed a bite of food, 'tell me everything.'

Hunro set down her golden cup. 'Well, little one,' she

said, 'first, you must know that your father is Pharaoh, King Rameses himself.'

Naunakhte's hand closed into a tight fist around the golden stem of the cup. She felt first cold all over, then burning hot. The blood surged up into her face, staining her honey-gold cheeks with a scarlet blush. Around her the girls drew back, whispering and rustling like a bed of reeds at dawn. Pharaoh was a living god, and his children carried the blood of gods in their veins.

But Pharaoh's wives and concubines lived in the palace, and his countless children lived there too. What had Naunakhte done to be exiled? She gazed at Hunro, and now her face was beseeching.

'Seventeen years ago, Naunakhte,' the Lady Hunro went on, 'there was a plot against King Rameses. Some of his chief ministers plotted to murder him and put upon the throne a man they could more readily bend to their will.'

'To murder Pharaoh?' gasped the listening girls, horrified. To kill Pharaoh was more than treason; it was sacrilege.

'They chose a boy in his teens, the son of Rameses's favourite concubine, the Lady Tiy,' went on Hunro. 'He was your full brother, Naunakhte. You are the daughter of the Lady Tiy and King Rameses. She was the most beautiful woman in the palace, and she bore Rameses many children.'

Naunakhte was trembling from head to foot. She set down her wine, lest the shaking of her hands spill it.

'I remember the day the plot was discovered,' said the Lady Hunro, and now her eyes seemed to look beyond Naunakhte and into the distance of the past. 'I was a visitor in the palace that day. They cried that there was poison in the king's drink. Everything was confusion. I heard later that they had taken the Lady Tiy and she had confessed to her part in the plot.' Hunro's eyes focused again upon Naunakhte. 'She was guilty,' she said softly. 'She had desired to be the mother of the new Pharaoh. She had carried the poison to Rameses with her own hand. The king could have had her executed by any means he chose, but he offered her the poisoned cup instead so that she might die with honour. By his order she gave the cup to her children also, not just her son, but all the children she had by Rameses, except you, Naunakhte.'

It was hard for Naunakhte to speak. She struggled with her shivering and at last whispered, 'I don't understand. Lady Hunro, why was I chosen?'

Hunro stretched out her hand and touched the mark of the god on Naunakhte's arm. 'When you came from the womb, Naunakhte,' she said, softly tracing the outline of the phallus shape with her finger, 'you carried this mark. The god Amun set his seal on you when Pharaoh's seed created you within your mother. The king did not dare kill you out of hand. He asked advice from the oracle of the god. It spoke clearly and said that you were destined to live and that you would be summoned when Amun desired it. So the king spared you, but he sent you out of the palace so that you would not be a reminder to him.' Her eyes softened. 'You see, Naunakhte, you resembled your mother, and Rameses had loved her. Her betrayal gave him great pain.'

So the god Amun had saved her life when she was not three years old. Naunakhte did not know whether to be sorry that she was the child of a wicked and treacherous woman, or pleased that she was the daughter of King Rameses, or in awe at the care that Amun had taken of her. At last she looked up with tears in her eyes and said, 'The god did not forget me.'

Now Hunro smiled. 'He did not forget. His oracle summoned you, and you are here. We must wait and watch to see what he has in mind for you now.'

Her smile became confiding and she stroked Naunakhte's cheek with her hand. The watching girls murmured again as they noted this mark of the high priestess's favour. Hunro's eyes darkened as she touched Naunakhte's smooth skin. 'Tonight,' she said, 'when night comes, we will offer you to the god. Beauty like yours will be most welcome to him. And in future, Naunakhte; in future, who knows?'

The Lady Hunro got up from her seat and stretched and yawned. 'It is hot,' she murmured, looking up at the burning noon sun above the screen of branches. 'I shall go and rest. We have much business tonight, and tomorrow at dawn you will attend me in the rite, Naunakhte. You should rest too. The girls will show you how things are here.'

She cast a fold of her white linen gown over her head and walked slowly away from the tree. Naunakhte watched her go, afraid to be left alone with these strangers. She looked around for the friendly face of Neferure, but could not see it. Instead she saw Tiy's bright hair and pale eyes, glittering with hatred.

'"In future,"' Tiy mocked, '"in future, who knows?" What do you think the Lady Hunro has in mind for you, daughter of a whore and traitor?'

'My mother was not a whore!' Naunakhte protested, leaping to her feet with her fists clenched.

'She was,' insisted Tiy. 'Everyone knows it. You are no more Rameses' daughter than you are the god's. Your mother, my namesake, had taken his chief minister for her lover. They meant to rule together. You are the child of two traitors!'

'The Lady Hunro did not say so,' retorted Naunakhte, determined to keep calm.

'The Lady Hunro admired your mother when she was a girl,' said Tiy scornfully. 'She would not like to believe ill of her. But we know, don't we?' She looked around, checking that the other girls were on her side. They shifted uncomfortably and would not meet Tiy's gleaming eyes, but not one of them spoke up to support Naunakhte.

'I know your plan,' hissed Tiy. 'You mean to usurp my place as the next Hand of Amun. It will not be so, Naunakhte, be certain of it.' Her face twisted with rage, losing its prettiness. 'I do not wish to resort to poison, as your mother did,' she snarled, 'but if I must . . .' The words hung in the air as Tiy turned and stalked away. One by one the other girls followed her. Some of them cast anxious glances at Naunakhte over their shoulders as they went, but all the same they followed Tiy.

Naunakhte stood in the shade of the palm, shuddering with anger and shame. What if what Tiy said was true? For a few moments she had believed herself daughter of Pharaoh. Was she now to find that she was the child not of one traitor, but of two?

It was too much for her. She sat down again on the cushioned couch and bowed her head as the tears came. She wrapped her arms tightly around her as if she could comfort herself.

Her right hand lay upon the mark on her arm. She opened her eyes and looked at it, and gradually her weeping ceased. Whatever the truth of her parentage, the god had not betrayed her. He had signed her before her birth and he had watched over her, and now he had called her to him. More than any man he had taken care of her.

She lifted her eyes to the sun. It glittered through the palm fronds and the remnants of her tears. 'Great god Amun,' she whispered, raising her hands in prayer, 'I will stay here, since it is your wish, whatever Tiy attempts against me. I am your servant, Lord Amun, as I was born.'

The memory came to her of the alabaster egg in the Lady Hunro's hand. It had slipped between the moist lips of her sex, opening her and filling her with fear and desire. Tonight the god would be offered the gift of her maidenhood. Perhaps Amun himself would take her, parting those same lips and this time not withdrawing but moving on within her, filling her, soothing her fears with his mighty presence.

'May it be so,' Naunakhte wished. She stroked the mark of the phallus on her arm and smiled at the sun. 'Oh Lord Amun, I am willing. Make me yours tonight.'

* * *

The last hour of daylight passed, and the sun sank swiftly towards the western horizon. Naunakhte lay stretched out on the cushioned couch beneath the shading palm tree, fast asleep. She dreamt.

In her dream the god came to her. He appeared as a young man in the flower of his strength, strong and shining like a bronze sword unsheathed. His dark hair hung around his broad naked shoulders, and the smell of him was like a garden of incense. When he cast his glowing eyes upon her, they pierced her like spears. She opened her arms to him and he stooped over her, brighter than the sun. He was weightless, and yet the weight of him smothered her and made her gasp. His hands touched her breasts and her nipples burned and froze. The pleasure was too much to bear. When Amun put his mouth on hers and thrust his tongue between her lips she knew that his embrace was mortal. He kissed her, and her spirit left her, driven from her body by the might of the god. She seemed in her dream to fly above herself. Her flesh lay soulless beneath the tree, and her spirit hung in the air, disembodied, to watch as the god Amun took her.

The god spread her hands wide apart so that her breasts were revealed to him. He made a sign with his hand, and her clothing vanished. She was naked, all of her exposed to Amun's eyes, to his hands and lips. The god's phallus rose up between his legs, hard as the granite of a statue, smooth as polished ivory. He took his penis in his hand and placed it against her body. Her spirit watched as the god took her maiden's flower. He thrust with his strong loins and his massive penis penetrated her, forcing the barriers of her body as in battle a ram forces a gate. She wanted to cry out, but her spirit had no voice.

Now the god Amun was moving, sliding his thick phallus to and fro within her. But she was helpless. Her spirit could see her body's pleasure, but could not feel it. In vain she tried to return to herself so that she could experience bliss as the divine Amun made love to her.

But only her body writhed and moaned, while her spirit hovered invisible in the air.

Neferure came and found Naunakhte tossing on the couch and crying out in her sleep. She shook her shoulder gently and whispered, 'Naunakhte, it is time. You must come and let us make you ready.'

Without a word Naunakhte got up and followed her. She could sense that between her legs the tender petals of flesh were wet with eagerness. Her dream had prepared her to meet the embrace of divinity, however it might appear.

Neferure led her to the tiring room, where some of the other girls awaited. A new dress hung on a stand in the light of a torch. It was magnificent; pleated and stitched and embroidered with gold. On the tiring table stood pots and jars filled with expensive perfumes and cosmetics. Beside them lay a massive collar of gold and turquoise and lapis, earrings that were great double discs of gold, and arm rings of gold inlaid with the god's phallic symbol in blue enamel. Before her dream Naunakhte would not have believed that these wondrous things were meant for her, but now she did not find it strange.

The girls undressed her. Neferure whispered in her ear, 'Tiy is very angry, Naunakhte. Everyone knows that her lover Panhesi took her virginity, and she is jealous that you have yours still to offer to the god. You must beware of her. When the Lady Hunro is not here she is very powerful.'

Naunakhte knew that Tiy would hate her whatever she did. She was grateful to Neferure for her warning, but she could not care for Tiy's malice now. Her whole being was focused on the rite to come. How much she hoped that the god would himself take the offering that she brought him!

One of the girls held a silver mirror and Naunakhte watched as her face changed beneath their careful ministrations. They dressed her abundant dark hair and placed over it a headdress of gold threads knotted into a fine web and hung about with beads of lapis and chrysolite. Powdered lapis coloured her heavy eyelids and black kohl outlined her eyes, making them look even larger. Her lips were stained scarlet with powdered carmine, and fragrant oils were rubbed into her skin until it gleamed. The collar of gold and lapis was heavy on her neck.

When they stood her up to place the dress on her she could no longer bear the suspense. 'Neferure,' she said, 'will the god himself possess me?'

Neferure recoiled, shocked. 'No!' she exclaimed, and her agitation increased as she saw the disappointment on Naunakhte's face. 'Of course not,' she went on quickly. 'Only the Hand of God herself may approach the image of Amun. It is her dancing, her loving of him, that calls the god into his statue. It would be the deepest sacrilege if one of us were to touch him. We sing and make music to please his ear, and sometimes we dance to amuse him, and we assist the Hand of Amun by arousing her so that she may better satisfy the god. Naunakhte, are you mad? Of course the god will not take you!'

Naunakhte bit her lip and turned her head away. Neferure thought that she was distressed, and to comfort her she added, 'Panhesi the chief priest will do it. It should be Merybast, husband of the Lady Hunro, but he rarely comes to the temple. But Naunakhte, the god will watch you. The rite will be performed before his statue. You are so beautiful it is bound to please him.'

Her words passed Naunakhte unheard, for Naunakhte was lost in her own thoughts. She was thinking of Tiy and her ambition. She did not doubt that Tiy wanted the position of Hand of Amun because of the power and state it would bestow, not to speak of the wealth of the temple. But now Naunakhte herself knew ambition. She wanted to be the woman whose task it was to submit herself daily to the power of the god. How could she bear to serve the temple and not know that pleasure?

At the doorway more of the temple girls appeared, carrying torches. Neferure set the folds of Naunakhte's dress with care. She said, 'It is time.'

'I am ready,' Naunakhte whispered.

She walked behind the torches out of the women's quarter and into the labyrinth of the temple complex. Pillars and columns and walls loomed before Naunakhte, engraved with the hieroglyphs that told the story of the first-born god Amun, creator of the world. Soon the priests joined them, dressed in white and carrying burning sticks of incense. The sweet pungent fragrance enfolded her and she remembered how in her dream she had been surrounded by the scent of the god.

Before her stood the doors of the sanctuary. She shivered at the sense of hidden power that seemed to come from behind them. It was as if she heard a mighty voice whispering her name, a rumble like the approach of chaos. Amun was calling her.

At the sound of his voice she forgot her disappointment and her ambition. She breathed deeply and her eyes glittered as a trance began to fall upon her. The priests and the temple girls saw that the god had dazed her, and they made good luck signs. It was an excellent omen that the sacrifice should enter thus into trance and go willingly.

The doors were open. Naunakhte walked forward into the sanctuary, and for the first time in her life she saw the golden image of the god Amun.

He appeared just as he had in her dream, mighty and shining. His face was familiar to her, as if she had known it all her life. His eyes and his brows were dark, inlaid with enamel upon the gold of the statue. She walked towards him, smiling, and as the torchlight flickered she saw the god return her smile.

On either side of the statue stood two figures dressed in white. They were the Lady Hunro and a man in priest's robes, the chief priest Panhesi. Between them stood a table of stone. When Naunakhte reached the table, two of the priests took hold of her arms and prevented her from going forward further. She stood still, gazing up at the statue with a face of wonder.

Panhesi stepped forward, staring. He was a young man, and it was clear from his expression that he found the sacrifice desirable. Beneath his breath he whispered, 'By Amun, she is a lovely one.' Aloud he said, 'You are Naunakhte. Speak now before the god Amun. Are you willing to offer him your body?'

His words floated through Naunakhte's consciousness. She heard the god's name and smiled as she stared up into the face of the statue. Very slowly she said, 'I am willing.'

'Disrobe her,' commanded Panhesi. Neferure and another girl came up to Naunakhte and unfastened the glorious dress, then drew it from her shoulders. Her oiled body gleamed in the light of the torches. Her round high breasts lifted and fell with her breathing, and already the rosy nipples that tipped them were erect and swollen with longing.

For this rite there was no music. In holy silence the girls guided Naunakhte forward and laid her down upon the cold stone of the table. She lay still, her eyes fixed on the face of the god. He looked down at her, and still he smiled.

Great Amun, Naunakhte prayed silently, my body is yours. Accept the offering.

The chief priest put his hands upon her ankles and parted her legs. The warm air of the temple caressed the lips of her sex. Her breathing deepened, for now her secret flesh was open, offered to the calm gaze of the god. She felt his eyes moving over her body as if they were hands touching her.

The Lady Hunro came forward also and with her slender soft hands touched Naunakhte's parted thighs. She slipped one finger into the moist folds between the girl's legs, exploring, and nodded as she felt the slick dew upon her fingers. Aloud she said, 'The offering is ready. Let the rite be performed.'

Panhesi raised his hands to the god in prayer. In one

of them he held a phallus, made of ivory and carved with holy texts. It was a copy of the god's penis, splendid in size and shape, and at its base it was encircled by the god's hand. Panhesi turned to face Naunakhte and placed the tip of the ivory phallus between the petals of her sex.

Naunakhte's lips parted as she felt the cool hardness there. She let out a whispering moan. Hunro frowned, afraid that Naunakhte had cried out in pain, and quickly let her hand rest on the dark cushion of the girl's pubic hair. Her fingers found Naunakhte's clitoris and began delicately to stroke and tease it. She signalled Panhesi with her eyes.

The gentle touch of Hunro's fingers filled Naunakhte with bliss. She closed her eyes for a moment, whimpering with pleasure. Then the presence between her legs began to move. The cold hardness was pushing its way inside her. She opened her eyes and gazed up into the god's face, breathing hard. It was the god that possessed her; it was his penis that she felt. A sudden stab of pain made her cry out, but she did not struggle or try to pull away. She welcomed the pain, because the divine being whom she loved caused it. She lay very still, and then she felt herself opened, penetrated and pierced by the power of Amun.

Nothing had prepared her for this sensation; for the feeling of helplessness and delicious vulnerability. She cried out in terror and ecstasy. The Lady Hunro's fingers fluttered against her quivering clitoris and the thick hard ivory slid into her flinching sex, deeper and deeper, until the god's fist rested against her vulva.

'Amun,' Naunakhte moaned. 'Oh Lord Amun, I am yours.'

Panhesi bared his teeth and withdrew the ivory almost totally from the velvet folds of Naunakhte's body, then thrust it in as hard as he could. Naunakhte wailed as once again she felt the god within her. It did not matter that Panhesi held the implement, for she saw the image of the god above her and knew that the phallus that filled her was the Lord Amun's. She began to writhe on the cold stone altar. Her fingers clutched at the slippery surface and could find no purchase. Her round hips lifted and fell, and in rhythm with her sensual movements Panhesi drove the ivory phallus in and out of her. It gleamed with her juices and at its base the god's white fist was smeared with hymeneal blood.

Now Naunakhte knew what bliss her body had felt when in her dream the god had laid himself upon her and thrust his penis inside her. She felt that bliss now and cried aloud with the pleasure of it. Great waves of joy surged up in her, each one mightier than the last. Never had she felt such ecstasy. She gasped out the god's name, calling on him as her lover, and at last the glory that possessed her was so vast that she could bear no more. Her body arched up from the altar, every muscle tense, and her breasts and her parted thighs shuddered with the pulsing of the climax that rushed through her. Her sight darkened, as if the brilliance of the god's golden face was more than she could bear.

Then the ecstasy faded. The god's presence withdrew from her, leaving behind it only emptiness and a shadow of pain. She moaned and flung one arm across her face. She had desired to float away on that river of bliss, deep and wide as the Nile. She would follow the river to its source and never return to the world of men.

'Accept the offering, Lord Amun,' intoned Panhesi. He lifted the phallus towards the statue, turning it so that the torchlight gleamed on the pale juices and the dark stain of blood. Then he laid the phallus at the feet of the statue and bowed, his hands crossed on his breast.

Naunakhte only half felt herself lifted and carried away. She knew that she had been taken from the god, and she felt grief and great fatigue. When they laid her down on a couch in a darkened room she moaned and whispered the god's name.

'Hush, Naunakhte,' murmured the voice of the Lady Hunro. 'All will be well. It is the fading of the trance that you feel. Your responses are very delicate, my little golden flower. Do not fear, all will be well. In the morning you shall see the rite, and that will recover you.' Soft lips pressed against Naunakhte's. The Lady Hunro slipped her tongue into Naunakhte's unprotesting mouth and fondled her breasts, tugging at the swollen nipples with her artful fingers. Naunakhte moaned again as the echo of pleasure shimmered through her body.

'There,' whispered Hunro, 'you see that the pleasure goes on, Naunakhte. Now sleep. I shall see you at the rite, and there – ' She kissed Naunakhte again with lascivious skill ' – there, you shall serve me.'

She left Naunakhte in silence and darkness. The girl was exhausted, and felt sleep tugging at once at her eyelids. But she lifted her hands and prayed.

'Oh Lord Amun,' said Naunakhte into the stillness, 'make me your servant. Let me feel you within me each day as I did today.' Her voice trembled with fervour. 'Great god, I long to serve you. Make me the Hand of Amun.'

Chapter Four

*O*ne of the temple cats sat in the corner of the small half-lit room, its green-gold eyes narrowed superciliously. Watching human beings copulate bored it, and it objected to the space that they took up on a couch that rightfully belonged to cats. However, these humans appeared intent on their pointless game. After some time the cat stretched and yawned, then curled itself into a ball and fell asleep.

Panhesi snarled as he caught hold of Tiy by her copper hair. He dragged back her head and sank his teeth into her throat like a wild dog. She cried out and struggled, beating her hands helplessly against his back, then raking her nails down his smooth flanks. He yelped and flung himself upon her, holding her down with his entire weight.

'Give in, you bitch,' he gasped, breathless. Tiy squirmed beneath him, her pale skin sliding deliciously under his as she twisted and wriggled. 'Give in.'

'No.' Tiy got one hand free and dug her nails into Panhesi's shoulder, making him wince. The sensation of her body under his, struggling as helplessly as a captured animal, was as intoxicating as wine. She arched her back to rub her breasts against the bare smooth skin of his chest. The little nipples that tipped them were as dark and hard as rubies. She scratched him again and said, 'You'll have to force me.'

'If you don't submit,' Panhesi hissed, speaking slowly and clearly into her flushed excited face, 'I'll turn you over and cram my cock right up your tight little arse. That'll make you squeal.'

'You wouldn't dare!' squealed Tiy, as if he were buggering her already. 'You wouldn't –'

'No?' laughed Panhesi. He heaved himself off her for just long enough to grab her by one shoulder and one thigh, lift her bodily off the couch and turn her over. He dropped her on her face and she gasped and tried to crawl away from him, but he caught hold of her by her tight high buttocks and held her still. With one hand he picked up the small flask of oil that stood beside the couch and let a thin stream fall on to the little hollow at the top of Tiy's bottom crease. She moaned, and he rubbed the oil slowly down the crease and around the taut puckered hole of her anus.

'Ah,' Tiy moaned, as Panhesi slowly eased one finger deep inside her. She cried out as though her bowels were turning to molten lead. 'Oh Hathor, help me.'

'Beg,' hissed Panhesi, leaning over her. His middle finger was deeply buried in her anus, wriggling slowly to and fro. The tight muscles of her sphincter clenched convulsively and he shuddered with pleasure to think of that strong grasp clutching at his ravenous penis. 'Beg for me to do it to you.'

'Please,' whimpered Tiy, 'oh please, Panhesi, put your cock inside my arse. Now, now.'

'Not yet.' Panhesi thrust in another finger beside the first and with his left hand reached around to find one of Tiy's dangling breasts. They were small and pointed, like hanging figs. He caught one little teat in his hand and fondled it brutally, tugging at the stiff nipple until Tiy yelped like a whelping bitch. Panhesi squeezed and tugged at her breast and slid his fingers in and out of her quivering anus, listening with pleasure to her shuddering moans. His stiff cock rubbed against the soft flesh of her buttocks. At last he withdrew his fingers and with both hands pulled the cheeks of Tiy's arse wide apart and feasted his eyes on the dark glistening crease and the puckered trembling hole. He lodged the head of his cock against the delicate orifice and thrust with all his strength.

Tiy flung back her head and screamed aloud as his thick penis penetrated her anus. 'Yes,' she cried. 'Yes! Oh harder, harder.'

'Bitch,' grunted Panhesi, thrusting into her so vigorously that his taut testicles slapped against her sex with an audible noise. 'Bitch, bitch, bitch.'

'Harder,' Tiy responded, heaving her buttocks up towards him and rubbing furiously at her clitoris and labia. 'Harder. Oh yes, yes, yes.'

She was orgasming already, her whole body shuddering as her anus spasmed and jolted around Panhesi's invading penis. He growled like a beast and clutched her hips tightly, pulling her back to meet his lunges. The pressure of her tight rear hole on his swollen cock drove him half mad with pleasure. After only a few more strokes he came too, snarling and writhing as his seed pulsed into her.

For a moment he hung over her limp body, panting. Then he withdrew and flung himself down on the couch, one arm above his head. 'I needed that,' he said.

Tiy stretched elegantly and sat down beside him, her pale eyes gleaming. 'Why?'

Panhesi looked at her for a little while without speaking, weighing up her likely reaction. Then he said, 'Ten days now since that new girl came. You know I want her, Tiy. Seeing her each day at the rite is driving me mad.'

The skin of Tiy's face tautened with anger and her nostrils flared. 'Am I not enough for you, then?' she demanded.

'Oh, come now.' Panhesi's voice was heavy with irony. 'Do I pretend that you stay faithful to me when I am away from the temple? You need regular servicing,

Lady Tiy. I heard that the last time I was gone three of the medjay took you at once. Have I made any trouble? And do you begrudge me a flash of desire for this new girl? By Seth, every morning I see her bending over to lick the Lady Hunro between her legs. I can see the whole of her woman's place, those pretty pink lips and that little tight hole. The only thing that has been in there is the god's ivory, Tiy, is that not so?'

Tiy had fallen silent when Panhesi referred in his offhand way to her exploits with the medjay. Now she looked thoughtful for a moment. At last she said, 'Nobody believes that Naunakhte has lain with any man.'

'By all the gods,' whispered Panhesi, 'I would like to have her. Just once, to push my cock up inside that tight little sheath and hear her cry out. She always looks so transparent, as if the god has entered into her.'

'The god!' exclaimed Tiy with scorn. 'You are as bad as Naunakhte. Do you really believe that she is the chosen of Amun?'

Panhesi looked uncomfortable. 'She bears his mark.'

Tiy pushed her lover back on to the couch and straddled him, holding his wrists to the linen. 'Listen to me, Panhesi,' she said, quick and low. 'Within the year the Lady Hunro will retire and adopt her successor. If she chooses Naunakhte, where then is your chance of succeeding Merybast?'

Doubt narrowed Panhesi's eyes. 'Do you really think she would choose Naunakhte?'

'Choose her? She is besotted with her. She talks to nobody else. Who serves her each morning at the rite? She used to say that she could wish for no tongue, for no hands other than mine. Now it is all Naunakhte. That village girl, that whore's misbegotten bastard daughter, means to take my place!' Tiy's voice dropped to a low purr. Her pale eyes gleamed as bright as the temple cat's. 'And if she takes my place, Panhesi, where does that leave you?'

For a moment Panhesi stared, frowning into Tiy's

49

face. Then he made an irritated gesture, pulled his wrists free of her grip and rolled over so that she was underneath him. With one hand he caught hold of her little pointed chin. 'Now then,' he said, changing the subject, 'about those three medjay. Is it true?'

Tiy smiled and raised her golden brows. With one hand she caressed the smooth skin of Panhesi's shaven head. 'What if it is?' she asked teasingly.

'What, three at once?' demanded Panhesi. 'Is it possible?'

Tiy wriggled lasciviously against him and fluttered her eyelashes. 'In fact,' she admitted in a little regretful voice, 'only two of them actually had me. The third one had one of the others. One in my sheath, one in my anus, and one of them buggering his friend while he did it to me.'

Panhesi looked unconvinced. 'Did you like it?'

'I screamed,' said Tiy, smugly. 'So did they.'

Her little hand slid down beneath Panhesi's body and found his slack resting penis. She grasped it gently and began to rub and tug. Panhesi shook his head and said, 'You deserve to be the Hand of God, Tiy. No woman I have ever known wants it as much as you do. You would give a dead man an erection.'

Her fingers tightened on his penis, making him wince. 'You are right,' she said. 'But if that is to be, we will have to be rid of Naunakhte.'

'Be rid of her?' Panhesi repeated cautiously. 'What do you mean?'

Tiy did not answer, but wriggled further down beneath Panhesi's body and began to kiss his stiffening phallus. He closed his eyes and breathed shallowly as her lips travelled up the length of the hardening shaft. When she reached the tip she extended her pink pointed tongue and began to swirl saliva across the thickening glans. Panhesi let out a soft, 'Ah,' as she flickered her tongue against the little eye at the very tip, then parted her lips and allowed his penis to penetrate her mouth.

She was skilled, and could so relax the muscles of her

50

throat that she could take the whole of his erection. He gasped and took hold of her hair, thrusting gently as he reached full hardness in the warm haven of her mouth. Tiy continued to suck him, flickering her tongue around his hot shaft and running her lips up and down, up and down, until Panhesi began to grunt and heave his hips towards her. Then, without warning, she pulled away.

'You little tease!' Panhesi exclaimed, reaching for her.

'If you want me,' hissed Tiy, 'you have to promise to help me get rid of Naunakhte.'

Her expression of contained malice made him shiver. She looked as beautiful and dangerous as a cat ready to pounce upon a mouse. He could almost sense the rippling of her fur, and as she watched him her green eyes darkened. He desired her desperately, but his uncertainty showed in his face. Tiy gave a little half smile and said, 'Of course, we could arrange things so that you could have her.'

Panhesi's eyes opened wide. Tiy caressed his aching penis and he found himself thinking of Naunakhte, of her tranquil, languid beauty, of the rapt adoration with which she gazed upon the god's statue. It was he who had taken her virginity with the god's ivory, and even then she had never once looked at him, never met his eyes. He wanted to hold her down and force her to notice him. She would pay attention soon enough when he pushed his stiff penis deep into that lovely body; that body that had never known a man.

'You say I can have her?' he asked, still cautious.

Tiy crouched beside him, her eyes gleaming. 'I promise,' she said.

Slowly Panhesi sat up. His erect penis stood up from his loins, stiff and eager. 'Suck me,' he said. 'I will help you.'

Obediently Tiy stooped down and drew his penis into her mouth. She sucked diligently and fondled with her little hands between his legs. She cupped and caressed his shaven balls and explored the naked crevices that on most men were hidden by hair. Her hands ran again

51

and again over his smooth oiled skin. He shuddered as she touched him and her warm lips slid over his hard penis, gripping him as tightly as her sex.

He wanted to come in her mouth, but before he was ready she let go of him and sat up. 'Fuck me,' she said, straddling him and offering her wet eager sex to his phallus. 'Fuck me, Panhesi. Make me scream. I will tell you about Naunakhte while you do it.'

She sank down on to him. As his thick shaft penetrated her she leant back, arching her spine until her breasts pointed towards the ceiling. Panhesi could not resist the appeal of her tight nipples, small as rosebuds. He leant forward and sucked greedily – first at one hard point, then at the other. Tiy rested her hands on his thighs and groaned, then wriggled her hips, clutching at him with the muscles of her vagina. He grunted with surprised pleasure.

'I have tried ... magic,' gasped Tiy, lifting her hips and then lowering them to impale herself again on Panhesi's avid cock. 'I have made spells to rob her of her beauty and make her sick. But they have not worked. The other girls begin to think that Amun himself protects her. But I know it is not so. She is a fool.'

She lifted and fell again, writhing with lewd pleasure as Panhesi's thick penis moved within her sex. He suckled and lapped at her swollen nipples, only half hearing her words. The sensation of her tight sheath milking his cock was so delicious that he could barely understand her.

'Naunakhte,' Tiy went on, licking her lips, 'Naunakhte is in love with the god. You see her face at the rite, Panhesi. She is enamoured of Amun himself! That way lies her downfall.'

'How?' gasped Panhesi. 'How?'

'Fuck me,' hissed Tiy, clutching at the nape of his neck and squirming on his deep-buried cock. 'I'll tell you if you fuck me.'

'Tease,' Panhesi hissed. 'Little bitch.' He caught her around her waist and stood up, carrying her with him, his penis still deeply imbedded in her quivering flesh. 'Tell me what you mean, you little bitch.' And he laid her down across the couch and wrapped her legs around his waist. Her shoulders hung off the couch, her arms were flung wide apart, and her head dangled limply, exposing her naked throat. Panhesi growled with pleasure and plunged his rampant phallus into her as hard as he could. His body struck hers like a blow. 'Tell,' he demanded, grasping her breasts as he shafted her. 'Tell me.'

Slowly the tale came out, broken by Tiy's groans of pleasure as his cock surged to and fro deep inside her. 'She has taken to ... leaving our rooms at night. Last night I followed her. Oh yes, Panhesi, yes, take me! Oh, that's so good!'

'Tell,' said Panhesi again, screwing his cock violently into Tiy's shuddering body.

'She went ... to the sanctuary. The guards were asleep. She went in and I followed her. I saw her touch the statue.'

Panhesi's shocked reaction broke the rhythm of his thrusts and Tiy grasped impatiently at his buttocks and pulled him deeper inside her. 'Don't stop. Fuck me, fuck me. She – ah, god – she took the god's phallus in her mouth. I saw her.'

'Sacrilege,' said Panhesi between his teeth. 'Sacrilege.' He closed his eyes and imagined walking into the temple and finding Naunakhte there, on her knees before the statue, her full lips parted to caress the great golden penis. He would come up behind her, kneel behind her, pull back her arms and penetrate her with his stiff cock before she could prevent him. Her cries would be smothered by the massive phallus crammed into her mouth. She would be at his mercy and he would screw her until she was limp as a rag. He would be her master, and not the god Amun.

'Go there,' hissed Tiy. 'Go there tonight, Panhesi. Take her in the act.'

'Yes,' Panhesi gasped. 'Yes, I will. I will take her, and then I will take her again.'

Tiy closed her eyes and let out a wild cry as her climax began. 'Sacrilege!' she screamed, as her vagina pulsed hotly around Panhesi's plunging penis. 'She will die for it. Ah, I am coming!'

Panhesi gave a final, desperate thrust, as if he would bury himself entirely within Tiy's twitching body. As the sensations of orgasm seized him and the semen spurted from his cock he heard Tiy's words and felt a shudder of delicious horror, mingled with his pleasure and heightening it, so that white sparks burst behind his eyes. Never had his climax come upon him with such strength.

After a moment he pulled Tiy up and shook her. She hung limply from his hands, sighing. When she opened her eyes her lids were heavy with satisfaction. Smiling her contained, cat-like smile, she said, 'It aroused you to think of her death.'

'No,' protested Panhesi, 'it did not.' But he knew he was lying.

That night Naunakhte waited, as had become her custom, until all the women of the temple were asleep. Then she got to her feet, moving like someone who walks in dreams, and went to the door.

She lived for these moments, when she was alone with only the presence of the god for company. During the day Tiy made her life miserable, constantly harping on about her birth and upbringing and making sure that none of the other girls in the temple were her friends for long. Naunakhte wished that she might ask the Lady Hunro whether what Tiy said was true, but she did not dare. Hunro clearly believed that Naunakhte's father was Rameses, and Naunakhte was afraid that she might give offence if she seemed to doubt what she had been told. So she bore Tiy's insults quietly, although they stung her like wasps.

Neferure had also told her, in muffled, secret whispers, that Tiy had tried to use magic against her to harm her or mar her beauty. The knowledge of Tiy's hatred and malice was with her always. It was like living in a house where scorpions bred beneath the floor.

But although she was lonely and unhappy she could not leave the temple, for the god had called her. His rite gave meaning to her existence. Naunakhte understood her part well. Each morning she aroused the Lady Hunro to receive the embrace of Amun. She was growing to love her mistress, and it flattered her that Hunro thought that her touch inspired desire, but even so it made her discontented to watch the rite. When she saw the high priestess moaning with bliss as she received the god's penis within her, all that Naunakhte could think of was how much she longed to be in Hunro's place.

Now, dressed only in her short simple kilt, Naunakhte moved through the temple complex like a shadow. Her hair was plaited behind her head and her eyes were unpainted. She wore no jewels except for the enamelled arm-ring that concealed the mark of the god, and whenever a servant or a medjay saw her he took her for a lowly serving maid, perhaps some captain's concubine on her way to attend her master.

Everywhere was quiet and still. The many servants of the temple were asleep, laid on pallets in corridors and corners. In a distant corner of the precinct, raised in a high tower, the watcher of the stars was waking, waiting to give the command which would rouse the god's people to perform the dawn rite. But the watcher's tower was far from where Naunakhte walked, silent on her bare feet.

She stood before the great doors of the god's sanctuary. As always, she stopped before them. For long moments she stood still, listening for the voice of the god. Every night she listened in case this time he should deny her, for in her heart of hearts she knew that what she did was wrong. But tonight, as before, she believed that she heard his voice, no more than a whispering murmur: *Naunakhte, come to me.*

The two medjay who kept the doors were asleep in their cubicles, their spears propped beside them. They did not hear when she silently coaxed back the great bolts and opened the door just enough to creep through. She pushed the door closed behind her and drew a deep breath as she beheld the face of her immortal beloved.

The sanctuary was dark, lit only by the moonlight filtering through the row of small single windows just beneath the roof. Within its cavernous shadows the image of the god gleamed as if it were lit from within. His calm, serene face looked down on Naunakhte as she approached him, and she thought his great dark eyes met hers with a look of tenderness.

'Oh Lord Amun,' Naunakhte whispered, 'I have come again to serve you. Accept my worship, great god.'

The statue towered above her, cold and impassive. She stepped up on to the pedestal and knelt before Amun, preparing to perform her own personal ritual of adoration, the rite which would make the god real for her.

First she kissed the feet of the statue. They were cunningly made, with every detail shown, even the tensing of the muscle in the arch of the foot, as if the god was ready to step down off the pedestal into the world of men. Her lips caressed the cold metal of the ankle, while her hands fondled the god's strong slender calves. She closed her eyes and began to tremble, because when she breathed she smelt the perfume of the god, the scent of divinity. That delicious fragrance permeated her limbs. Her lips were soft and heavy with longing and her breasts ached with desire. She took slow, shallow breaths, and the trance of the god began to fall upon her. Her eyelids fluttered over her half-closed eyes. Her pupils were wide and black.

She set her lips to the god's golden knees and with her hands explored the tender hollows behind them. Her fingers probed and stroked, delicate and irresistible.

As she touched the statue she felt it coming alive. Where her hands moved, there the golden skin flushed and became warm with the pulsing of divine blood. Metal became flesh and flesh throbbed with life. She kissed the god's strong thighs and sensed his skin yielding to the pressure of her lips.

Now Amun's phallus reared up before her, grasped firmly in his powerful fist. Naunakhte lifted herself up on her knees and let her head fall back. Her lips parted and she gave a little moan of anticipation. The points of her round breasts were tight and hard with longing. She swayed her body forward so that her erect nipples chafed against the god's golden thighs, and she spread her legs so that she could rub her body against his strong calves. She pressed her face against the golden penis, smooth metal against smooth skin, sensing its potency and power. Then, very slowly, she extended her tongue and licked the god's phallus from the root to the tip.

To Naunakhte it seemed that as her tongue slid along that splendid length, Amun's penis became warm and real, pounding with the hot blood that stiffened it. The finely traced veins quivered beneath her lips, the skin was soft as down and the flesh beneath it hard as ebony. Above her she sensed the god breathing, his mighty chest lifting and falling as he took pleasure in what she did for him. Her body was soft with desire. She pressed her mound of love close against the god's legs and squirmed up and down like a beast, smearing the glittering gold with her juices. Then she clutched the god's muscular buttocks in her hands and opened her mouth wide.

The god's phallus slid between her lips, filling her mouth. She moaned as she licked and sucked. Her own pleasure mingled in her mind with the pleasure of the god, and she trembled as if a thousand fluttering wings brushed against her flesh from head to heel.

Her moment was coming; that moment when the god would grasp her with inexorable power and make her his. She uttered a smothered cry and pressed her body more tightly against the god. Her lips tingled and stung and the points of her breasts felt ready to burst.

Then, without warning, hands seized her arms and pulled them behind her. At once the hot pulsing penis in her mouth became cold metal as she woke from her erotic trance. She gasped in shock and tried to scream, but the god's golden phallus gagged her and kept her silent.

One of the hands reached down to lift her kilt, then thrust between her legs and roughly explored her warm moistness. Two fingers thrust into her vagina, making her gasp. A voice hissed in her ear, 'You are ready for me.'

With a desperate wrench Naunakhte pulled free of the clutching hands. She writhed her head away from the statue of the god and twisted up to her feet, then flung herself towards the door. But a strong hand caught her arm and swung her around. She looked into the face of Panhesi, the chief priest.

'Sacrilege,' said Panhesi softly. 'Sacrilege, Naunakhte. This is a killing offence.'

Naunakhte could not speak for fear. She knew that what Panhesi said was true.

'Do you know the punishment for sacrilege?' Panhesi's voice was still soft, but his eyes glittered like black jewels and his penis was erect, standing up thick and stiff beneath the white linen of his kilt. 'Not just death, Naunakhte, but death for ever. You will be tied down to the desert sand and they will heap hot coals upon you until you are burned to ashes. There will be nothing left of you to enjoy the afterlife. Your shade will wander the earth for ever, homeless and weeping.'

His words conjured up an image of such horror that Naunakhte let out a little wail of fear. Her foster father Ammenakht and his men had worked all their lives to make tombs in which the bodies of Pharaoh and his nobles might be preserved to live again after death. Now Panhesi promised her a death that was permanent, irrevocable, terrifying. She tugged helplessly against his clutching hand and moaned, 'The god called me. He called me.'

'How dare you?' demanded Panhesi. 'How dare you set yourself above the god's wife, the Hand of Amun? Who are you to presume?'

'Please,' Naunakhte whimpered, 'let me go.'

There was a silence. Panhesi's face changed. His expression became greedy and his fingers dug into the flesh of her arm. With his other hand he reached out and took hold of her breast, ignoring her gasp of shock. 'Perhaps I will let you go,' he said softly. 'Submit to me, Naunakhte. Let me have you.'

'What?' Naunakhte could hardly believe what he said. Was he not Tiy's lover? Why should he want her?

'Submit,' said Panhesi again. He pushed his kilt aside and revealed his erect penis. Like all priests he was pale, and the thick stiff rod of flesh was white as a fish's belly and tipped with angry scarlet like a carbuncle. It rose proudly from naked shaven testicles.

The sight of it horrified Naunakhte. 'No,' she moaned, writhing.

'You are as wet as the Nile,' hissed Panhesi. 'Kneel down, Naunakhte, put that peach-like arse of yours in the air. My cock will slip into you so easily, you will love it. I will fuck you better than ever that statue did.'

His crude words sounded in her brain like brazen gongs. They filled her with confusion and sudden furious anger. She beat at him with her fists, shouting, 'No, no! You are the sacrilegious one, not me. You are as bad as Tiy. This is all her doing. I will never submit to you!'

'Be silent,' he hissed, but it was too late. The doors were open and the medjay were running in, spears in their hands, wild eyed. Panhesi cursed and tugged down his kilt. 'Medjay!' he snapped, in a voice of cold command. 'Arrest this woman!'

The medjay ran to Naunakhte and caught hold of her, their strong hands hard on her arms. She stood shuddering, staring at Panhesi with disbelieving fear. He ran his hand over his shaven scalp and said, 'I found her in the act of sacrilege. She dared to . . . approach the statue of the god. Take her to the prison. Tomorrow she will suffer the punishment.'

'I have done nothing wrong,' Naunakhte protested, though she knew it was hopeless.

Panhesi took a step towards her. She tried to move away, but the medjay held her tightly. The chief priest looked into her face for a long moment, then put his hands on her body and began to run them over her golden skin. She closed her eyes, trying not to feel him. He weighed her breasts, pinched her nipples between finger and thumb, squeezed her slender ribs, lifted her kilt and probed between her legs. Naunakhte turned her head away from him, but she could not restrain a helpless moan as his fingers parted the lips of her sex, found and titillated her erect clitoris, then slid deep into the moist well of her sheath.

'A whore,' he said at last, as if his lewd fondling had been some sort of judicial examination. He lifted his fingers to his nose, looked at the shine of her juices upon them, then smelt them voluptuously. 'She is ready to serve the god with her body. She can have no defence. I found her with her mouth upon his penis.'

The medjay gasped as if they had been struck and stared at Naunakhte in horror. One of them made the sign against evil. Panhesi smiled, then said again, 'Take her away. In the morning she will die.'

Without a word the medjay hustled her towards the door of the sanctuary. She strained to look over her shoulder, praying silently to the god beneath her breath, 'Amun, Amun, if you love me, help me now.' But the god's golden face was still and his voice was silent.

Outside the door the guards glanced at each other. Like many medjay, they were both big men, dark-skinned and Nubian looking, dressed in short white kilts with fringes of coloured wool. The whites of their eyes shone in the gloom. The taller of them pushed his hand through his tight curly hair and said in a low voice, 'The prison?'

'You heard what Panhesi said, Menneb,' said the other.

'Come on, then.' The one called Menneb looked at Naunakhte as if she were a dangerous snake. 'Sacrilege,' he whispered, shaking his head. 'By the Hand of Amun, she is a bold one. In the sanctuary!'

'I didn't – ' Naunakhte began, but the medjay raised his hand threateningly.

'Don't you say a word,' he said. 'You'll put a spell on us. Come on, Hori. Don't listen to her.'

Menneb and Hori towed her through the dark passageways of the temple. At first she struggled, but they were strong and pitiless, and after a while she went where they guided her. They left the temple proper and emerged into the open air. Behind them the bulk of the hypostyle hall reared up against the dark-blue sky, black against the brilliant stars. A little way away stood a cluster of low buildings – granaries for the temple's riches of food and dormitories for its people – and beyond them was the precinct wall, twenty feet high and smooth as glass.

Above Naunakhte the stars burned like hanging lanterns. She looked up at the sky and remembered how not twelve days since she had gazed up into that infinity of light and begged for guidance. The god had called her and accepted her worship, but now it seemed that he had abandoned her. She turned her head away from the brilliance of the stars, smothered with agony at Amun's betrayal of her trust.

The medjay had stopped. She realised that they were speaking to each other over her head, talking in low voices. Hori said to Menneb, 'I just think it's a shame, that's all.'

'It's the law,' said Menneb. 'That's the punishment.'

'But to burn her? There'll be nothing left. If they just killed her with the noose, at least the embalmers could have some fun with her body.'

Their words filled Naunakhte with horror and the fear of death. She looked wildly from one dark face to the other and burst out, 'Please, don't take me to the prison! Panhesi only wants to get rid of me to please the Lady Tiy. It's all her doing; she hates me.'

'The Lady Tiy?' said Menneb, slowly.

'She hates me,' Naunakhte repeated desperately, 'because I am the favourite of the Lady Hunro. She wants Panhesi to kill me. Please, please, let me go.'

There was a silence. Then Menneb said quietly to Hori, 'Do you remember the Lady Tiy, Hori? That copper-haired she-jackal? She sucked us dry and then had us beaten for her pleasure. I swear I still have the scars.'

'How could I forget her?' said Hori dryly. 'You have scars on your back, Menneb. I have them in another place altogether. She bit me.' He caught Naunakhte's face in his hand and looked down into her eyes. 'Are you lying to us, little witch?'

'No,' Naunakhte insisted. 'No, I swear by the god.'

'You don't care much for the god,' said Menneb, 'if what Panhesi said was true.'

I do care for him, Naunakhte thought, more than anything in the world. But how could the Lord Amun have allowed this to happen to her? Why had he not intervened? He must have forsaken her.

Hori stroked his hand down Naunakhte's face, then muttered to Menneb, 'She's a slippery little thing. She could have got away from us. She could pay us, Menneb.'

'Pay you?' Naunakhte repeated faintly. 'I have nothing.'

Menneb's voice was like the purr of a lion. 'Pay us with your lips, little witch. Do for us what you did for the god.'

Naunakhte's stomach lurched with understanding. She stood very still, breathing shallowly, her eyes running up and down the glossy bodies of the medjay who held her arms. They were handsome, these two big men, and they reminded her of Psaro. How she had longed to lie with Psaro, to take his penis in her hands! If the god would not save her, then she must save herself.

'If you release me,' she said steadily, 'I will do what you wish.'

For a moment the medjay spoke with their eyes. Then Hori tugged at her arm. 'Over here, in the shadow of the gateway. Come quickly.'

She followed them into the gloom. Hori said, 'Me first,' and Menneb nodded and turned to keep watch, leaning on his long spear like a statue. Hori propped his spear against the wall, grinned at Naunakhte and opened his kilt. 'On your knees, little witch,' he said.

Obediently Naunakhte dropped to her knees. In the darkness she could barely see Hori's nakedness, but she could smell him. He smelt musky and strong, of dry sweat and cheap scent and maleness. The smell lodged in her throat; she could hardly swallow. Where was the erotic exaltation that filled her when she knelt before the god? Now she was faced with reality, without even a trance to protect her.

'Hold it,' hissed Hori. 'Suck it, little witch. Suck it.'

Naunakhte was trembling. She did not know if fear or excitement were stronger in her. She put her hands on the medjay's thighs. They were sturdy as pillars, warm and smooth. Where they joined there was a mat of curling hair, strong and coarse, and then a soft dangling pouch, wrinkled and heavy, laden with two swollen eggs of flesh that filled her exploring hand. This was a real man; flesh and blood, lust and desire. Naunakhte's hand moved up from the hanging purse of Hori's testicles and found his penis.

It was soft and thick and long, and as she touched it it lurched against her hand so that she gasped. She wrapped her fingers around it and shivered to feel it actually growing, swelling and changing shape; becoming as stiff and strong as the phallus of Amun's statue. The starlight gleamed from its glossy head. Shaking with anticipation, Naunakhte leant forward and opened her mouth.

At once Hori caught hold of her head with both his big hands and thrust hard. She gagged, half choked by the thick shaft of his erect penis. The taste of him overwhelmed her. She staggered and would have fallen, but his hands were wrapped in her thick hair and he held her up as he slid his cock in and out of her slack unprotesting lips.

Naunakhte moaned, overcome with pleasure and horror. She licked with her tongue at the great glossy head of Hori's penis and he grunted and pushed harder into her mouth. Something moved behind her, and then Menneb's hands were on her breasts. He clutched at them, squeezing them like fruit, and her nipples were trapped between his strong fingers. Naunakhte began to pant in rhythm with Hori's thrusts, utterly consumed by the delicious sensation of his penis moving between her lips. When Menneb released one of her breasts and reached down to push his hand between her slack thighs she let out a little whimpering cry of disbelief. He found her clitoris and began to stroke and tease it as his fingers pinched and pulled at her tormented nipples. A great wave of pleasure flowed from Naunakhte's loins through her whole body. She tensed, every muscle taut and straining, her lips helplessly parted, and as she shook with the onrush of her climax Hori's fingers knotted in her hair and his penis shuddered in her mouth and gushed his hot seed into her open throat.

She slumped backward, limp and reeling. Menneb laughed and pushed her to the ground, then straddled her shoulders with his strong thighs. 'Open your eyes, witch,' he grunted. 'Look up.'

Naunakhte forced herself to lift her heavy eyelids. She saw Menneb's penis above her, not a foot from her face. He was masturbating, his strong hand sliding quickly up and down the rigid shaft. 'Look,' Menneb gasped, rubbing faster and faster. 'Look, look, look.'

She looked, riveted. He groaned with pleasure and

the rough hairy pouch of his balls rubbed against her chin. His thighs tightened on her face and as her mouth opened in a gasp of protest the white semen spurted from the tip of his jerking penis and fell on to her lips, her cheeks, and her eyelids. She moaned and lay still.

After a moment Menneb stood up, still panting. He glanced at Hori and muttered, 'What now?'

'We have to get her out of here,' whispered Hori. 'We can't climb the wall. Quick, if we go now we may find the tradesmen's gate unguarded.'

They lifted Naunakhte to her feet and half carried her between them through the dark buildings, going at a stealthy run. She was dazed with pleasure and shock and hardly knew where she was. After an indeterminate time they stopped by a tiny gate in the wall. Menneb glanced anxiously from side to side, then opened the gate. The hinges squealed and both of the medjay hissed with fear.

'Out you go,' said Hori, gesturing at the open gate. 'Go on, run.'

'But – ' Naunakhte said. How could she leave? Where would she go?

'Go on, if you value your skin,' hissed Menneb. 'It'll be dawn soon, and then Panhesi will be sending for you. Do you want him to burn you alive? Run!'

The name of Panhesi reminded her of Tiy, and of her fear. She pulled free of the medjays' hands and ran through the gate. They closed it silently behind her. She stood on the sands of the desert, trembling beneath the stars. The temple precinct was shut. There was no way back for her now.

Chapter Five

*I*n the dark before dawn Naunakhte staggered away from the temple of Amun. The harsh desert sand scraped her bare feet and the night wind was cold, so that she actually shivered and wrapped her arms around herself. Once only she stopped to look back at the temple. Then her eyes filled with tears and she put her hand over her face and turned away.

She was forsaken. The god had abandoned her. All her belief of Amun's desire, and her hopes and ambitions to succeed the Lady Hunro, now seemed like so many dreams. The only thing that seemed real was Tiy's hatred. That malign resentment had driven her out, and if she was captured she knew that Tiy would seek her death. Everything was turned to poison. She was sure now that Tiy was right to call her a bastard, misbegotten child of a whore and a traitor. If she had been Pharaoh's true-born daughter, why would her fate have been so bitter? The gods had been playing with her as adults play with children, calling her from her village to the temple and dangling a life of joy before her, only to pull it away from her as if it had never been.

So she was outcast. Where could she go? She clambered up on to a great red rock and looked out across the valley of the Nile.

On her right lay the temple precinct. On her left was Waset, a dark smudge speckled with lights like the marsh-lights of evil spirits. Naunakhte had never been to Waset, but her foster father had often told her of its wickedness and advised her to avoid it. A huge city, a crowded city, street after street of cramped mud-brick houses and tawdry bazaars, narrow alleys filled with the dung of people and beasts, taverns where men grew drunk on beer and swore over the gaming boards and fornicated with prostitutes. What would become of her if she went there?

Beyond the city the banks of the river were studded with great houses – the villas of the rich and noble. Naunakhte knew she was beautiful. Perhaps if she could find her way to one of those houses, a nobleman might desire her as his concubine. Could she be safe there, within the walls of the women's rooms?

For a moment she stared into the darkness, tense with hope. Then she laughed bitterly and shook her head. She was dressed like a servant in a plain white kilt, with no perfume, no jewels, no wig, no eye paint. Who would desire her as she was? And even if she could find herself a nobleman, he would hand her over to the temple authorities as soon as they sought her.

In the east a faint streak of grey turned to gold. Naunakhte looked at the sky and shuddered. Within the temple the watcher of the stars would be striking the little bell that called the servants of the god to the rite. Soon her absence would be noticed and they would begin to hunt for her. She must hide herself. But where?

As if from nowhere the answer came to her. 'Of course!' she cried, and she leapt down off the rock and began to run across the shifting sands towards the green lands that bordered the Nile. 'Home. I will go home!'

Her foster mother would already be up, busy making the flat bread for the family to eat that day. The children would be running about, getting underfoot, and Harshire would be lying still in bed, waiting for his mother to bring her first-born son something to make his waking more pleasant. Naunakhte heard the bustle of the house, the sounds from the neighbours, the shouts of the men meeting in the main street as they went up the hill towards the valley of the tombs. Her feet flew across the sand.

When she reached the green farmlands she stopped, her breath heaving, and glanced from side to side. There, a little way away across the flat green valley, was the pier where the Nile ferry tied up. It was on this side of the river, waiting for its first load of passengers. Naunakhte brushed her hands down her kilt, cleaning off the stains of sand as best she could, and smoothed her hair. As she walked on she passed a channel carrying water from the Nile to irrigate the fields. She held her cupped hands in the stream of water and splashed her face, trying to wash away the remnants of Menneb's semen.

As the sky brightened to pink she approached the ferry. She felt lighthearted, as if she had been released from a prison. Soon she would be home. How amazed her parents would be to see her! They would understand that she had done nothing wrong and hide her, even if the medjay came to seek her. The village was such a warren that nobody could find someone there who wanted to remain hidden.

She stood for a moment under a stand of date palms, breathing deeply. The ferry lay before her. Its owner was leaning on his paddle and chatting idly to one of his passengers, an old man with a wrinkled shrunken belly that drooped over the waistband of his kilt. The ferryman said something that made the old man laugh, and Naunakhte giggled behind her hand at the way the wrinkled skin shook.

Then the ferryman stood up straighter and pointed, frowning, at a man who ran swiftly along the riverbank path towards his boat. Naunakhte shivered and drew back behind the tree, for the running man was a medjay, a young athletic man carrying a naked sword.

'Amenhotep!' called the medjay. 'News from the temple.'

'What news?' replied the ferryman.

'A prisoner has escaped,' panted the medjay. 'A girl, guilty of sacrilege. Her name is Naunakhte. She is tall and slender and she has a mark on her left arm, the god's mark, a phallus. If you find her bring her to the temple; there is a reward. You have not seen her, have you?'

The ferryman shook his head mutely.

'Praise Amun,' said the medjay. 'Her home was over the river, and I was afraid that she might have crossed already. Well, if you see her, Amenhotep, you know where to come.'

He turned and hurried away, sword in hand. The ferryman and his passenger watched him go, then fell into eager conversation. Naunakhte pressed her hands over her mouth, ready to weep with fear and frustration. But weeping would not help her. She clenched her fists and set her jaw, then slipped away down the riverbank. The medjay had gone away from the city, so she went towards it. Perhaps she might find a fisherman on the bank who would be prepared to take her across. She could not cross the Nile without a boat; the crocodiles would take her before she was a stone's throw from land.

She was too late; the fishermen were already out on the river, casting their nets to take the fish as they rose in the dawn. Naunakhte barely stopped herself from cursing in the name of Seth. She glanced behind her at the looming mass of the temple, and as she set her eyes on it she heard the trumpets.

They had raised the alarm now in full. The whole might of the temple would be raised against her, pursuing her as jackals pursue an antelope. She gave a gasp of fear and began to run towards the city. Perhaps she might be able to hide herself there, for a little while, just until it was safe to cross the river.

A little further down the bank there was another ferry

station. The sun had risen now and the station was busy, thronged with people waiting for the boat. They were chattering and laughing together. The ferry was approaching, gliding over the surface of the glittering river like a swan in the golden light. There were several passengers on board. The ferry drew into the bank and the passengers began to disembark.

The last of them caught Naunakhte's eye, distracted as she was. It was a man, dressed in a fine white pleated kilt with a heavy fringe of gold bullion. His sandals were bound with gold and studded with jewels, and they flashed as he jumped down from the boat. A great collar of gold and faience lay around his neck and broad gold arm-rings clasped his muscular wrists. His wig was in the latest style, plaited and parted and drawn away from his high brow with strands of gold filigree, and he wore a long sword on a baldric made from the skin of a leopard. A cloak of scarlet wool hung behind him, embroidered with blue and gold. He was neither young nor old, but in the prime of manhood, carrying perhaps 30 years on his broad, tanned shoulders. His face was shaven smooth as a woman's and his eyes were painted with grey antimony. He glittered with splendour among the peasants like a drake among dowdy ducks.

Naunakhte could not help wondering what a young nobleman was doing on the Nile ferry at such a time in the morning. Returning from an assignation, perhaps? What a paragon his mistress must be, like a lily-flower floating upon clear water. For a moment her anxious mind relaxed, filled with the memory of the love songs that the village boys and girls sang to each other.

The man had been chatting to the ferryman and one of the waiting passengers. Now he had finished his talk, and he nodded politely and turned towards the city. The queue of people began to crowd towards the ferry. Naunakhte moved closer, then hesitated, biting her lip and wondering whether news of her had come so far.

She had been running fast: could she have outstripped the medjay messengers?

It was worth a try. She pursed her lips and whistled, trying to look as if she had not a care in the world, then walked towards the ferry. The crowd opened to admit her, taking no notice. The river was before her, the boat waiting.

Then she heard two of the passengers talking together. They were men, dressed in the rough loincloths of manual workers. Dirt and dust was ingrained beneath their nails. One of them said to the other, 'I hope I find her. They say the reward is enough to make you rich for life!'

'They say she's beautiful, too,' said his friend. 'Catch her first, screw her until you're tired of her, and then sell her to the priests. You can bet that all of them will get between her legs before they send her to punishment.'

'Too right,' said the first. 'Priests are all the same.'

A cold fist of fear grasped Naunakhte's belly, squeezing until she could barely breathe. She stopped walking and the crowd pressed in behind her, cursing her. With a whimper of terror she pushed her way free of them, then flung back her hair and turned towards the city.

As she walked a figure stepped in front of her, so suddenly that she could not stop. They collided, and strong hands caught her arms. She struggled and tried to pull away, but she could not free herself. Lifting her eyes, she found herself looking into the face of the young nobleman. He was nearly a head taller than she, and his shoulders and his naked chest were broad and strong. He looked as powerful as a panther.

He smiled at her, showing teeth that were sharp and white. 'Well, now,' he said, 'what have we here?'

His fierce face terrified her. She drew breath to scream. Quick as flickering flame he hissed, 'If you scream, I will denounce you to the medjay!'

Naunakhte fell silent, staring at him and shaking with terror. His sharp smile broadened as he saw that his

71

threat was effective. 'Well, then,' he said in satisfied tones, 'now I know who you are.'

A few hopeless tugs proved to Naunakhte that his hands were as strong as they looked. She closed her eyes as sobs of despair rose up in her throat and choked her.

'Let us check,' said the voice, and one of the strong hands shifted the ring on Naunakhte's left arm to reveal the mark of the god. Her captor drew in a long breath. 'Well,' he said again, 'what a valuable object I have in my hands. What shall I do with it?'

Naunakhte forced away her tears and looked up. She could not free herself, but she could plead. She looked into the man's painted eyes, concentrating. His irises were pale brown – an unusual colour for Egypt. 'Please,' Naunakhte whispered, 'don't take me to the temple. Let me run away to Waset. Please.'

'To Waset?' Her captor looked as if he would laugh.

'I will hide there. Please, let me go.'

Now he did laugh, throwing back his head with abandon. 'Hide in Waset? A girl like you wouldn't get through the gates in safety. How many men would you like to be raped by, pretty one?'

Naunakhte turned her head away in despair. She could see from his face that he did not mean to release her.

There was a silence. The man slid one hand up Naunakhte's arm, across her shoulder, up her long throat. His brown fingers were cool and hard. Something about the way he touched her, something deliberate and masterful, stirred her. He took her chin in his hand and lifted her head so that he could look into her eyes.

'Tell me your name,' he said.

'Naunakhte,' she whispered.

His eyes were hot beneath their shadowed lids. He glowed like the collar of gold around his neck. His look made her tremble. 'Naunakhte,' he repeated. 'Well, Naunakhte, it seems that the priests are hunting you. I am not fond of priests, parasites that they are. If I say

72

that I shall hide you in Waset and keep you safe, will you come with me?'

She shook her head and tried to pull away from him. 'No. Why should I trust you?'

'Why indeed? Why should you trust anyone? All men are traitors.' His voice should have been light and pleasant, but it had a sharp, bitter edge to it which chilled her. She looked at him again and saw that he was smiling, but it was a cruel smile. 'You will trust me, Naunakhte, because you have no choice. Come with me now, or I will call those men from the ferry and give you into their hands. Don't you think they would seize the opportunity?'

Still she hesitated. 'Why should you help me? Why?'

Again he gave his sardonic laugh. 'Are you really innocent, pretty one, or are you just pretending? Why should any man help a woman? I desire you, and I am taking you back to where I live so that I may enjoy your body.'

He spoke so coldly that she felt herself blushing. It was clear that she had no choice, but she was afraid. She trembled between his hands like a captured dove, and he laughed again to feel her fear.

'Come, pretty one,' he said, taking off his cloak. He slung it around her, wrapping it over her head and shoulders so that her face was almost hidden. 'Come, no one will know you. Come with me.' He put one arm around her, beneath the shelter of the cloak. His strong cool fingers lay on her spine. The touch of his hand made her shiver, and the points of her breasts tautened. He looked down and saw her nipples protruding through the fabric of the cloak and he smiled his ironic smile, then began to lead her towards the city.

Naunakhte felt herself in the grip of fate. She looked up at the man's strong face and flinched at what she saw there – anger and bitterness. 'Please,' she whispered, 'what is your name?'

His brown eyes fixed for a moment on hers and a smile touched his lips. It was a different smile, warm and confiding, and for a moment it lit up his face with kindness. He said softly, 'I am Khonsu.'

They walked together towards Waset as the sun climbed in the sky. Naunakhte wanted to ask her captor where they were going and who he was, but she did not dare. His hands held her, one on her wrist, one in the small of her back. They were capable, managing hands. She was certain that she could not escape them.

When they came to the gates she knew he had been right to warn her of the city. The guards there were not well-spoken, well-dressed men like the medjay she knew. They were rough and fierce and at first they called out to her to unveil. But then Khonsu turned and stared at them with his cold eyes and loosened his sword in his sheath and they fell silent. One of them muttered, 'The Lord Khonsu! I apologise, lord.'

The Lord Khonsu? That puzzled her. A nobleman should have servants attending him, and he should live in a great house away from the noise and smells of the city. But Khonsu led her on into the labyrinth of tiny streets, guiding her through the chaos of the bazaars and the filth of the alleys with unhasty confidence. How did he know his way so well in such a vile place? As they went people recognised him and called out to him or bowed with hand on brow, as if he were a lord indeed. But these people were not respectable merchants or well-born scribes – they were surly, slinking villains and women so crudely painted and bedizened that they must be whores. Who was this man who looked like the son of Ramesses himself, yet was at home in the mire of Waset? Into what hands had she fallen?

Once, only once, Khonsu spoke to her. They walked beneath a window and three young women leant out from it and waved at him, calling out eagerly, 'Khonsu! Khonsu, come up to us! Look at you, where have you been? Did the wife of Pharaoh welcome you last night?'

Naunakhte glanced up and saw that the young women were dressed in nothing but their tawdry jewels and their eye paint. Their breasts dangled into the warm morning air and their nipples were stained dark red. She gaped, shocked, and Khonsu glanced down at her and said with his chilly smile, 'I do not usually walk the streets so bedecked. Normally my cloak would cover all. They are surprised at me.'

He said not another word until they reached a small, quiet street, a respectable place lined with the shops of coppersmiths and potters. The bright morning sun shot a bar of golden heat down one side of the street, reflecting off a myriad copper cooking pots set out on display. It felt like home to Naunakhte, being so like the main street in the tombmakers' village. Only the fetid buzz of the city over the rooftops reminded her that they were in Waset. Khonsu pushed open a little door and guided Naunakhte into a narrow, dark stairwell.

'Upstairs,' he said softly. 'All the first floor is mine, and the roof garden.'

The first floor of a little house in a tradesmen's street for a man who wore enough gold to ransom a prince? Naunakhte was consumed with curiosity, but she was also consumed with fatigue. She had been awake all night, and now she was exhausted. As Khonsu steered her up the stairs she staggered and almost fell.

'Are you all right?' he asked her sharply, leaning over her to help her to her feet.

'Yes,' she managed to say, though her voice was unsteady. 'But so tired – '

'Ah.' He opened the door at the top of the stairs and led her into a large room. It was very clean and almost bare. A large clothes chest and a soft reed pallet lay against one wall. There was a single window, through which a brilliant square of sun poured into the room. Underneath the window there was a scribe's mat, and beside it was a writing set and a little heap of papyrus scrolls, tied up with scarlet cords. In one corner was a small table and on it were a number of beautiful objects: a granite statue of a cat with gold rings in its ears, a little naked woman made of ivory with her eyes and lips and nipples painted in, a series of cosmetic bottles made of alabaster and chalcedony and agate, and a silver mirror. In another corner stood several vessels of clay and wicker for food, and glazed jars for water and oil. Sunlight also filtered down also through the stair-well which led to the roof.

It was a room such as a poor young scribe might have inhabited, except that the things in it were rare and beautiful. Naunakhte stared about her, utterly puzzled and very weary.

'Come,' said Khonsu, his voice both mocking and gentle. 'Lie down. You will need to practise, if you want to stay awake all the night.' He unwound the cloak from her hair, led her over to the sleeping mat and handed her down on to it. Then he very gently laid the cloak over her and whispered, 'Sleep. You will be safe.'

There was no reason at all for her to believe him, and yet she did. His voice was no longer cool and mocking, but soothing as a lullaby. She closed her eyes and took a deep breath and felt sleep welling up within her. As she fell asleep she sensed Khonsu moving about the room and wondered what he was doing, but she was too tired to open her eyes to find out.

She woke slowly, feeling half stunned. After a moment she realised that it was the sun that had awoken her. As it descended in the sky it had crept across the floor of the room and now a broad band of red-gold light was falling directly into her eyes. She murmured in protest, shaded her eyes with her hand and turned over.

And gasped, because Khonsu was lying on the mat beside her, watching her with the intensity of a leopard waiting at the riverbank for its unsuspecting prey. Without meaning to she drew back a little, clutching his scarlet cloak against her. The bright gleam of his brown eyes discomfited her. As she drew back she realised that he was naked, and the nearness of his nude body made her tremble with heat and cold together.

Khonsu said nothing. He was lying on his front, his

chin propped on his hands. Naunakhte stared, breathing shallowly, drinking him in. He wore just his great gold arm-rings, and he had removed his wig and eye paint. His straight black hair was cropped short and it lay against his well-shaped head as sleek as the pelt of a gazelle, and without the paint his brilliant eyes were even more striking. They were set deep, beneath heavy, arched lids, and his black brows were as strong and straight as if a scribe had drawn them with a brush. He smiled a little when he saw her gazing, but he did not move. She clutched the cloak more closely around herself, because his nakedness made her painfully conscious of her own body.

He was astonishingly beautiful. Naunakhte had seen many men naked, from her foster father and brothers to the fishermen who worked the Nile, but she had never seen in the flesh a man whose physique approached the divine beauty which sculptors sought to show in their statues of the gods. Khonsu had that perfection. He was well muscled, but not bulky and ill balanced like a labourer. Every part of him was in its due proportion; wide, strong shoulders tapering to lean waist, thighs and calves that blended power and slenderness, and buttocks so perfectly arched, so deliciously rounded, that they seemed to beg for hands to grasp them. His skin was tanned all over to a deep, rich brown and he gleamed faintly with oil, whose slight fragrance heightened the natural warm smell of his body. He was as relaxed and unselfconscious as a desert beast; like a tawny lion or a prowling panther, perfect and strong and dangerously quiet.

Presently he smiled. The smile lifted his wide, fine-cut lips to show his sharp, white animal's teeth. 'You look at me as if you would eat me,' he said, 'or as if you were afraid that I might eat you. Are you hungry, little goddess?'

'Hungry?' Naunakhte repeated, and at the word she began to salivate. She nodded her head eagerly.

'I thought you might be.' Without another word he

got to his feet. He turned away from her, but not before she had seen the thatch of dark hair in his loins and the soft penis hanging there. She swallowed hard and pulled the cloak more tightly about her, watching his lovely back, the muscles moving in his shoulders and buttocks as he crouched to open the basket where he kept his food. Why did his nakedness perturb her? Why should looking at his beauty make her tremble?

Because, said something within her, *because he is as beautiful as the god Amun.*

She turned her head away, shocked at her own unspoken sacrilege. She heard him come back across the room, but she did not look. He sat down on the mat beside her and said, 'Here, Naunakhte. Eat.'

He put food before her: new bread, honey, fresh cow's milk, dates and figs, a pomegranate, a dish of baby gourds stuffed with meat. She did not hesitate, and the food was so good that she did not even look up at him as she ate it.

'That is better,' he said, when the panicky speed of her eating slowed.

Naunakhte burped. She glanced up with a shy smile, saying, 'I have eaten well,' as her mother had taught her.

'You have,' said Khonsu, returning the smile. 'Enough for two skinny temple girls.' He picked up the dishes and moved them off the pallet.

Naunakhte felt uncomfortable, as if he were taking away some barrier that protected her from him. She remembered suddenly what he had said to her on the road from the ferry: I desire you, and I am taking you home so that I can enjoy your body. She shivered, and when she looked up at him again her skin came out in goosepimples. He was so strong. What would it be like if he . . . had her?

He handed her a linen towel to wipe her hands, then cast it away behind him. He was sitting cross-legged, like a scribe. The powerful muscles of his thighs were flexed and his feet were tucked in neatly, hiding his genitals from her. His naked body filled her with fear and desire.

As if he sensed her confusion, Khonsu changed position. He unfolded his legs and spread them apart and propped his elbows on his raised knees. In the shadow between his thighs the golden flesh of his penis gleamed faintly against the dark cushion of his pubic hair. It was not erect – it lay slack as a piece of rope – but it drew her eyes. Her breath came more quickly, chilling her parted lips. She stared, trembling.

'Naunakhte,' said Khonsu sharply. She gasped and lifted her face to his. His eyes narrowed, the lower lids lifting sensually. 'By Seth and chaos,' he whispered, 'you are lovely.'

Naunakhte looked away at once, terrified by the way he linked her beauty to the dreaded name of Seth. Did he mean to curse her? She said nothing, and presently Khonsu spoke again. His cool voice made her shiver. 'You look at me like a virgin,' he said. 'Are you a virgin, Naunakhte of Amun's temple?'

She was silent. 'Answer me,' said Khonsu, and now his voice was sharp with command.

How could Naunakhte deny him, when he held her life in his hands? She met his eyes for a moment, then looked away, because the intensity of his expression burned her like a brand. She felt that she must be truthful. 'I have never . . . known a man,' she whispered, 'but I am not a virgin.'

There was a little silence, then Khonsu laughed, flinging back his head and showing his white teeth. 'Riddles now!' he exclaimed. 'Are you trying to make a fool of me, little goddess? Explain yourself.'

'Explain?' whispered Naunakhte helplessly.

'Tell me,' he ordered her. 'Tell me what became of you in the temple. How can you be a virgin and not be one? And why are they pursuing you to the death?'

Slowly, hesitantly, the story came out. Khonsu listened quietly, though sometimes his eyes narrowed and his lips tightened. When she finished, 'And so I was on the road, trying to find my way back to my village,' he stroked his hand thoughtfully over his chin and regarded her with a look of cold detachment. She would almost have thought that he disapproved of her, or that he had not believed her story.

'So,' he said at last, 'the priests behave as we all expect. Those drones, those parasites! They take half of everything the land produces, they live on others' labour, and they even take the most beautiful virgins for their barren pleasure!'

Naunakhte said swiftly, 'You have not understood. I was offered to the god Amun.'

'The god Amun?' repeated Khonsu, his voice heavy with irony. 'Why should a god be interested in you, Naunakhte, when there are goddesses with immortal beauty to slake his lusts?' He laughed. 'Come, don't play games. The chief priest deflowered you, you said as much. He just didn't do it himself, the madman. He's probably a sodomite, half of them are. No, that's not right, either; you said he was your enemy's lover. Well, he was a fool. If it had been me, I should have taken you myself and said I stood as the god's deputy. That's as good a tale as anything they can imagine.'

'No,' Naunakhte protested. His caustic disbelief hurt her more than she could have believed possible. 'Khonsu, you don't understand. The god called me. He called me to serve him. I went because I loved him.'

Suddenly Khonsu's face was very still, only his lips moving faintly, as if he wanted to speak and could not. His eyes burned, bright as glowing coals. Naunakhte could hardly bear to look at him, but she could not look away. She saw lust and anger in his face, and the sight of his lust awoke hers. Beneath the cloak her breasts lifted and fell, aching for the touch of his hands. With a shock she realised that between his legs his penis was stirring, lifting all by itself, thrusting forward with mysterious power.

'You loved the god,' said Khonsu, and his voice was a soft whisper of rage. 'You loved a statue, Naunakhte.

Believe me, the gods care nothing for men. No god called you. You gave yourself to a thing of metal and wood.'

'No.' She shook her head, ready to weep. Amun had forsaken her, but she loved him still, as a woman will love her husband although he beats her. 'I know what I felt, Khonsu. The god came to me. I know it.'

'A thing of metal and wood,' he said again. 'Temple girl, it is time that you learnt what it is to give yourself to something made of flesh.'

He reached forward and caught hold of the cloak, then pulled it away from her and flung it violently into a corner of the room. The fading sunlight shone on her half-naked body. She breathed fast and made as if she would leap to her feet and flee, but he caught her by both arms and pulled her towards him. Her head fell back and Khonsu lunged towards her and buried his lips against her golden throat.

His breath was hot and damp and between his open lips his strong tongue lashed her skin. She cried out, shuddering. He pulled her close and with one hand ripped away her crumpled kilt. His mouth travelled up her throat and found her mouth and he kissed her with such ferocity that she could not breathe. His lips crushed hers and his tongue coiled and twisted within her open mouth. She felt as if she were drowning in the depths of the Nile, and it was such bliss that she wished that she might never breathe again.

Her naked body was pressed against his, close and tight; golden limbs against bronze; taut nipples against smooth bare skin. He pushed his way between her legs and moved her into his lap so that her thighs were wrapped around his waist. His big hands held her shoulders and buttocks, folding her against him as if he wanted to make them both one flesh.

He lifted his lips from hers. 'Did the god kiss you?'

She could say nothing. 'Did he kiss you?' demanded Khonsu fiercely. 'Did he put his mouth on to your mouth, Naunakhte? Did he bite your lips? Did he give you his tongue to suck?'

If she said no she would deny the god. She turned her head helplessly and whispered, 'Kiss me.'

Khonsu hesitated, then pressed his mouth back on to hers with such passion that she moaned aloud. He moved one hand down to her waist and with the other pushed her shoulder so that she bent away from him, offering her swollen breasts to his eager lips. He cupped her left breast roughly in his hand and took her right nipple into his mouth, licking, sucking, biting, making her utter little desperate cries of astonished pleasure.

'Did Amun suck your breasts?' Khonsu asked her, pulling her back into his arms and speaking straight into her wide eyes. He was shaking with emotion and his hands gripped her so tightly that they hurt her. 'Did he lick your nipples and make them swell? What did the statue do to you, Naunakhte?'

'Don't,' Naunakhte whimpered, racked with guilt and desire. 'It's sacrilege. I mustn't speak of it. Don't.'

He shoved her violently away from him. She fell back to the pallet and stared up at him in shock and fear. He knelt over her, towering with his rage, his penis so swollen and erect that it brushed against his flat muscular belly. A single transparent tear stood on its tip.

'Open your legs,' said Khonsu coldly.

'No,' Naunakhte whispered, terrified. She longed for him, and her whole body quivered with need like a single string plucked and vibrating a long note of music. But his fury filled her with fear; she did not understand it.

'Open to me!' Khonsu roared, and he thrust his knee between her thighs and drove them apart with a jerk. She lifted her hands to fight him off, but he flung himself on to the pallet between her legs, caught her buttocks in his hands and pressed his mouth to her sex.

'Oh!' Naunakhte cried in horror and delight. His strong pointed tongue was sliding between her labia, while his lips were kissing and caressing the little delicate stem of flesh that was the heart of her pleasure. With his hands he pressed her thighs wider apart, exposing her secret heart. She ceased to struggle and lay panting, held open to his lascivious fondlings, shuddering as beat after beat of ecstasy pulsed through her.

He licked her with as much skill as the Lady Hunro and his strong fingers squeezed and stroked at the tender flesh of her inner thighs, stimulating her so unbearably that she began to cry out regularly and arch her back. She touched her own breasts, gripping the soft mounds tightly in her hands and pinching at her nipples. Delicious sparks of pleasure flickered between her breasts and her belly, like little fish swimming among waterlilies. Khonsu began to tease her with his fingers, tracing the entrance to her silken sheath and trickling her juices back and back until he could stroke and stimulate her quivering anus.

'Oh help me!' Naunakhte moaned. She was enfolded in the sensations of approaching orgasm. Divine glory hovered around her, buffeting her like an eagle with its mighty wings. 'Help me!' she cried aloud. 'The god is coming!'

At once Khonsu pulled away from her, panting. She shuddered violently and whimpered as the feelings withdrew, leaving her empty and unsatisfied. She opened her eyes and looked up at him, holding out her hands in supplication. 'Please,' she whispered.

Khonsu knelt above her, still breathing hard. His mouth was shining with the juices of her body and his rigid penis quivered as if it yearned for her. His nostrils flared like a stallion's. His whole taut body spoke of how much he desired her, but when he spoke his voice was icily controlled. 'The god was not coming, Naunakhte.'

She breathed fast and said nothing. Khonsu leant over her, propped on his knees and his hands, awing her with his size and power. The muscles of his arms flexed and swelled as they took his weight. 'You were coming, little goddess,' he whispered, 'coming to your moment of pleasure. I was taking you there, not the god. Do you understand me?'

Naunakhte could not speak. Her body still shook with longing and need and her mouth was dry. At last she mouthed almost silently, 'Please. Please.'

A bitter smile touched Khonsu's lips. 'What do you want, Naunakhte?'

She lifted her hands and touched the smooth warm skin of his arms. He was poised above her like the sky goddess Nut arched over the earth; infinite, heavy with might. She wanted to feel his power; to be crushed by his weight, to be conquered and beaten down beneath the body of a living man. She spread her thighs wider and lifted her hips towards him, writhing with unconscious lewdness as she offered herself. 'Please,' she whispered again. 'Khonsu, please. Love me.'

'I am real,' Khonsu replied softly, lowering his beautiful mouth towards hers. 'I am here, Naunakhte, ready for you. Take what you desire. Put your hand on my cock and guide it. Feel how thick it is, how much it craves you. Put me inside you, Naunakhte, if you want me.'

Her breathing was quick and shallow. She was suddenly afraid, as if he were as dangerous as a poisonous snake. But her longing was so great that she reached down tentatively with one shaking hand and touched his penis.

Smooth, hot, dry, hard as a sun-warmed stone, but softer to the touch than the finest sand slipping over her fingers. She hesitantly explored its length, and Khonsu closed his eyes and bared his teeth. The feel of his readiness made her shake with desire. Timidly, because she did not know what she was doing, she guided the broad shelving head to the lips of her sex and lodged it where she felt the most empty. It nudged at her, twitching with a life of its own, and she moaned.

Khonsu opened his bright eyes. 'Command me,' he whispered. 'Little goddess, beautiful Naunakhte. Tell me what you desire.'

'Take me,' Naunakhte whispered. 'Oh Khonsu, Lord Khonsu, put your cock inside me. I beg you.'

'Yes,' he breathed, and his strong hips tensed and he thrust, slowly and deliberately. She flung back her head and gasped as his penis gradually slid up inside her, filling her so beautifully, soothing all her longing and yet burning her with an even greater need.

'Did the statue do this to you, Naunakhte?' hissed Khonsu. His arched buttocks tautened as he withdrew from her, then slowly, steadily lunged again. Their loins met; the rough curling fur above his penis ground deliciously against her, the soft insides of her thighs cradled his flanks, and her heels rested on the tender hollows behind his knees. She remembered suddenly how she had caressed the statue of the god, fondling those same tender hollows with her fingers, how she had felt his flesh coming alive as she touched him.

The memory and the sensations joined in her mind, indecipherable. She cried out with pleasure and caught hold of Khonsu's buttocks, pulling him closer against her. 'Don't stop,' she moaned. 'Don't stop, Khonsu. Oh, I feel it.'

He took her unhurriedly, strongly, every thrust revealing his power. Naunakhte writhed beneath him, held his prisoner, impaled and squirming upon the piercing shaft of his swollen penis. She moaned and tried to lift her head to kiss him, but the sensations of penetration were too strong for her. She subsided, shuddering, driven into submission by the fierce thrusts of his muscular loins. When her climax came it was as if she was being torn apart by wild beasts, consumed by fire, trampled by pounding feet and flung aside. She cried out, a lonely dying wail, and Khonsu snarled and drove his jerking penis into her tense, rigid body with savage strength. Even through the smoke and flame of her orgasm she felt him throbbing within her, a potent dangerous presence.

He rested his hands on her breasts and looked down into her face. His throat and shoulders shone with sweat, his body stuck to hers. She thought that he would demand again that she forswear the god, but she was wrong. He smiled at her, a quick ironic smile, and brushed his forehead against hers to wipe away the sweat. His passion seemed to have vanished, replaced by cool, mocking humour.

'Well,' he said after a moment, 'I shan't be turning you in for the reward, not at once, in any case. You will stay with me and I shall ... educate you.' His smile broadened. 'Also,' he added, 'I will find some sort of an occupation for you. I can think of one already.'

How could he talk of educating her, of putting her to work, while his softening penis still lay buried deep in her moist body and they were both panting and gleaming with the effort of satisfying their desire? Naunakhte looked up at him, astonished. But he seemed to want an answer from her. His eyebrows were lifted quizzically and his mouth was quirking. She swallowed, then managed to say, 'But what do you do, Khonsu? What sort of man are you?'

Khonsu toyed idly with her swollen nipples, making her gasp. He smiled lazily at her reaction. 'All in good time,' he said.

Chapter Six

That night Naunakhte slept like the dead. When she woke Khonsu was gone. She waited within the house, trying to occupy herself by examining Khonsu's possessions. They were so beautiful. The comb for his wigs was made of ivory and his cosmetic sticks and brushes were of gilded bronze. The silver mirror was an heirloom fit for a prince. Feeling very daring, Naunakhte took the mirror to the sunlight and combed her hair and used Khonsu's own paints to colour her eyes. She looked at herself in the mirror and put her head on one side. The shock of Amun's betrayal and her flight from the temple did not seem to have marred her beauty: she had seldom seen her eyes so bright, her lips so moist and appetising. Something told her that this was because Khonsu had made love to her. She remembered the ecstasy his body had bestowed on her and shivered with delight.

Then it was as if a mist came between her and the sunlight. Her eyes darkened. An invisible hand seemed to brush her neck and warm breath touched her ear. A deep voice whispered, 'Did you gain more pleasure from giving yourself to him than from serving me, Naunakhte?'

Naunakhte set down the mirror, feeling sick and cold.

Yes, Khonsu was beautiful. But how could she so quickly forget the god, and the trance-like exaltation of spirit that had filled her when she knelt to serve him with her mouth? Perhaps all of this was nothing more than a trial, a test set by Amun to prove her worth.

Footsteps crunched on the stairs. Naunakhte jumped up in fear, but when the door opened it was Khonsu. He was wearing ordinary clothes today, a plain shoulder-length wig and a heavy white kilt, with no more adornment than a pendant of lapis hanging from a leather thong in the centre of his chest. In his hand he carried a bulky basket. He smiled to see her holding the mirror. 'Very nice,' he said, stroking one finger along her shadowed eyelid, 'but I think malachite would suit you better. I will get you some tomorrow.'

'Could I not go out and buy it?' Naunakhte asked timidly.

Khonsu chuckled. 'By all means, if you would like to encounter half a dozen of the temple medjay. They are everywhere, searching for you. The people hereabouts would turn you in for the reward. Stay within doors, Naunakhte.'

'Stay here?' Naunakhte sounded disbelieving. 'Alone?'

'I will be here sometimes. And I have brought you some pastimes.' He set down the basket and revealed several lengths of linen, thread and bone needles, and four or five coiled bundles of wicker. 'I imagine a girl with a village background could usefully employ herself making baskets and suchlike.'

Naunakhte looked at the linen and wicker with barely concealed dismay. Was this what he had meant, when he talked of employing her?

Khonsu must have read her face, because he laughed again. 'Don't worry, little goddess,' he said, 'I know you are good for more than this. I'm working on an idea or two. I will tell you. All in good time.' He brushed dirt from his hands, took her by the chin and lifted her face to kiss her. His lips were very soft, and for long moments he did not seek to enter her mouth with his tongue. When he did, it was so sweet that Naunakhte could not keep in a moan of simple pleasure. She returned the kiss eagerly and lifted her hands to catch hold of his shoulders and hold him to her, but he brushed her away, grinning, and turned to the door. 'Now, I have things to do. I'll be back before sunset.'

He vanished. Naunakhte listened to his receding footsteps and swallowed.

So the medjay were seeking her in the streets, were they? Khonsu had smiled when he said it, as if he knew that she would not dare go outside to see if what he had said were true. She could not leave his house. Was he her rescuer, her protector, or her captor? Could she trust him?

That would depend on what sort of a man he was. He had said he would tell her, all in good time. She was already beginning to fear that she would not like the answer.

Over the next few days the answer became clear to her, and it was as distasteful as she had feared.

By night Khonsu left the house, sometimes dressed as a nobleman, sometimes slipping like a shadow wrapped in black. When he returned he would be carrying gold, and sometimes his clothes were mussed and there was drying blood on the blade of his bronze sword. By day all sorts of disreputable men came in ones and twos to his house, asking for instructions and guidance or reporting in whispers details of deeds that made the hairs stand up on Naunakhte's neck.

It seemed that Khonsu was indeed a lord, but a lord of such people as she had hardly known existed. His world was the bottomless sink of Waset's law breakers. He was a master of thieves and cut-throats. He did not seem remotely ashamed of what he did. He did not speak about it to Naunakhte directly, but he made no attempt to hide it.

What should she do? Her foster father had always

told her that thieves and murderers were the hyenas of the human world, beasts to be spurned at every turn. But now she was at the mercy of a king among those beasts, and worse, she was beginning to enjoy her captivity.

For Khonsu was not only beautiful, but charming. He was quick witted and made her laugh with almost everything he said, and he flattered her and brought her gifts, perfumes, jewels and fine clothes to make her look lovely and render her confinement more acceptable to her. She waited for his footsteps on the stairway with eager anticipation, longing for his presence. After that very first encounter he did not try to browbeat her with her love for the god, he simply ignored it. He treated her like one of his precious objects, to be cherished and admired.

Nor did he restrain himself simply to possession of the eyes. By day and by night he possessed her body also. She learnt all the delights of physical love: the giving and taking of pleasure, the ecstasy that is doubled because it is shared. His body was like a thing of magic to her, strange and perfect and delectable. She never tired of stroking his bronzed skin, of exploring the soft, warm hidden places of his neck and armpits and buttocks, of nuzzling the strong flat muscles of his chest and belly.

In short, she was happy. She knew that she should despise Khonsu for what he was – certainly a thief, certainly a liar and perjurer, possibly a murderer – but she could not. To her he was gentle, and his ardent physical passion enchanted her.

On the evening of the tenth day since Naunakhte fled the temple she lay with Khonsu in the warm twilight upon the roof. The roof of Khonsu's house was as carefully furnished as the single room. It had its own sleeping pallet of soft rushes, hung with a fine fishing net to keep off the mosquitoes, and plants in pots stood in every corner so that it was almost like a garden. It was a fine place to make love.

Khonsu was skittish that night. He teased her. He touched her breasts until they swelled and ached, he caressed her throat and shoulders until every part of her was tingling with erotic warmth, and then he began to tickle her until she gasped and shrieked. He kissed her between her legs, lapping and stroking with his long tongue until she was almost at the point of orgasm, and then he pursed his lips and blew on her warm flesh, chilling her and making her scream. When she protested and tugged at his cropped hair and tried to hit him with her palm he laughed and held her away from him at the length of his arms, so that she raged and fumed quite impotently. 'Go on, fight,' he said, still laughing. 'You look so lovely when you rage, Naunakhte. Hit me, go on, go on! Look at the way it makes your breasts move!'

'You beast!' Naunakhte spluttered. 'Teasing beast!'

'A beast, am I?' he asked, grinning. 'Fight the lion, then, before it eats you.'

He flung himself upon her. She struggled and writhed, but he was too strong for her. In moments she was pinned beneath him, flailing helplessly at his broad back with her hands. He grinned down into her furious face, and without a word he found the entrance to her sex and thrust himself into her.

'Beast,' gasped Naunakhte. 'Beast!'

She grunted with shock as he lunged, forcing himself inside her with all his strength. 'We are both beasts,' he hissed. 'Do you know what beasts do, little not-quite-a-virgin? Beasts fuck. I am fucking you, Naunakhte. Feel it.'

The surging movement of his penis within her filled her with ecstasy. She moaned and ceased to struggle. She knew his words were filthy, but they inflamed her. She felt like a beast, indeed – a copulating animal, dirty and lewd and delicious.

'Fuck,' whispered Khonsu, and his body struck hers again with a soft voluptuous sound. 'Naunakhte, Naunakhte.'

It was no longer enough for Naunakhte to hear the

words. She wanted to say them. She dug her nails into Khonsu's buttocks and groaned, 'Yes, Khonsu. Fuck me.'

As he thrust deep into her he laughed, his body shaking. 'That's it, temple girl. Tell me what you want.'

A sense of wild freedom seized Naunakhte. She flung her arms wide apart and drummed with her heels on Khonsu's labouring buttocks. 'Fuck!' she shouted. 'Yes, yes, Khonsu, I feel your cock inside me. We're fucking!'

He drove into her again and again, and the pleasure was so great, the relief of her sexual tension so tremendous, that she screamed like an animal as he writhed and jerked and snarled his satisfaction and his penis pulsed within her.

Then from the next rooftop a voice shouted, 'Seth curse you, you foul-mouthed pair of copulating hippos! People here are trying to sleep!'

And Naunakhte and Khonsu laughed so hard that his phallus slipped out of her and they lay on the mat clutching each other and roaring like a pair of idiots.

After a little while Khonsu got up. 'I have to go out,' he said.

Naunakhte bit her lip. She hated it when he went out at night. The blood on his sword made her fear for him. But she said nothing.

Khonsu grinned at her, then dropped a papyrus scroll by the bed. 'While I'm away,' he suggested, 'look at that. It's pictures, not just writing. They may amuse you.'

Naunakhte was intelligent, and as the child of a scribe she had learnt enough of the hieroglyph alphabet to read moderately well. But no man would suspect this of a woman, and Khonsu unrolled the scroll and pointed with a smile to a picture before he picked up his everyday sword, a businesslike affair slung on a strong linen baldric, and went to the stairs.

Amuse me? thought Naunakhte. The pictures were crudely pornographic and she thought they were disgusting. They showed a whore and her client in a number of different positions, and there were simple captions: *Oh, you're huge tonight, lover*, and similar vulgar statements.

But the positions in themselves were ... interesting. What could this one mean, *come behind me with your love*? She turned the papyrus upside down, squinting in the faint light.

Soon the twilight faded and she could no longer read. She composed herself to sleep as the stars came out.

Just as she prepared to close her eyes, a shooting star streaked overhead. Naunakhte lay as if stricken, her hand unconsciously clutching at the god's mark on her arm.

A sign from the god! Why should he send one to her now? She was beginning to be, if not happy, at least content. If Amun did not want her, could he not at least release her from his service?

She turned her head away from the glowing sky and shut her eyes tightly. She tried to think of Khonsu. They had laughed together that evening and he had given her pleasure.

But he had left her. Beneath her happiness she knew that what he did was both dangerous and wicked, and she feared for him. Her spirit rebelled, and when she slept, she dreamt of the god.

A few hours after darkness fell Khonsu returned to his house. He was not alone, but at his whispered order his shadowy companions left him beside the door. The moonlight glittered on their drawn weapons as they went away.

He went silently up the stairs and opened the door, whispering, 'Naunakhte.'

The bed was empty, illuminated in a bright square of silver light. Khonsu smiled and unslung his sword. He drew it from its sheath with a long, soft hiss and checked that it was clean, then stowed it in the chest where it belonged. He took off his wig and put it carefully in its wicker basket, then unfastened his kilt.

The pleated linen was stained with blood and there was a long gouge on Khonsu's thigh. His mouth tightened briefly as he inspected the wound, but it was not serious. The bleeding had stopped. Khonsu screwed up his kilt and wet it with water from the jar, then gently wiped away the dried blood. For a moment the wound opened again, but it was already beginning to scab and there was only a little more bleeding.

Khonsu dropped the stained kilt and went to the little staircase that led to the roof. For a moment he stood at the bottom of the stairs, leaning his head upon his upflung arm and smiling up at the moonlight.

It was strange and wonderful to him to have Naunakhte to return to. He had become accustomed to living alone. When he had first come to Waset and had money to spend he had bought himself company – one whore after another to warm his bed and keep his house, but he had not found them to his taste. They were loud and crude and they demanded things of him he was not prepared to give.

But Naunakhte was different. It was as if a white bird of the sea had come to him, bringing a breath of the cool sea air to the dark close atmosphere of the city.

It was not just her beauty, although Khonsu knew his own worth and had always been selective in his choice of woman. It was something else about her, something he could barely name, let alone explain. She was young and inexperienced, and yet she was calm, almost serene. She welcomed his body, and yet she seemed to preserve an aura of remote purity, like a goddess on a mountain. She was transparent. Khonsu scorned her love for the god Amun, but to himself he admitted that if the god were to choose any mortal woman to receive him, it would certainly be Naunakhte.

Khonsu went slowly up the stairs, thinking. He could not remember any time when a woman had made him feel so moved. And how did he respond to her? By mocking, by joking, by speaking filthy words to her and encouraging her to speak them too, like one of the

94

bazaar whores he despised. Why did he try to destroy the very thing about her he found most intriguing?

You are afraid of her, said a tiny voice within him. *You fear her love for the god.*

But Khonsu would not admit that he feared anything, not even to himself. He ran up the last few steps on to the roof and stood in the flooding moonlight looking down at Naunakhte, sleeping naked beneath the net.

The pale light turned her long limbs to silver. She lay on her back, one slender arm flung up above her head, her lips slightly parted. Khonsu drew in a deep breath and wrapped his arms around himself, resting his chin on his clenched fist. The words of an old poem came to him: *Look, she is like the star goddess arising at the new year, brilliantly white, bright skinned, with beautiful eyes for looking, with sweet lips for speaking. A long neck and white breasts, her hair of lapis lazuli, her arms more brilliant than gold, her fingers like lotus flowers, her full buttocks and slender waist. Her thighs offer her beauty . . .*

He pushed the words impatiently aside and lifted the net. He would prove to himself that he could love her without trying to deny what she was. He would love her without even awakening her.

Very softly Khonsu knelt down on the mat beside Naunakhte. He leant over her and with infinite gentleness put back a straying strand of her strong black hair. She did not stir. He smiled, and with the tips of his fingers he grazed her throat, her shoulder, the curve of one tender breast.

Naunakhte took a long breath and let it out in a sigh. Khonsu's hand moved on, lighter than a moth, hardly touching her silky naked skin. The points of her breasts hardened and she took another long deep breath.

Now he touched her with both hands, still as delicately as in a dream, fluttering his strong fingers over her throat, her ribs, her belly. Naunakhte smiled in her sleep and her head rolled back, tensing her shoulders and offering her white breasts to the white moon. Khonsu shuddered, astonished and aroused by the simple sensuality of her response. He leant forward and with the tip of his tongue he licked the swollen tip of one breast, and Naunakhte's whole body undulated like the leaf of a waterlily when a boat passes by.

She was still fast asleep. Emboldened, Khonsu gently drew her nipple into his mouth and sucked at it. It swelled between his lips and Naunakhte sighed again and again, regular whispering moans of pleasure. Her body twisted and her lush thighs opened, revealing the delicate petals of flesh between them. Khonsu sat up, smiling to himself, and touched the soft skin of her inner thighs.

Naunakhte's hips began to lift up towards him, heaving like the waves of the Nile. Her head moved from side to side and she breathed more quickly. Khonsu let one hand stray to the dark cushion of her sex and found to his delight that she was already as moist and ripe with juice as a bursting fruit. The little point of flesh that was the secret of women's pleasure was swollen and stiff with her sleeping desire. He licked his finger and touched the little point, so gently it was hardly a touch at all.

At once Naunakhte's body tensed as if she had received a mortal wound. Her spine curved like a bended bow and her lips opened wide, gleaming. She let out a long moan, and now there were words in her sigh. 'Oh Lord Amun. Amun, great god.'

Khonsu drew back his hand as if he had laid it upon a scorpion. He knelt beside Naunakhte shivering with shock and fear. Before her he mocked the gods, but now even as he looked at her with desire in his heart he saw that she was in the possession of Amun, that the god himself lay with her, invisible and powerful.

He did not dare touch her when the god was present. The revenge a jealous god might take upon a foolhardy man made him quail. His hands clenched into fists and he watched with wide anguished eyes as Naunakhte's body rippled and her lips parted and closed again with the increase of her sighs.

'Amun,' she moaned again, 'Lord Amun.' Her closed eyes tightened and she gave a little shuddering cry, as if she was overwhelmed by pleasure. Her hands opened, her fingers stretched and tensed, and her lips drew back from her teeth. The breath hissed in her open mouth. The god Amun was with her, bestowing immortal pleasure upon her mortal flesh.

Khonsu covered his face with his hands. Fear and jealousy warred within him, making him shake. He could not bear to watch Naunakhte quake as his divine rival brought her to the moment of climax. Her sighs burned in his ears.

At last she was silent and still. Khonsu drew his hands from his face and made a sound that was almost like a sob, then without hesitation pressed his naked body against Naunakhte's. He entered her at once, gritting his teeth as her warm moistness surrounded his aching erect penis. She was wet with the seed of the god. Furious and wretched, he caught hold of her slender wrists and held her down. She gave a little gasp and awoke, her dark eyes staring up at him, a tiny moon reflected in each pupil.

'Khonsu,' she whispered, soft as breathing. 'I thought – '

'What did you think?' he hissed, thrusting into her and withdrawing. The pleasure of possessing her surged through him; rich warmth from his buried penis, tingling softness from the touch of her body against his.

'Nothing,' murmured Naunakhte. She closed her eyes and sighed with pleasure as his phallus slid in and out of her clasping sheath.

'Did you think I was the god?' Khonsu mocked, smiling harshly at her sudden look of shock. 'Am I Amun now? Take flesh and blood, little not-quite-a-virgin.' He drove himself into her with all the strength he could command. Her body rippled as his loins struck hers and he rejoiced to see her wince with pleasure and pain. 'You are mine,' he told her as his thrusts built up to a steady, driving rhythm, powerful and relentless. 'Mine, Naunakhte, mine.'

She did not fight him. Her body twisted and writhed as he penetrated her, her breasts swelled beneath his clutching hands, and her cries met and mingled with his as he worked his penis to and fro within her. He took her with the roughness of a slave master breaking in a new girl, determined to subdue her and compel her to admit that he was her lord. But even at her climax, even at the moment of his ultimate possession, her face was rapt and glazed as if Amun was still within her. Khonsu sensed the god standing behind his shoulder, smiling condescendingly at his pathetic efforts.

'Mine,' he cried hopelessly, as his penis spurted his seed. 'Mine!'

Afterwards he lay with his head on her breast, exhausted. She stroked her fingers slowly through his hair, then fell back into her drowned sleep. He closed his eyes and listened to the steady double beat of her heart.

How could he challenge a rival who was invisible, all powerful? What could he offer this strange, remote, pure young woman, to make her feel for him as she did for her lord the god?

One thing is certain, Khonsu told himself with conviction. I shall not put myself within her power. Neither she nor the god shall know that I love her.

Chapter Seven

Naunakhte awoke in the cool sweetness of the dawn from dreams of the god Amun. She looked up at the sky, pale coral-pink with burgeoning daylight, and sighed with longing.

In the god's sanctuary at this very hour the rite was taking place. The Hand of Amun was dancing before the statue, arousing the god. Soon she would moan with pleasure as the priests lifted her and offered her to the possession of Amun. The handmaidens would watch with dry mouths as the god's magnificent golden phallus slowly penetrated the moist vulva of the high priestess.

Last night the god had come to Naunakhte and loved her. As she slept he had parted the secret lips of her body with his powerful penis and filled her with such bliss that she sobbed. Nothing compared to the ecstasy which his might bestowed upon her.

But he had forsaken her, allowed her to be driven from his temple. Naunakhte closed her eyes against tears of bitter grief. 'Oh Lord Amun,' she prayed beneath her breath, 'if you will not have my service, at least release me. Release me.'

Beside her Khonsu stirred and sighed. Naunakhte jumped, startled by his sudden movement. She looked down at him and frowned. He was fast asleep, his head pillowed on his hand, relaxed as a child. His penis was erect, warm and pulsing with morning eagerness. Naunakhte looked at his splendid silky phallus and licked her lips. Last night, had he not come to her, too? She was uncertain; everything was confused in her mind. Did she not remember him lying above her, pounding urgently into her, his face contorted with lust and desperate need? Had he not given her pleasure, just as Amun had?

It was as if he had come to take her mind from her loss of the god's favour. Her face lit with pleasure and gratitude and she leant over Khonsu to kiss him.

Then, before her lips touched his, she drew back. Her breath came fast. On his thigh was a bloody scab the length of her forearm. It marred his smooth bronzed skin as blight mars a flower. It mocked her with knowledge of his mortality.

Naunakhte closed her eyes to shut out the sight of Khonsu's wound. She crouched over him and leant down and with her extended tongue caressed the soft veined underside of his stiff penis.

He tasted delicious; salty and sweet, of her juices and his combined. The deep musky odour of his body filled her nostrils. As she licked, his phallus jerked up towards her open mouth, demanding her instant attention. It was like a petulant child begging for sweets. Naunakhte smiled and tolerantly parted her lips.

The glossy, swollen tip of his penis slid into her mouth. Her belly and sex clenched in upon themselves as if this penetration of her lips were a penetration of her sex. She moaned, and as she slipped her mouth steadily up and down the glorious glistening length of Khonsu's erection, her inner muscles tensed, gripping helplessly at emptiness.

He woke. The texture of his skin changed, becoming springy with life. Naunakhte could not keep away the memories of Amun's statue, and how its golden skin had turned to warm flesh beneath her caresses. She whimpered and sucked harder, probing with her soft tongue into the tiny eye at the tip of Khonsu's velvety glans. She heard him moan and felt his hands in her hair, steadying her bobbing head.

It was blissful to serve him thus. Naunakhte slipped one hand between Khonsu's strong thighs to cup and stroke the soft hairy sac of his testicles. He was sensitive there, but even more sensitive beyond, in that dark secret crease between his strong buttocks. Her fingers squirmed and probed, carrying her warm slippery saliva to forbidden places.

Khonsu cried out and heaved his loins towards her face. Naunakhte smiled even as his erect penis filled her mouth. She pressed with her index finger at the tense quivering ring of his anus. He moaned and tightened his cheeks against her, but she would not be denied. Her finger pressed, slipped, then eased its way inside him. Khonsu groaned in protest and delight, then began to lunge up towards Naunakhte's lips. Every time he thrust she pushed her finger deeper within him, until it was buried its full length and gripped by the strong muscles of his sphincter. She clasped with her lips at the head of his penis and her cheeks hollowed as she sucked. Khonsu gave one last desperate cry as his orgasm struck him. Within her mouth his penis throbbed, and his spasming anus clutched feverishly at her penetrating finger.

At last he relaxed and she released him. Her mouth was filled with the warm, salty taste of his semen. She licked her lips and swallowed, then wiped her mouth with her hand and sat up.

He was smiling. 'Ah,' he said with approval, 'that's the way I like to wake up in the morning.'

She returned the smile, but tensely. 'Khonsu,' she said softly, gesturing at his thigh, 'what made that wound?'

Khonsu looked down, raised his black brows and grinned at her. 'A sword,' he said carelessly.

Naunakhte turned her head away, because his words made her think of violence, of death, of glittering blades

101

whirled in darkness, and she was afraid. Khonsu made a face when he saw her concern. 'Don't worry,' he said, 'it's nothing. Look, it's scabbed already.'

She lifted her face to his. 'Who did it to you?'

'It doesn't matter,' said Khonsu easily. 'I killed him.'

Naunakhte stretched out one hand and very gingerly touched the dark scab. Khonsu watched her in silence, not flinching. Around the dried blood the flesh was alternately bluish and pale and dark, unhealthy red.

'Khonsu,' Naunakhte whispered at last, 'what would I do if one night you went away and you did not return?'

He caught her hand then and looked into her face with such intensity that she was breathless. She thought he was about to say something serious, something that would comfort her. But before he spoke his face assumed its usual expression of ironic humour. 'If it worries you,' said Khonsu, 'then you will like my latest idea all the more.'

Naunakhte gave a little sigh, then returned his smile. 'What idea?'

'For your occupation. You will enjoy it, Naunakhte, we both will. It will be a success, I promise you, and it will make us laugh.'

She raised her eyebrows. 'What can it be?'

'Magic,' said Khonsu, in a stage whisper.

'Magic,' Naunakhte repeated hesitantly. The word chilled her with possibilities. She withdrew a little, stifling a shiver.

'Don't look like that,' said Khonsu irritably. 'I mean mock magic, Naunakhte, everything pretended. People will come because they are fools, not because it is true. Imagine!' He jumped to his feet, naked in the dawn sunlight, waving his arms in excitement. 'Who would not buy a love potion from you? You are so beautiful, everyone will believe that it will work. Besides which, when they see the ingredients that go into it they won't be able to resist. And as for fortune telling, it's easy, Naunakhte. I know something of everyone in the city –

I will be able to tell you what they want to hear. You will make it sound convincing, I know. It will be easy.'

Naunakhte shook her head slowly. She felt cold, as if a trickle of water were running down her naked spine. Everything within her cried out against Khonsu's plan. But how could she explain? Very cautiously she said, 'Khonsu, magic calls upon the gods. I would . . . I would be happier if I did not need to do that.'

For a moment his face was very still. Then he shook his head angrily. 'You need not call on anyone,' he told her. 'Just use your sense, Naunakhte, and what I have told you, and everything will work perfectly well. Listen, just listen, you will love it. Listen to what I have in mind for a love potion.'

He caught her shoulder and pulled her close to him, then whispered in her ear. She turned slowly and stared up into his face, her mouth open in disbelief and unwilling excitement. 'What,' she said, 'in front of them? In front of the people who were buying it?'

He arched one eyebrow. 'Is it any more shameless than what the high priestess does in the temple of Amun?'

She opened her mouth to deny it, but he put one finger on her lips. 'Hush,' he said. 'I can see you want to try it. I will be with you, Naunakhte, all the time. Nobody will harm you. And just imagine. If this is as successful as I hope, soon I may not have time for gadding about at night. That would make you happy, wouldn't it?'

His eyes were bright and shallow, like the sun on a pool of water. She did not believe him for an instant. But he was so eager, like a child, and although she would have liked to deny it she too was tingling with excitement at the thought of trying out his plan. She fought with her qualms and finally subdued them.

'All right, Khonsu,' she said. 'We will try what you want.'

* * *

Khonsu was proven right. Magic was an excellent way for Naunakhte to earn her keep.

She was astonished at how many clients came. But Khonsu did not seem remotely surprised. He just smiled and continued to bring men to the house, one after the other, all of them prepared to pay deben upon deben of copper or even rings of gold to take away with them a small phial of Naunakhte's love potion. It was tiring making the potion, and eventually she had to ask Khonsu to restrict the number who came each day, lest she become too exhausted to perform adequately. After each client had gone she and Khonsu would laugh as they imagined how he might intend to administer the potion to the object of his desire and what the result might be.

For a few days Khonsu went to bed with Naunakhte when darkness fell and lay with her until the morning, holding her. It was bliss to lie in his arms all night. She believed that his presence kept the god from her. She began to hope that her success might continue to keep Khonsu with her. But she hoped in vain. After not many days of domesticity he dressed one evening in his nobleman's clothes, slung his best sword on its leopard-skin baldric over his broad smooth shoulder, and left without a word. He did not even look behind him as he descended the stairs.

So, a fig for his promises. Naunakhte went sadly up to the roof and crawled beneath the net under the glittering stars. She turned on her side and sighed with the rueful resignation of a woman who has expected her man to disappoint her all along. Then she closed her eyes to sleep, for she was very tired.

Sleep eluded her. She imagined Khonsu stalking the streets of Waset in the darkness, with daggers and spears awaiting him in every doorway. Or perhaps he had dressed in his finery to visit some noblewoman, his mistress. When he returned, would he again carry a wound, or would he smell of his mistress's perfume?

At last she sat up, shaking her head. Aloud she asked the stars, 'Why am I giving myself such pain?'

Her intuition supplied the answer, unbidden. *Because you are falling in love with Khonsu.*

Naunakhte lifted her hands and closed her eyes as if she could shut out her feelings. 'Lady Hathor,' she prayed, 'goddess of love, have mercy on me. Let me not love him. He will break my heart.'

When she awoke Khonsu was asleep beside her. He was unharmed and smelt of his own fragrance. Only the dark shadow of antimony on his heavy eyelids showed that last night had been anything but a dream.

He woke slowly, as was usual with him, and looked up smiling into her anxious face. 'A client this morning,' he said, 'for the love potion. And then this afternoon, someone wants you to do some divination for him.'

'Divination?' Naunakhte shook her head. 'No, Khonsu. You know I don't like to do it.'

Khonsu caught hold of a handful of her hair and tugged at it gently, as if he were playing with a puppy. 'Little goddess, be reasonable. I am not asking you to communicate with the gods! All I want you to do is make what I tell you sound specious. Bahematun wants to know what's in his father's will, that's all. He wants to know what the old man has left him. There's half a dozen sons – we could say anything. Draw blue lines on your eyes and mutter – you know what to do.'

'No,' Naunakhte insisted. 'Khonsu, you don't understand. It doesn't matter that you tell me what to say. Whenever you ask me to tell a fortune it's the same.' She shivered at the memory of the last time. 'I can feel that I shouldn't do it. It is dangerous, Khonsu. It is against the will of the gods.'

Now Khonsu looked really angry. He caught hold of another handful of hair and held her head still so that he could look into her eyes. 'Naunakhte,' he said very softly, 'I am not even telling you to lie. We are just

105

making something up, like a story. What can be wrong with that?'

She shook her head against the pressure of his strong hands. How could she argue against him, when all she knew was that to make divinations *felt* wrong? 'Please,' she said, 'don't make me do it.'

Khonsu's face hardened. 'Look. Bahematun is ... influential.' He did not specify in what circles the man's influence was exercised, but Naunakhte thought she could guess. 'I would rather not disappoint him. He has power, and he bears grudges. So dress yourself prettily, little goddess, and do what I tell you.'

She knew that she ought to hate him for forcing her to do what she knew to be wrong. But she could not hate him, and it frightened her that she could not. She got up without another word and went downstairs to prepare herself for her first client of the day.

The client knocked on the door while the morning was still fresh and cool. Khonsu, dressed as an acolyte in plain kilt and a collar of lapis, leapt down the stairs to admit him. He was a middle-aged man, whose corpulence showed that he was wealthy and successful, and he hurried through the door as if someone might be watching him.

'Will she see me?' he asked Khonsu eagerly.

'She is ready,' said Khonsu without a smile. 'But you must be prepared for anything. Have you brought the cockerel?'

The client nodded, chins wobbling, and held out his right hand. In it he held a black cockerel, dangling by its feet. Its beak was tied shut with string to keep it quiet. The black wings flapped forlornly.

'Good,' said Khonsu. 'Come.'

The man followed Khonsu up the narrow stairway, breathing hard. The room at the top of the steep stairs was dark and quiet. Even the noise of the coppersmiths, tapping away in the shops along the street, seemed muted. Khonsu withdrew and faded into the shadows, leaving the client alone.

For a moment he stood with his eyes narrowed, blind from the sun. He stared about him, lips moving faintly as if he would have liked to speak but did not dare.

Naunakhte stood still as a statue, covered from the crown of her head to her ankles in Khonsu's voluminous black cloak. Though she could see nothing, she could sense the growing tension and fear of the disorientated client. She judged her moment just so. When the poor man actually gibbered from anxiety she flung back the cloak and said in her most compelling voice, 'I am here.'

In the background Khonsu lifted the covers from a pair of bright lamps. The light flared up, revealing Naunakhte standing with her hands raised, dressed in a long gown of white linen so fine that her rose-pink nipples and the dark fur at the join of her thighs showed through like shadows seen in a dream.

'What do you want of me?' asked Naunakhte softly.

The middle-aged man ducked his head as if she were a great lady and held out one hand in a gesture of supplication. 'Great mistress,' he said huskily, 'I seek a potion to make a woman fall in love with me.'

'What woman is it whose love you seek?'

The man shifted uneasily. 'It is . . . a girl within my house, lady,' he muttered at last. 'She denies me. And I want her.'

Naunakhte concealed a smile. Something told her that her client spoke the truth, and many men would have taken a reluctant serving girl by force. It pleased her that this tubby rich man had not. She would make the potion for him with a good will.

'Bring the vessel,' she said, lifting her hands again.

Khonsu emerged from the shadows behind the lamps, carrying a deep earthen pot glazed with golden sand. He set it on the floor before Naunakhte and brought the lamps to set at either side of it. The little flames shivered, sending trembling sparks of light bouncing from the gold that Naunakhte wore at her throat and wrists. The discs of gold that hung in her ears shook like leaves in a breeze.

'You have the bird,' said Naunakhte to her client. 'Kill it. Let its blood fill the bowl.'

The man hurried to obey. He pulled his knife from the waist of his kilt and hacked at the cockerel's throat. Naunakhte nodded, then said to Khonsu, 'Let the blood be mixed with honey. And bring me the magic stone.'

Khonsu bowed to her and scurried away. Naunakhte lifted her head and gazed on nothing, making herself look beautiful. She still wanted to smile. One of the best things about being a sorceress was that in his character as faithful acolyte Khonsu had to give her complete and immediate obedience. This was a novel and delightful experience, and she made the most of it.

Khonsu approached, holding out a heavy object on the palms of his hands. It was a phallus, cunningly carved of gleaming granite, rose-pink and freckled with dark red like specks of drying blood. He knelt before Naunakhte, holding up the phallus.

'Let it be given to him,' commanded Naunakhte.

The client looked startled, but he lifted the heavy stone from Khonsu's palms and held it between both hands. His eyes met Naunakhte's and he swallowed.

Naunakhte allowed herself a little smile. Then she unfastened her gossamer robe and pushed it from her shoulders. The tubby man gasped as the fine linen fell to the ground behind her, revealing her lovely body naked and gleaming in the light of the lamps, adorned only with gold.

'If she is to love you,' Naunakhte whispered, 'your body's juices must enter her together with those of a woman. You have come to me for my help, and my juices shall be yours.'

The client's eyes gleamed with eagerness and he stepped forward, clutching the phallus tightly. Its shape was mirrored by the shape of his own penis, lifting up beneath the linen of his kilt. But before he could touch Naunakhte, Khonsu was between them, holding up one hand in a gesture of stern negation. The tubby man fell back, chastened.

'You may not touch me,' Naunakhte said. 'It is forbidden. None but my servants may touch me.' She sensed Khonsu's smile and avoided meeting his eyes. 'But you shall wet the magic stone with your saliva, and I shall draw forth the milk of my body with it. It shall be the weapon which serves you in your battle.'

He looked at the stone phallus, eyes wide, then back at Naunakhte. 'And as for me, mistress?'

'Even as the god Amun created the world,' said Naunakhte with a sweet smile, 'let your own hand call forth your seed. Let it fall into the bowl. There it shall blend with my juices. The power of such a mixture will not fail you.'

The client bowed his head, then hesitantly opened his mouth to lick the stone phallus. Naunakhte touched Khonsu's shoulder and said to him, 'Anoint me.'

For a moment, Khonsu's eyes met hers, bright with amusement and arousal. Then he returned to his knees before her and lifted a little jar of scented oil. He poured the oil into his hands and began to smooth it on to her golden skin.

Naunakhte stood very still, arms outstretched. In the temple of Amun she had anointed the Lady Hunro each day before the rite, and the touch of her fingers had driven the high priestess into the trance of the god. Now, as Khonsu gently spread the perfumed oil over her calves, her thighs, her belly, she also felt the trance begin.

She could not permit herself to fall into the possession of Amun. She must keep herself whole, in the present, able to perform as her client required. She fought away the strange floating sensation that threatened to engulf her. But the touch of Khonsu's hands was so wonderful, so deft and delicate, that it took all her control to remain upright.

He poured more oil into his palms and reached up to her breasts. His eyes glittered. As always, this ritual aroused him almost as much as it did her. Beneath his kilt his penis was in strong erection, thrusting forward as eager as a hound on the scent. His hands cupped the soft roundnesses and his fingers met on her nipples, pulling them out into long buds of taut ecstasy. She let out a little helpless moan.

'Oh, gods,' whispered the hapless client. He was still holding the granite phallus in one hand, but now he dragged up his kilt and took hold of his penis and began to rub at it, hauling away with desperate urgency. His belly shook with the rhythm of his tugging.

'The stone,' Naunakhte whispered. Khonsu turned to retrieve the phallus and she let herself slide to the floor, her oiled body glistening. In a moment she would open her legs and show herself to this stranger's gaze. The delirium of total abandonment began to fill her. She could resist the trance no longer.

The base of the phallus was heavy and cold in her hand. She let it rest between her breasts, relishing its smoothness and weight. She wanted to feel it within her. Gradually she drew it down her body, tracing a faint line across the soft rounded swell of her belly, parting the dense curls of dark hair at her loins. She nudged the tip of the stone between her closed thighs. It caught against the erect stem of her clitoris and she moaned with pleasure.

It was time. Naunakhte arched her back and let her thighs fall apart, loose and soft. The moist petals of flesh between them gleamed in the light of the lamps and the frantically masturbating client let out a long gasp of delight and disbelief.

For a moment she stimulated her clitoris with the cold tip of the phallus, teasing and rubbing the little bud until her breath was shaking. Then she edged the broad stone head between the lips of her sex and began to ease the full length of it into her.

Its coldness was like the coldness of Amun's statue before her caresses brought it to life. It was unrelenting, harder than a man, divinely determined. With one hand

Naunakhte thrust it deep within her, and with the other she rubbed and rubbed at her aching clitoris. Her hips lifted and lowered as she worked the smooth granite slowly to and fro in her snug sheath. She began to cry out and shake as the wonderful sensations mounted within her.

She heard the client groan as if he were in another world. Nothing was important now but her own pleasure and satisfaction. The phallus within her was Amun, the divine lover of her dreams. He showed himself to her in his godhead. She was surrounded with the fragrance of the god; her senses were drowned in it. She cried out again and gripped with her inner muscles at the smooth, cold shaft of the granite phallus. Her whole body tensed and shook as her orgasm possessed her.

Then she lay still, breathing slowly as she returned to reality. She felt the phallus gently withdrawn from her and made herself concentrate.

She sat up and took the phallus from Khonsu. It gleamed in the lamplight, coated with her milky juices. She met the client's eyes, then leant forward and slowly stripped the creamy fluid from the phallus and let it drop into the mixing bowl.

'It is done,' she said, leaning back as if she were very weary, which she was. 'It is completed.' And she pulled the black cloak towards her to cover herself.

She heard Khonsu say, 'There are prayers you must say to accompany the potion. I will tell them to you. They are very important.'

Naunakhte smiled beneath the shelter of the cloak. Khonsu was a consummate fraud. If for some reason the potion failed to work and the client returned to complain, he would be able to blame a fault in the prayers rather than in the potion. She took a deep breath, fatigued by the trance and her orgasm. It was easy to allow herself to fall into a light doze.

She woke with a start. The cloak was being dragged from her and it was dark. Khonsu's voice whispered,

111

'Wake up, sorceress. Another satisfied customer. I've taken the cockerel to the cookshop; they'll roast it for us.'

'Oh,' Naunakhte murmured, still half in a daze. 'Has he gone?'

'Yes.' Khonsu's hands caught at her, turning her so that her back was towards him. 'By Seth, little witch, you inflame me. Ordering me to anoint you and then pleasuring yourself! I'll teach you a lesson.'

He pulled her on to her hands and knees. Naunakhte shook her head, blinking.

'Remember that picture?' hissed Khonsu. *'Come behind me with your love?'*

Naunakhte remembered, vividly. She shivered as Khonsu poured a stream of the fragrant oil directly on to the cleft of her buttocks, then began to stroke and fondle the delicate flesh between them. 'What are you doing?' she whispered.

'Coming behind you with my – ' Khonsu broke off in mid-sentence. His hand pressed and pushed at her anus, at last opening her. One finger slithered inside her and she cried out with shock and delight at the sudden dark pleasure that flooded through her.

'You have had your fun,' hissed Khonsu in her ear. 'Time for mine.'

The smooth hot head of his erect phallus nudged between the cheeks of her arse and lodged itself in that secret hole. He withdrew his finger and replaced it with the head of his cock, keeping up a steady, powerful pressure. Naunakhte moaned, wanting to resist him and at the same time wanting to feel him within her.

'Gently,' whispered Khonsu, and at that moment she relaxed and his stiff penis began to enter her anus. Once the head was within her Khonsu chuckled and caught hold of her arms, then thrust harder. Naunakhte gave a groan of protest and tried to pull away, but now it was too late to stop him.

'Bend over,' Khonsu ordered her. He twisted his hand into the mass of her dark hair and pushed her head forward so that her buttocks were offered lewdly up towards him. He grunted with satisfaction and drove himself slowly and deliberately into her. 'In the name of chaos,' he gasped, 'that's good. That's tight. Ah, Naunakhte, you are a witch indeed. You make me want you. Ah, gods.'

He was shaking with urgent lust. He began to thrust himself into her anus quickly and powerfully, wrenching her with sensations so extreme that she could not keep in cries half of pleasure, half of pain. 'Please,' she whimpered, 'you shouldn't, Khonsu, stop.'

'No,' Khonsu snarled, and then he gave a great shout of consummation and his strong hands clutched tightly at her naked buttocks as he succumbed to orgasm.

At once he was contrite. He withdrew very gently and kissed her bruised flesh tenderly, whispering endearments. She moaned and clung to him. 'Hush,' he soothed her. 'Did I hurt you, little one? I'm sorry. Hush.' He poured a little more of the perfumed oil on to his fingers and began to massage it into her, gently coaxing away the hurt. His other hand stroked her breasts softly.

Presently his delicate fondling overcame her pain. She sighed and turned over in his arms, looking up at him in the half light. His eyes glittered and the expression on his face made her catch her breath. She could almost believe –

No, she could not believe that he loved her. If he loved her, how could he bear to hurt her? How could he make her do things which she did not wish to do? He was cold and manipulative and he wanted her only because she was beautiful.

It was against sense, to love this amoral, ruthless man. He would use her and then be rid of her. And yet the beauty of his strong face moved her, and the pleasure of feeling his arms around her was almost enough to make her forget the god Amun. It was too late for sense.

'Khonsu,' Naunakhte whispered, reaching up for him. He stooped his lips to hers and kissed her. Their tongues met and parted in their open mouths and it was both sweet and sad.

He withdrew a little and whispered her name, then kissed her again. His lips were as soft as the petals of a flower, and as relentless as the creepers of a vine which can split the walls. His hard hands pressed against her back, holding her close against his smooth powerful body. Naunakhte clung to him, hardly knowing that she was weeping.

Chapter Eight

Noon came and went. Naunakhte sat by the window, resting. Khonsu had always accepted that the performance of her magic tired her, and now he moved smoothly and silently around the room, making things ready for the next client.

The wooden blind that kept out the sunshine while she made magic was lifted and the brilliant golden light poured into the room. Naunakhte watched Khonsu as he moved here and there, admiring the play of muscles under his golden skin. The scar on his thigh was no more than a shadow now.

Beside her lay one of his papyrus scrolls. She put her hand to it and unrolled it, hardly thinking. The writing caught her eye. It was the tale of Bata. Naunakhte remembered her father telling the tale, and she ran her finger along the words, smiling as she read.

Bata went to the stable and loaded himself with barley and wheat and carried it outside on his shoulders. His brother's wife said to him, 'How much is it that you have upon your shoulder? Five sacks in all? You are very strong. Every day I see how strong you are.' And she desired to lie with him as a woman lies with a man. She arose and took hold of him and said, 'Come, let us sleep together for an hour!'

A shadow fell over the papyrus. Naunakhte jumped

and looked up, almost ashamed to be discovered. Khonsu was standing over her, frowning down. After a long moment of silence he said, 'You can read?'

He sounded utterly disbelieving. Naunakhte nodded and said uncomfortably, 'My father was a scribe. I learnt by watching him.'

Khonsu sat down beside her, legs crossed. He took the papyrus from her hand. He read a little, then smiled at her. 'There we are the same,' he said softly. 'My father was a scribe, too.'

In all the time she had been with Khonsu, he had never mentioned his childhood or where he came from. Now Naunakhte felt as if she walked on a slender bridge of papyrus reeds over a bottomless marsh. She said in a carefully casual voice, 'Where was that, Khonsu?'

'At Memphis, in the lower kingdom,' said Khonsu. His fingers moved slowly over the surface of the papyrus, tracing the swirling lines of the cursive hieroglyph script. He glanced up at Naunakhte. 'Tell me about your father.'

'My foster father,' Naunakhte said. 'He works at the royal tombs – he is a servant in the place of truth. He used to be a tomb painter before he was promoted and became a scribe. He liked to paint; even after he was made the scribe, he went on painting, for the tombs of friends and so on. It is very skilled work.'

'Yes, it is,' Khonsu agreed softly. He seemed to be lost in memories. 'I would have liked to have been a painter,' he said at length. 'At least when you paint there is something of creation to be done. But writing ... I was supposed to follow my father in his profession. But his mind was small. He worked in the accounts office of the royal palace. I could not have borne it.'

Naunakhte looked into his face, breathing shallowly. His eyes were veiled, as if he shut her out. She tried to imagine him as an ardent young eighteen-year-old, full of energy and enthusiasm. Who would have tried to pen him up in the musty, silent labyrinth of a palace

116

accounts office? It would have been like caging a desert leopard.

'Khonsu,' she said softly. He looked up, and his expression was both hesitant and vulnerable. Her heart moved, and she opened her lips to say that she loved him.

Below them someone beat on the street door, a thundering tattoo that made them both jump. Naunakhte shut her eyes, not sure whether she should be frustrated or relieved that she had not been able to speak.

'Bahematun,' said Khonsu. He glanced down at the scroll in his hands, made an angry face and thrust it away from him like a youth found playing with his old toys. He jumped to his feet and lowered the blind, shutting out the sunlight. 'Get yourself ready, Naunakhte,' he ordered. 'Quickly.' Then he was gone, vanishing into the stairwell without another word.

Naunakhte took a deep breath and seized the silver mirror. Her eyes stared back at her, glittering in the half light. They were heavily painted for her magic – green with malachite and black with kohl.

'She is making ready.' Khonsu's voice on the stairs, procrastinating. 'Let me go before you.'

Then another voice – a deep harsh snarl that chilled Naunakhte's blood. 'If she is a diviner, she knows already that I am coming.'

She stepped to the head of the stairs, suddenly determined that this villainous associate of Khonsu would not awe her. In a commanding voice she said, 'Bahematun.'

Khonsu stopped on the stairs and looked up at her with admiration and approval in his face. He moved aside and Naunakhte saw the man standing behind him. She stiffened her shoulders against her immediate, instinctive reaction to recoil.

Bahematun was a few years younger than Khonsu. He was thin and wiry, tanned mahogany brown by the strong sun of Egypt, and his eyes were as black as ink. His heavy wig fell to his shoulders and was tipped with

117

beads of glittering black and gold, his wrists were clasped with broad gold bracelets brightly enamelled with the figures of beasts and birds, and around his neck was a great collar of coloured glass – red, blue, white and yellow. His clothes were like any wealthy man's, but as he advanced up the stairs with his eyes fixed on Naunakhte's face, he exuded an aura of such concentrated menace that it took all of her willpower to remain where she stood.

'So,' said Bahematun as he entered the room. His dark gravelly voice sat ill with his narrow-shouldered, skinny frame. 'This is the beautiful sorceress who has ensnared Khonsu.'

Naunakhte had never considered what the effect of her arrival might have been on Khonsu's life, but now was not the time to react or to ask questions. She drew herself up to her full height and was pleased to see that she was a little taller than Bahematun. 'You want me to make a divination for you,' she said coldly.

'Yes.' Bahematun's eyes glittered. He looked her up and down as if he would strip her naked. She determined at once that for this performance she would remain clothed throughout.

'Sit,' she said, gesturing at the small folding stool in the centre of the room. Bahematun raised his brows and smoothed his kilt before he sat down. Naunakhte drew a deep breath and knelt before him, opening the palms of her hands like a statue from a tomb. 'Khonsu,' she said softly, 'bring me the drink.'

The drink was nothing more or less than strong, unwatered grape wine, but all diviners took something to drive them into trance and clients expected it. Khonsu held the cup to her lips, ignoring Bahematun's undisguised sneer.

Naunakhte looked at the thin man's scornful face and felt a sudden wave of fierce protective anger. He was mocking Khonsu! She swallowed the wine and its strength flooded through her. 'Why have you come here,' she said coldly, 'since you do not believe in my powers?'

She must have spoken Bahematun's thought, because he looked uncomfortable. In the shadows Khonsu gave a satisfied nod. Bahematun licked his thin lips, then said, 'I . . . am prepared to listen to what you say.' The lamplight caught in the whites of his eyes. 'They say you have the power of the gods,' he added, speaking more softly.

His face was cruel and harsh and Naunakhte feared him. She wanted to shiver at the touch of his cold eyes. How could Khonsu bear to associate with men like this? Controlling herself, she said, 'Tell me what you want to know.'

Bahematun leant a little forward. His hands clutched the air as if they would squeeze the life from it. 'My father has made his will,' he said softly, in a voice like feet crunching over the desert rocks. 'Tell me, sorceress, what is in it. I have brothers. Tell me what he has left to me.'

His eyes met hers. They were blacker than a moonless night. Naunakhte stared into his face, resisting the urge to shudder. She hated this role that Khonsu had forced upon her, and she feared Bahematun. There was death in his face.

Amun, she prayed silently to herself, *great lord, protect me*.

She closed her eyes. She meant to pretend to be in a trance, to mutter and writhe and speak nonsense the way Khonsu had shown her. Then, when Bahematun believed that she was in the power of the god, she would say what Khonsu had advised, that his father had left him property equally with all his sons. That, after all, was the most likely outcome.

But suddenly her mind felt very clear and cool and remote, as if she were standing on a mountain top in the desert dawn. Behind her closed eyelids she saw light, a rosy flush like the sun rising. For a moment she bathed in a sensation of inexplicable bliss, and then she knew that the god was with her.

Naunakhte, said the voice of Amun, *do not fear. I will be with you.*

She heard her own voice as if from a great distance. It sounded strange, cold and far off. 'Your father has made his will, Bahematun, and he has left you nothing.' In the corner of the room Khonsu leapt to his feet, eyes wide, and made a quick gesture across his throat with the flat of his hand. But Naunakhte ignored him. The cloak of the god was spread over her, and she spoke under his protection. 'Your father hates you. He has left you nothing.'

Bahematun leant forward on the stool, his right hand knotted into a fist. His knuckles were ugly white and red. 'You lie,' he hissed.

Naunakhte shook her head. She felt very light, as if she were made of filmy cloud. The god Amun stood behind her and stroked her hair. His touch crackled through her like summer lightning. 'I do not lie,' she said calmly.

There was a silence. Khonsu stood in the shadows, staring and breathing fast. Bahematun got slowly to his feet and looked down at Naunakhte as she knelt before him. She returned his gaze, her face translucent, and her whole body radiating limpid calm.

At last Bahematun said in a harsh, clotted voice, as if he spoke through blood, 'Sorceress, tell me what I must do to change this. What spell shall I say? How may I change what is written?'

There was no doubt that he believed in her now. Naunakhte's conscious mind smiled with triumph. She got to her feet, her hands still raised as if she called on the god. Amun's presence was with her, unshakeable. 'And if I told you,' she asked coolly, 'what then?'

'I will give you gold,' said Bahematun quickly. His face lit with urgency and greed. 'Name your price.'

Khonsu stepped forward, about to speak. But Naunakhte cut across him. 'First,' she said, 'swear that you mean no harm to your father. If his will were in your favour, what would you do?'

'Nothing,' protested Bahematun, too quickly. 'I honour him. I only want to know what he intends, so that I may plan accordingly.'

'Swear,' repeated Naunakhte. 'Swear by the Lord Amun.'

'I swear,' said Bahematun, holding up one hand, 'by the name of Amun, that I mean my father no harm.'

The presence of the god towered up within Naunakhte, filling her. She flung up her head, gasping as divine strength poured through her, and both Bahematun and Khonsu took a step backward. For a moment she struggled for breath as words tried to tumble one on top of the other from her lips. Then the god withdrew a little and she could speak.

She shook back her hair and fixed her eyes on Bahematun. She glowed with such fierce anger that he held up his hand in the gesture that wards off the fury of the gods. 'Bahematun,' she said, and her voice shuddered with power, 'you have lied. You have sworn falsely by the god Amun.'

'Naunakhte, no!' called Khonsu urgently.

She did not hear him. The god's words filled her mind and she spoke them at once. 'You came here with murder in your heart. You mean to kill your father. The god sees you, oath breaker!'

Bahematun let out a curse and reached for the sword at his hip. Naunakhte stood quite still, watching without reaction as Khonsu cried out and leapt forward to struggle with Bahematun. She felt as if nothing could touch her.

'You bitch!' Bahematun shouted as Khonsu at last wrested the sword from his hand. 'Foul-spoken whore!'

Naunakhte extended one hand as if she flung fire at Bahematun. Her eyes flashed as if with lightning; she was the might of the god revealed. Bahematun whimpered and recoiled, throwing up his arm to protect himself. 'Oath breaker,' she said again. 'May the god show you his power. May he punish you for the evil in your heart. Your false oath upon your own head!'

Her voice shook in the rafters. Bahematun cried out as if she had struck him with a whip and ran for the door. As he scurried away he cried out curses and promises of vengeance.

Evil was gone, and within Naunakhte's mind the god faded. She sank to the ground and covered her face with her hands. All around her was darkness and emptiness. She was alone, bereft.

'Naunakhte.' Hands on her shoulders, shaking her. 'Naunakhte, Naunakhte! Seth take you, wake up!'

She forced her eyes open and saw Khonsu before her. He was pale and his eyes were stretched wide open as if he were in great fear. 'What possessed you?' he demanded furiously, still shaking. 'Seth and chaos, what have you done? Bahematun will never forgive such an affront. He could destroy us!'

'It was not an affront,' Naunakhte said unsteadily. Her voice sounded faint and weak without the power of the god in it. 'It was the truth.'

'The truth?' Khonsu shook his head violently. 'Naunakhte –'

'The god spoke,' Naunakhte whispered. 'I called him and he came.'

'The god!' Khonsu's voice was fierce and scornful. 'What did he do, whisper in your ear? Enough, Naunakhte, enough!' He pulled her up from the ground and caught her in his arms. His lips were trembling. 'I will share you with no one, Naunakhte, man or god,' he said softly. 'Why did you call on him?'

'I asked for his protection,' said Naunakhte. She turned her head away from what she saw in Khonsu's eyes: anger, terror, grief.

'Why?' Khonsu demanded, shaking her as a mongoose shakes a snake. 'Was I not there to protect you? By Seth, I disarmed the rat-faced bastard! Ah, gods.' His voice choked and he let go of Naunakhte and turned violently from her, one arm flung up to cover his face.

122

He reeled to the wall and leant against it, his head hidden in the crook of his arms. His shoulders shook.

Naunakhte could barely believe that Khonsu could weep. She heard his harsh sobs and a great pain filled her, as if her heart were breaking. She stood for a moment, silent and uncertain, then crossed the room and laid her naked palm to Khonsu's naked back. He tensed and smothered the sounds he made, but he did not turn to her.

'Khonsu,' she said very softly, 'I am sorry that I hurt you.'

At that he turned and faced her. His eyes were brighter than the flames of the lamp and the paint around them was smudged by his tears. 'I made you do it,' he said brokenly. 'You warned me, and I forced you. And then the god took you and you were gone. I looked in your eyes, Naunakhte, and you were gone.'

'Hush,' Naunakhte whispered. She stroked her hand down Khonsu's cheek and ran her fingers over his beautiful mouth. 'Hush,' she said again. 'I am returned to you.'

Khonsu's broad chest lifted and fell with his quick breathing. Naunakhte leant against him, her head resting at the base of his strong throat. The smell of his skin filled her nostrils and she closed her eyes in ecstasy. Her hands traced the lines of his face, his jaw, the corded muscles of his neck, the long smooth curves of shoulder and arm. His heart beat strongly and fast and he swallowed and murmured something inaudible, then slid his hands beneath the weight of her heavy hair and caressed the nape of her neck.

Love for him threatened to overwhelm her. She felt as if every limb were melting, like warm wax or hot honeycomb. In a moment she would turn all to liquid and pour herself into him, sliding into every pore of his skin.

'Khonsu,' she said, lifting her face. She did not open her eyes, but stood very still, her mouth turned up to

123

his. For a moment there was silence, and then he pressed his mouth on hers.

The kiss was so deep that Naunakhte would have fallen had Khonsu's strong arms not held her up. She gasped and shivered as his long tongue traced strange patterns within her mouth, caressed her palate, and explored the insides of her lips. She sucked lasciviously on his tongue, moaning. Arousal flowed through her, making her hollow and empty with yearning. She pressed her body against Khonsu, parting her legs so that she could rub herself against the hard muscle of his thigh. Her breasts ached for his hands.

He lifted his mouth from hers and now he was smiling. 'When I kiss her and her lips are open,' he quoted, 'I rejoice without even having drunk any beer.'

She was relieved to see him restored to good humour so quickly. 'So,' she said archly, 'I am better than beer, am I?'

'You are better than wine,' Khonsu whispered. He pulled back her head by the hair and kissed her long golden throat until she cried out. Then he stooped and quickly caught her up into his arms, lifting her without effort. She put her hands around his neck, rejoicing in his strength. 'There is nothing I would rather drink than you, my mistress,' he said. 'Let me show you.'

He carried her across to the reed mattress and laid her down. She lifted her arms above her head and looked at him with love. It was blissful to lay the burden of her pleasure in his skilful hands. He would please her and he would take pleasure himself. They would cry out into each other's mouths and their sweat would mingle and they would forget about Bahematun and the god and the dangers of divination.

Khonsu tugged at the knot on his kilt, released it and flung it away. His phallus stood up between his legs, erect and swollen and glistening. Naunakhte's mouth was dry as she looked at it. She reached out to take hold of it, but Khonsu smiled and pushed her hand away. 'Not yet. You must be naked too, little goddess.'

He knelt down beside her and unhurriedly reached for the ties that held her complex pleated gown closed across her bosom. As he unfastened them he brushed his fingers very gently across the points of her nipples, standing up through the fine linen as hard as the stems of a fruit. Naunakhte sighed with bliss.

The gown parted and Khonsu pushed it gently away from her breasts and belly, revealing the length of her slender, golden body. 'Beautiful,' he whispered. He put his hands on her shoulders and ran them down to her breasts, taking their soft, round weight in his palms and pushing them together so that Naunakhte's nipples stood up directly before her like sentinels, eager and proud.

'Your breasts,' he said softly, 'are like lilies, little goddess, lilies growing on the Delta of the Nile. Your body is the stem, your breasts are the flower. Let me graze for honey on the flowers of your breasts.'

He lowered his lips and took her right nipple into his mouth. He lapped at it and sucked it, until it swelled even further and the whole areola flushed and darkened. Naunakhte cried out at the sudden rush of ecstasy from the caress of his lips.

Khonsu lifted his head and smiled at her. 'Here is nectar,' he said. 'But to drink from the honeycomb itself I must seek further afield.'

He kissed the skin between her breasts, then his lips travelled slowly down her body. His open mouth pressed to her ribs, her abdomen, the softness of her round belly. Behind his lips his tongue moved, swirling delicately over her smooth skin. Naunakhte pressed her palms flat against the wall and arched her back, groaning with delicious anticipation. Her thighs parted by themselves, offering her soft, moist and secret heart to Khonsu's searching kisses.

Gently he nuzzled the crisp cushion of her pubic hair, then laid his cheek against her belly. She waited for a tense moment, then let out a little moan of complaint.

Khonsu looked up at her and laughed softly. 'What do you want, little goddess? Why do you whimper?'

'You know well what I want,' Naunakhte moaned, and she tried to push his head further down with her hand.

'Oh, I know.' He kissed her navel lightly, a moth's kiss. 'And I want it too, little goddess.'

Moving with sudden decision, he wheeled his big body round until his head was pointing towards her feet. Then he lay down and caught hold of her hip and pulled it towards him. Naunakhte opened her eyes, startled, and found herself lying on her side with his erect penis directly before her face.

She let out a breath of amazement and delight and reached out for him at once. Her mouth opened wide to allow the swollen, downy glans to slip between her lips. She embraced his loins with her hands, sliding one arm between his thighs so that her hands could fondle and admire the strong resilient curves of his buttocks. The taste of his penis filled her mouth. She sucked at it greedily, laving the glossy head with her tongue, and with her fingers she teased and caressed the delicate membrane behind his tightly drawn-up testicles. He gave a sigh of pleasure and she felt his nose and lips nuzzling at her closed thighs. His arms encircled her hips and he slid his hands between her legs from the back and with his palms pressed her thighs apart. Warm air kissed her sex and she moaned with longing.

Then, at last, she felt his face between her open legs. She cried out and folded her full thighs around him, holding him there, and sucked harder at the stiff, wet shaft of his penis. Her body clung to his, breast to belly, belly to breast. His breath was cool on the soft lips of her sex and he opened his mouth and drew in the whole of that moist swollen mound of flesh. Naunakhte's body tightened against him as he began to lick and suck gently and steadily at her swollen clitoris.

They played each other's bodies like musical instruments, a delicate duet of ecstasy. When Naunakhte wished to be sucked hard and brutally, she clasped Khonsu's penis strongly in her hand and moved her lips rapidly up and down. When he desired to slow the tempo of their mutual pleasure, he withdrew a little and titillated her clitoris with the most delicate strokes of his tongue. They embraced each other, hands sliding over the skin of thigh and buttock and waist. As the sensations increased, their bodies tensed and became as taut as reeds which have been bent for bird nets. Naunakhte's hands clutched and clung, then fluttered helplessly as she lost control. Khonsu was parting her buttocks, easing one finger gently into her anus. The addition to her pleasure was almost more than she could bear. She knew that soon her moment would come, and she wanted him to come with her. He was telling her without words what he wanted her to do to him. She moaned and thrust her hips towards his face and let her lips glide more and more swiftly up and down the slippery length of his quivering cock, and with one finger she stimulated the tender cleft of his arse. Khonsu lapped harder at her clitoris and thrust his finger deep within the snug crevice of her anus. Her ecstasy increased and she sucked furiously at Khonsu's penis, moaning with pleasure to feel him moving between her lips as strongly as if he took her sex. Her orgasm flooded over her and her hands clenched and then opened and caught at Khonsu's thighs, pulling his loins towards her, taking in his phallus so deep between her shuddering lips that the jerking head touched the back of her throat. Her finger drove deep into him and he cried out, his voice smothered against her sex, and within her mouth his penis throbbed as the salty seed sprang from its tip.

They lay there as the sensations faded, suckling as gently as babies. Naunakhte moaned and smiled to feel Khonsu's penis softening within her mouth. A trickle of his semen ran from her lips and she sought it out with her tongue and lapped it up with libidinous care. Khonsu's hands were squeezing her buttocks and stroking the soft skin of her inner thighs, and his long tongue was buried deep in her vagina, slowly and thoroughly exploring its softness, not sparing a drop of her juices.

At last he lifted his head and let her fall on to her back, then leant over her, smiling. 'Better than wine,' he whispered, licking his glistening lips. 'Kiss me.'

She kissed him, shivering with lewd pleasure to taste her secretions on his mouth and tongue. He would be able to taste his own semen too, and the knowledge made her squirm with delight.

Khonsu searched her mouth with his tongue until she moaned. His fingers fondled her breasts, tweaking her stiff nipples. Then he leant against the wooden headrest of the bed and waved his hand in a lordly manner. 'Sing for me,' he commanded.

'What?' Naunakhte was startled.

'Sing for me. You said the temple women sing for the god, to arouse him. Sing for me, Naunakhte. Arouse me, take your pleasure with me.'

His face was bright with humour. Naunakhte was glad to see him so free from bitterness. She jumped to her feet, saying apologetically, 'I have no instruments. There should be harps, and a sistrum, and the finger cymbals – '

'You have your hands,' said Khonsu with another lordly wave. 'Clap the rhythm, temple girl, and sing for your master.'

'My master!' repeated Naunakhte with some heat. But she did not deny that Khonsu was her master. After all, she loved him. She thought for a moment, then remembered a love song that Neferure had sung to them as they sat around the lily pond in the slanting evening sunlight. Her body swayed to the unheard rhythm and her thick black hair swept to and fro like the reeds in the wind. Her eyes closed as she heard the tune within her own head. She took a slow step to one side, bent gracefully towards Khonsu, then arched back, supple and sleek as a gazelle.

Oh my god, my lotus flower, she sang. She lifted her

hands and clapped the rhythm, subtle and slow, like the beating of two lovers' hearts.

Oh my god, my lotus flower!
I love to go out and bathe before you.
I allow you to see my beauty in a dress of the finest linen,
Drenched with fragrant unguent.
I go down into the water to be with you,
And come up again with a red fish lying splendid on my fingers.
I place it before you.
Come, look at me!

She began to hum the tune and dance. Her arms swayed like the palm leaves in a high wind, and her breasts shifted with her movements. She danced as if she were in a trance, but she was very much there, in the present, aware of Khonsu's bright eyes watching her. He leant against the headrest in an attitude of negligent relaxation, but his lips were parted and he breathed shallowly as he watched her every move. She met his eyes and advanced a little towards him, undulating her hips lasciviously. Khonsu's eyes were fixed on her shimmering flesh – on the quivering skin of her belly and loins, the shifting shadows nestling in her pubic hair. He licked his lips, and between his legs his penis began to stir again, lifting towards her like a snake dancing to the charmer's pipe.

Naunakhte flung back her head. The thick curtain of her blue-black hair swept against her buttocks. She lifted her arms, reaching up with her hands as if the delight of the world hung above her head, just out of reach. She was moved by Khonsu's silent attention, his instant, aroused reaction to her dancing. Her shoulders heaved, thrusting forward her breasts, and her nipples swelled, tender succulent points of desire.

Now Khonsu shifted uneasily where he sat, as if he were trying to take the pressure off his freshly engorged cock. Naunakhte stepped towards him, looking down at him from beneath her heavy shadowed lids. She jerked her hips towards his face and watched his nostrils flare as he caught her scent. Then she drew her hands slowly, teasingly up her thighs, leant backwards and showed herself to him, parting her lips and revealing to him her secret rose, fresh and glistening.

'By the gods,' Khonsu hissed, 'come here, Naunakhte.'

'No,' she breathed, whirling away from him and clapping her hands again above her head. Her hair swung forward, concealing her nakedness. She arched herself over backward like a tumbler, reaching with her hands for the ground behind her head. She, too, was aroused by her dancing. She was wet and ready and she wanted to touch Khonsu's penis, to hold it and feel its length and stiffness, to guide it into her and rejoice as she felt herself penetrated and possessed. But first she wanted to make him want her.

Again and again she turned, clapping her hands and singing the last line of the song. 'Come,' she sang, flashing her eyes, 'come and look at me.'

'Seth and chaos, Naunakhte!' cried Khonsu, reaching out for her. 'I am looking! Come here to me!' His hands caught at her thighs and at his touch she could resist him no longer. She swung herself down towards him and straddled his lean hips and caught hold of his penis. The hot smooth tip of his erection slipped between the lips of her sex and she gasped and let herself sink slowly down. Her head fell back and she cried out in ecstasy as he entered her. All of a sudden he was there, within her, filling her everywhere. His arms were around her, her nipples rubbed against his chest, and his lips were upon her throat. She was complete.

'Oh my god, my lotus flower,' Naunakhte breathed. She shifted herself gently, sighing with bliss as she felt Khonsu's thick penis moving deep within her. 'I allow you to see my beauty. Look at me, my lotus flower.'

Slowly she leant back. His phallus was inside her, stiff and unyielding. She rested on his knees and let her arms hang loosely so that her breasts were offered to his searching mouth. He leant forward and suckled at her nipples, gentle and insistent.

'Khonsu,' she moaned, and slowly she rose and fell. The wonderful pillar of his phallus slipped out of the clasp of her tight sheath, then back to its rightful place. His hands gripped her buttocks, taking her weight, and he rose a little to thrust into her. They moved like a boat upon rippling waters. Naunakhte's eyes were open, gazing up into the half darkness of the room. At this moment, sharing love with Khonsu, she could think of nothing that would please her more. She was with him, and nothing else mattered.

Khonsu held her tightly and gritted his teeth as he forced himself into her, again and again. She hung above him, suspended as if in nothingness, whimpering as his thick penis slid slowly, deliciously to and fro within her. 'Little goddess,' whispered Khonsu, 'now you look at me.'

With infinite effort Naunakhte lifted her head. Her hair swept against Khonsu's thighs. She swung forward and gazed down into his face, gasping as the feelings swept over her. He returned her gaze, and the brilliance of his glittering eyes was shadowed by his half-closed, languid lids. He was so beautiful that as she looked at him she felt the sensations of her climax sweeping through her, filling her with such bliss that she cried out aloud. Khonsu reached up and caught hold of her hair, holding her head still so that as she reached her moment of infinite ecstasy she had no choice but to look into his eyes. He thrust up from the bed towards her, his face tense and trembling with the effort of driving himself towards his own orgasm.

'Khonsu,' she gasped, and as he bared his teeth and shuddered she plunged her mouth down on to his and kissed him with all the fervour she felt.

They clung together, their skins glistening and slippery with sweat. Gradually their breathing slowed. Naunakhte rested her cheek against Khonsu's, rejoicing at the soft smoothness of his body against hers. He was

131

relaxed, every muscle at rest, like a great cat stretched out in the sun. She was very relieved that they had left their disagreement and fallen straight into the shared pleasure of lovemaking. When they lay together she could forget all the things that made her afraid: the might of Amun, her own unfathomable power, and her fear that beneath his charm and gloss Khonsu did not love her.

Khonsu ran one finger down her cheek and smiled at her. 'Little goddess,' he whispered. 'Say that I share you with no one.'

She looked at him and shivered. No doubt he meant to be kind, but his words only made her think of what she feared. She turned her head away.

'Naunakhte!' Khonsu's voice was sharp. 'Say it. Say you are mine.'

Naunakhte could not remain silent, but nor was she prepared to lie to him. She lifted her chin and looked into his eyes. 'I am yours,' she said, 'as long as you do not ask me to make divinations.'

His body tautened, becoming hard and rigid as bronze. The cords on his neck tensed and stood out as he set his jaw. 'And if I ask you to?' he demanded coldly. 'What then?'

His physical rejection, so quick and so unfair, hurt Naunakhte deeply. She pulled away from him and got up, then reached for the crumpled rags of her dress and put it on, as if she needed to shield her body from him. He sat up on the bed and stared at her, challenging her with his eyes. His nakedness seemed only to increase his strength and confidence. 'Well?' he insisted.

Naunakhte fastened the dress. 'If you ask me to make divinations,' she said slowly, 'I am putting myself in the hands of the god. I cannot resist him.'

Khonsu leapt to his feet, quick as a panther. He looked enraged, and Naunakhte fell back, truly afraid for a moment that he would strike her. 'Cannot!' he shouted. 'Will not. It is all your dream, Naunakhte. There is no god in you. You are in love with yourself.'

There was a long, unbelieving silence. Naunakhte fought against tears of protest and fury. When she was calm enough to speak she said in a voice that trembled, 'Khonsu, you do not mean that. Amun – '

'That for Amun,' scoffed Khonsu, flinging up one hand in a gesture of fierce obscene dismissal.

'Don't.' Naunakhte caught his hand and pulled it to her lips, but he wrenched it angrily away. 'Khonsu, do not play games! You believe in the gods, I know you do. You may not worship them, but you believe in them.'

'Do I?' He looked down at her with cold eyes.

'You must,' whispered Naunakhte, taking a step back as the enormity of his suggestion began to break upon her.

'Must I?' His voice was as cold as frost upon the stones of the desert. 'Listen to me, Naunakhte, and understand. There is only one god that I believe in, and that is Seth.'

'No.' Naunakhte shook her head again and again in futile protest.

'I believe in chaos,' said Khonsu, his voice strengthening. 'I believe in darkness and evil and lust. Seth rules on earth, Naunakhte. The fact that you stand here with me proves it.'

Desperately, Naunakhte searched for an answer to his bleak vision. 'Perhaps,' she said at last, 'I stand here because . . . because we were fated to love each other.'

For a moment Khonsu looked at her in silence. His lips were trembling, as if he were in the grip of a powerful emotion. But then he flung back his head and let out a harsh laugh. 'Love!' he cried. 'What is love, Naunakhte?'

'It is – ' she began hesitantly. 'It is when you want the other person's good as much as your own.'

His laughter went on, loud and humourless. 'Listen to me, temple girl. Nobody does anything except for themselves. What is love? It is nothing more than an itching of the parts. When you want me to fuck you, when you want to feel my cock inside you, when you want my mouth on yours and my hands on your breasts, that is love.'

It was as if he sought to destroy everything that mattered. How could he bear to hurt her so? She fought against tears, but she could not stand before him and listen to his bitter words. 'You are a child of Seth indeed!' Naunakhte burst out, holding up her hands as if to protect herself from his baleful look. 'Amun will shield me from you.'

'Seth take the name of Amun!' roared Khonsu. He leapt towards her as if he would seize her and shake the life from her. She ducked, dodging his grasping hands, and flung herself towards the door. He cursed and ran after her, but her feet were already on the stairs.

'Naunakhte!' he shouted. But she was pulling open the door to the street.

Outside it was twilight. Naunakhte cast about wildly, wondering where to run. Then she heard Khonsu pounding after her and she took to her heels.

Within a hundred paces she skidded to a gasping stop. Advancing towards her with torches flaring in their hands were three of the temple medjay, and behind them was the thin, wicked face of Bahematun. 'That's the one you seek!' he cried.

Naunakhte was betrayed. She turned, the breath sobbing in her throat, and pelted back the way she had come. Khonsu stood in the narrow street before her, blocking her path. He was naked and furious, like an angry god. 'Khonsu,' she wept, 'help me!'

He saw the medjay and his face changed. As she got up to him he caught her arms and put her behind him. 'Run,' he said. 'Run away, little goddess.'

The medjay were armed and he was naked. 'Khonsu –' Naunakhte began.

'Run,' he hissed, thrusting her away from him. His face was alight with determination. 'Don't look back.'

'Catch the witch!' yelled Bahematun, and the sound of his harsh voice filled Naunakhte with such terror that her feet fled faster than the wind. She looked once over her shoulder and saw one of the medjay lying on the ground. Khonsu had a sword now and was swinging it like Pharaoh smiting his enemies, but the other two medjay were pressing him hard. With a moan of horror and grief she fled away into the twilight, quite alone.

Then she stopped. Her heart pounded and her breath sobbed, but she forced herself to stand still and think.

Khonsu had offered himself for her. He had protected her with his body, though it could mean nothing but death for him.

How could she have doubted his love? And was it thus she repaid him?

She knew what she must do. Without hesitation she turned and ran back the way she had come. She stopped at the end of the street of the coppersmith's, panting. Blood was staining the dust of the street, and a single figure stood outside the door to Khonsu's house. It was Bahematun. The sight of him lurking there like a vulture drawn by death made Naunakhte's head swim with terror and loathing.

As she approached, Bahematun turned and stared at her. His eyes were like pits. She hated and feared him, but needed what he knew. She came to within a few feet of him and demanded in her most arrogant voice, 'Where is Khonsu?'

His face showed that he was considering telling her a lie, but then he seemed to think better of it. 'Taken,' he said. 'They have taken him to the temple. He will die for what he has done. He will wish that the medjay had killed him.'

Naunakhte swallowed hard. 'You seek revenge on me,' she said flatly. 'You may have it. Take me to the temple of Amun and claim the reward.'

Bahematun's face became narrow and pinched with a smile. 'To the temple?' he repeated with a horrid, cold chuckle in his voice. 'All in good time. The reward will wait until I have had my cock inside you, you whore of a sorceress.'

Naunakhte rallied her courage. She stood still, staring

135

him out. 'If you lay your hands on me in lust,' she said with conviction, 'the god Amun will hound you to your death. I am his chosen one. I carry his mark.' And she tore the ring from her arm and showed him the phallus of the god, clear upon her golden skin as if it were painted there.

Bahematun took a step back, making the sign against the evil eye. Naunakhte's lips writhed back from her white teeth in a snarl. She looked like a beast defending her young from the hungry lion. 'I promise you,' she hissed, 'the curse of death and agony, if you touch me.'

For a long moment Bahematun stared at her, muttering under his breath. Then he clenched his fist in anger and frustration. 'Well,' he growled, 'the reward, then. To the temple.'

Chapter Nine

Naunakhte had no intention of letting Bahematun reap the reward for her return to the temple. She needed him only because she could not have reached Karnak without protection, and she thought that if Khonsu were cautious of Bahematun, the rest of Waset's low-life would be.

She was not wrong. Bahematun led her through the labyrinth of Waset's streets without any interference whatsoever. He did not touch her, though occasionally he glanced at her with a mixture of loathing and cupidity.

By the time they reached the temple precinct it was quite dark. Two great torches flared on either side of the massive pylon gateway. When they were still a full arrow's flight away from the gate, Naunakhte shot one quick look at Bahematun, then broke into a run.

'Hey!' he shouted. 'Come back here, curse you!'

He lunged for her. His clutching hand brushed her shoulder. She turned as swiftly as a striking cobra and spat upon his wrist. 'I am the one who curses you, oath breaker,' she cried, 'in the name of Amun!'

Bahematun fell back, clutching at his wrist and white with fear. She turned her back on him and covered the distance to the gateway in a flash. 'Let me in!' she cried to the medjay. 'I am a servant of the Lady Hunro!' She looked wildly over her shoulder. 'This man is pursuing me!'

They opened the gates at once and she ran through, then turned to laugh at Bahematun, who stood, still pale and trembling, staring after her. 'The god hears you, oath breaker,' Naunakhte shouted as the great gates closed. 'His anger is on your head.'

Another medjay stood within the gates, looking at her curiously. He was a middle-aged man with a kind face. She said quite calmly, 'I am Naunakhte, the proscribed servant of the god. Take me to the Lady Hunro.'

His eyes widened in amazement. 'The Lady Hunro is sitting in judgement with the Lord Merybast,' he said at last.

If they were sitting in judgement, it must be upon Khonsu. 'Take me there at once,' Naunakhte commanded loftily.

The medjay narrowed his eyes in disbelief. 'Lady,' he said after a moment, 'your death is pronounced. Do not return to the temple!' He looked from side to side as if he was afraid that he would be overheard, then leant forward and whispered, 'Hori and Menneb are my friends, lady. They told us all what happened. We know you did nothing evil, we know it was all the doing of the Lady Tiy. Come with me, and we will hide you.'

Until this moment Naunakhte had thought only that she must save Khonsu, even at the cost of her own life. His sacrifice demanded recompense. But now the name of Tiy brought her to reality with a cold shock. She saw her death in the medjay's kind, dark eyes, and she felt terror. Her heart thumped within her breast, fast and irregular, and her bowels were chilly and cramped with fear.

Then calmness enveloped her mind like a cool breeze on a scorching day. The anxious face of the medjay seemed to recede and fade, despite the bright torchlight. The god's presence was with her. She closed her eyes and lifted her hands to him in welcome.

Trust me, Amun whispered.

And then he was gone, but she was no longer afraid. Had he not given her power over Bahematun, so that she could be brought to the temple without danger? He would not fail her. He would tell her what to do.

'I must go to the Lady Hunro at once,' she said to the medjay. 'Amun commands it.'

The man bowed his head in sadness and submission. 'Follow me,' he said.

The great expanse of the hypostyle hall was aglow with light. The lotus and papyrus columns flung shadows upon the walls, the roof, each other; a tangled jumble of brilliance and darkness, as complex as the reedbeds in the marshes. The medjay led Naunakhte in and gestured with one hand, then withdrew. She stood in the shadows, breathing shallowly.

At the far end of the hall there were people. Naunakhte saw servants of the temple holding torches and medjay carrying spears and naked swords. As she made her way through the columns she saw also the Lady Hunro, seated on a tall throne beside an imposing man whose own greying hair showed beneath the edges of his black wig. This must be the Lord Merybast. He was leaning his head towards the Lady Hunro, listening closely to her murmured words.

Before them a naked man knelt on the stone floor. Naunakhte moved silently forward, her fist pressed to her breast as if to hold in her pounding heart. She would have known Khonsu's back among ten thousand. His elbows and wrists were pinioned behind him with harsh sisal ropes. Dark blood crept from a wound on his arm.

The Lord Merybast straightened upon his throne. 'Khonsu,' he said, and Khonsu flung up his head. 'Your sentence is death.'

'No!' said Naunakhte. Her clear voice echoed among the columns and the medjay flung themselves around to search for the interloper. Naunakhte put back her shoulders and walked from the last row of columns towards the little group of people around the tall thrones.

Khonsu looked around at her. His face was bruised and blood ran from his lip, but he looked as fearless as the desert lion. But then he saw her face revealed in the flickering torchlight and his expression twisted into a mask of denial and grief. Naunakhte could not bear it, and she looked away.

'Lord Merybast,' she said. She was intensely aware that every eye was fixed upon her. 'I am Naunakhte, the servant of the temple. You have condemned Khonsu for hiding me from you. I am here. I offer myself to you in return for his freedom.'

The Lady Hunro spoke in a disbelieving whisper. 'Oh, Naunakhte.'

'No!' Khonsu's voice was frantic. He leapt to his feet, every muscle taut. But before he could take more than a step the medjay seized him and forced him to the ground. One of them struck him hard around the face and they pinned him painfully down over his bound arms. A bronze spear point hovered before his throat.

The Lord Merybast had not spoken. He looked steadily at Naunakhte with dark, deep-set eyes. She felt her confidence falter. 'Lord Merybast, I offer myself in his place. I beg you to release him. He did nothing but try to protect me.'

'He resisted the temple medjay,' said Lord Merybast in a slow, deep voice. 'One of them lies gravely wounded because of him. That in itself merits death.'

Naunakhte took a step forward, moving close to the tall thrones. 'Lord Merybast, you never sought Khonsu. It was me that you sought. I stand here, Lord, ready to offer myself for judgement. Give him mercy.'

Merybast looked deep into her eyes for a long moment. She felt that he was reading her soul. At last he said, 'Naunakhte, your death is certain. Why should this man, who was your lover, I have no doubt, not die as well?'

Words escaped Naunakhte. She closed her eyes, listening for the word of the god, but Amun was silent.

Silent to her, but not silent completely. When she opened her eyes again she saw the Lady Hunro touching her husband's arm. Merybast leant towards her and they conferred in quiet voices. Hunro seemed to be urging something. Naunakhte shivered with awe, certain that Amun was moving the Lady Hunro in her cause.

Merybast looked at Hunro, then turned away from her. He seemed to be deep in thought. After a long silence he said, 'Naunakhte, the Lady Hunro has argued your case to me. I should not let this young man go, but in the circumstances, since you have returned voluntarily to accept your punishment, I am prepared to show mercy. He will be taken to the gate of the temple and released.' He jerked his head at the captain of the medjay. The man caught hold of Khonsu's arm and pulled him to his feet.

'May I speak to him?' asked Naunakhte. She wondered why she felt so calm, as if the constantly reiterated threat of her death was laughable or meaningless.

'Here,' said Merybast. 'Not in private.'

Naunakhte bowed her head towards the throne, then walked slowly across until she stood in front of Khonsu. He looked down into her face. His eyes were cold and bleak, as if he were hiding from her. The muscles on his neck and shoulders stood out, tense and twisted because his arms were so cruelly pinioned. Naunakhte wanted to soothe and caress him; she also felt strangely remote from him, as if everything they had shared had been no more than a dream.

Still she wanted to comfort him. 'Khonsu,' she said gently, 'do not fear for me.'

He shook his head. 'Naunakhte,' he whispered, 'your death is pronounced. How should I not fear for you?'

Suddenly Naunakhte knew the answer. 'The god will protect me,' she said. Her face was bright with faith. 'I will commit myself to his oracle. He will save me.'

Khonsu's mouth twisted as if he had eaten bitter

herbs. 'I was ready to give my life for you,' he said. 'And even now you would rather trust yourself to a dream!'

Without another word he turned away from her and signalled with a jerk of his head that he was ready to leave. Naunakhte watched him for a moment, biting her lip. But she could not really feel his emotion. The presence of the god was with her, and her soul was alight with consciousness of his majesty.

But there was something Khonsu needed to know. She called, 'Khonsu,' and he hesitated, then turned and looked at her once more. 'Khonsu, it was Bahematun who brought me here. He may still be outside the temple. I cheated him of the reward. Beware of him.'

Khonsu's beautiful face twisted into a cold, ironic smile. 'Bahematun? If I meet that jackal, he is the one who will have to beware, even if I am naked and he has a sword in his hand.' He let out a short, bitter laugh. 'You deserve an attendant to accompany you into the afterlife, Naunakhte. Now, goodbye.'

He went silently into the darkness and shadows of the columned forest. Naunakhte watched until she could see him no more. Then she turned to face the Lord Merybast and his wife.

Hunro was weeping. 'Oh Naunakhte, why did you return? I cannot save you.'

Merybast looked at his wife as if he disapproved of her grief. To Naunakhte he said, 'Naunakhte, the chief priest Panhesi has accused you of blasphemy and sacrilege. His word cannot be doubted. You must die.'

Naunakhte's mind was as clear as cool water. Words dropped from her lips as if the god himself had spoken them. 'Lord Merybast, I am a servant of the temple. I carry the mark of Amun. Once before, when I was a child, the oracle of the god spoke to save my life. Now I claim trial before the oracle. Let the question of my sacrilege by put to the god. If Panhesi is right, I will be shown guilty and I will accept my death.'

'You claim trial by the oracle?' Merybast's deep voice was slow and hesitant.

'Let the god pronounce my guilt,' said Naunakhte. 'I give myself into his hands.'

There was a long silence. Merybast drew down his grey brows and stared at her as if his dark, glittering eyes could extract the truth from her. Hunro sat very still upon her throne, and the lapis beads that tipped her heavy wig glittered and swung as she trembled. Naunakhte waited, secure in the protection of the god. She was certain that Amun would watch over her.

At last Merybast sat back on his tall throne, one hand pressed to his lips. He said steadily, 'It shall be done. After the rite tomorrow, Naunakhte, you will be submitted to trial by the oracle of the god. Panhesi will be present, and your other accuser, the Lady Tiy.' He gestured to the captain of the medjay. 'For now, imprison this woman. Tomorrow the oracle will speak before the sacred lake.'

The medjay encircled Naunakhte, ready to escort her to the secret bowels of the temple. She went with them, silent as if she were in a dream, and Amun walked beside her.

Khonsu tried to keep his feet as the medjay flung him from the temple gateway, but they were violent and he fell to his hands and knees upon the harsh stone. As he pushed himself up, the gates slammed behind him.

He wanted to run to the gates and beat his fists against them, demanding that they let Naunakhte go free. He wanted to bring a great ram to batter his way into the temple, to save his woman from the priests who would take her life. But he was powerless. He stood with his eyes closed, fighting tears.

She was lost, no doubt of it. Khonsu had faith in nothing but evil. Naunakhte had offended people of power, and no god would protect her against their anger. He would never see her again.

Naked, and distracted with grief, Khonsu wandered

mindlessly along the broad road that ended at the temple gate. The warm stars hung over his head close enough to touch, but he did not see them. He was remembering other nights, happier nights, when he had held Naunakhte in his arms and caressed her; when the peaks of her breasts had risen to meet his searching fingers, when her sweet lips had parted to emit little trembling cries of ecstasy as his body penetrated hers. And then those lips had surrounded him, slipping delicately up and down his penis, coaxing it back to full hardness. He had moaned as he thrust his face between her loosened thighs and her sex had opened for him like a flower, parting its petals in the moonlight and filling the night with its fragrance. He had sucked her nectar and rejoiced at her taste – sweet but not cloying, more delicious than manna.

The road led down to the Nile, where it crossed the wide, dusty track that led to Waset. Khonsu stopped at the riverbank and looked down into the waters fringed with reed and lilies.

Among the blue shadows something stirred, something longer than a man with a carapace like armour. A crocodile, surely. Khonsu watched it moving, vaguely considering that if he stepped a little closer, a little nearer to the river, the lurking beast might take him. Would not death be preferable to life without Naunakhte?

Then he tensed and swung round, knowing without thinking that someone was behind him. His eyes widened and his breath stopped as he saw Bahematun. He crouched like a beast ready to spring. He was naked, and Bahematun carried a sword and was dangerous. Khonsu tensed and prepared to fight for his life.

But Bahematun staggered like a drunken man and his eyes were unfocused and wandering. He took a couple of shaking steps towards Khonsu and stretched out his hand. For a moment Khonsu wondered what could have become of Bahematun to unman him so, but only for a moment.

Snarling with hate, he lunged. Bahematun's hesitant fingers reached uncertainly for his sword and Khonsu lowered one shoulder and charged. Bahematun fell to the dust, sprawling, and Khonsu leapt on top of him and dragged the sword from its sheath. Then he put his foot on his enemy's throat and stood back, lifting the sword, ready to kill.

'No,' whispered Bahematun. 'Khonsu, mercy! The witch cursed me.'

Khonsu stared down, shuddering. Had Naunakhte's curse robbed Bahematun of strength and sense? It terrified him to think that he had lain with a woman of such power. He pushed the thought aside and remembered his vengeance.

'Oath breaker,' he said thickly. 'Her curse will kill you, not me.'

The sword hissed down. Bahematun screamed as the blade struck not his neck, but his wrist, severing his right hand. The stump spouted glistening blood. Khonsu reached down and seized Bahematun by the throat, pulled him up and dragged him towards the river. Bahematun struggled weakly, but there was no strength in his wiry limbs. It was as if Naunakhte's curse had softened his very bones. Khonsu gripped his nape hard and flung him into the still water.

The splash echoed from the banks and Bahematun wailed and flopped feebly in the shallows. His blood spread around him, darkening the water. For a moment he struggled alone among the reeds. Then from the darkness a dark ripple arrowed towards him.

The crocodile lunged and Bahematun arced from the water, shrieking. Khonsu watched until his enemy could no longer scream. Then he turned and walked on towards Waset.

This time the medjay did not pity Naunakhte, nor offer her her freedom. They led her deep into the temple complex, to a small, heavily guarded building without windows. One of them spoke a password and the door opened.

Within were a number of small cells, dark and airless. The medjay put Naunakhte into one of them and closed the door. Bars and bolts crashed down.

It was completely dark. Naunakhte felt her way across the room, moving her bare feet hesitantly across the cold stone. She found a sort of ledge, heaped with dry straw. It was not as uncomfortable as might have been expected. Naunakhte lowered herself gently to the straw, folded her hands and looked up into the darkness.

She was not afraid of the ordeal which would face her in the morning. She could still feel the presence of the god, like warm breath down the back of her neck. The presence felt benign, like a parent watching over a sleeping child. Naunakhte implicitly believed that the oracle would find her innocent.

But she was scared of sleeping alone, in this dark enclosed space within the precinct of the temple. For many days now she had slept under the stars, with Khonsu's strong, smooth body warm beside her. Sometimes she had woken in fear from dreams of vague horror to find Khonsu holding her, cradling her head against his shoulder and whispering comfort in her ears.

Khonsu! She remembered how he had looked at her, his face set in its old lines of defensive mockery. Her heart ached for the love she had felt for him. But she had survived; her heart was not broken. In this, as in other things, the god had protected her. He had seen Khonsu for what he was – a follower of Seth. Her foster father Ammenakht had been accustomed to reading to his children from a papyrus written by one of his predecessors, scribe Kenhirkhopeshef. The papyrus had described the followers of Seth. How could a man who lived two generations ago have known Khonsu?

The god in him is Seth. He is one dissolute of heart on the day of judgement. He is beloved of women through the magnificence of his body and the greatness of his loving them. Though he be a royal kinsman, he is like a man of the people.

He makes no distinction between the married woman and the whore. He destroys any man who opposes him. He will not pass into the afterlife, but is placed on the desert as a prey for the rapacious birds . . .

Khonsu was gone, and she was better off without him. A servant of Amun should not associate with a follower of Seth. But he had comforted her when her dreams had made her afraid, and now she was to sleep here in the temple prison and she knew that dreams would come. In her sleep she would be exposed to all the powers of the other world, and she could not be confident that Amun would protect her in that world as he protected her in this.

She tried to keep her eyes open. But the darkness of the cell crept into her brain and the exhaustion of the day lay heavily upon her, and she did not even realise that sleep was coming until it was too late.

The door of the cell opened and light streamed in, impossibly brilliant. Naunakhte lifted her head and got up. The light flooded over her with tangible power. It swept away her crumpled garments as if they were water. She stood quite naked, her golden skin glowing like the heart of a furnace.

A figure appeared in the doorway, silhouetted blackly against the light. Naunakhte smiled with sad sweetness, for she saw that it was Khonsu. He came towards her, holding out his hand.

'Come,' he said. 'I am still a god and now you are a goddess. Come, little goddess. Your worshippers are waiting.'

She wanted to say that she had not realised that Khonsu was a god, but her lips seemed to be sealed. In silence she followed his outstretched hand. Beyond the doorway was the open air. It was dark, and a great moon hung like a ghostly face over a lake surrounded by palm trees. Before them stood a tall altar and on either side of it stood people, ranks and ranks of people. They were all faces that Naunakhte knew. There was

147

the Lady Hunro, hand in hand with her husband. There was Psaro, the village medjay, and her brother Harshire. There was her friend Akhtay, holding to her breast the child that had killed her. There were Hori and Menneb, and there was Tiy, standing beside Panhesi. When they saw Naunakhte walking towards them, naked in the brilliant moonlight, the people let out a long sigh, soft as the dawn breeze.

'Lie upon the altar,' said Khonsu, waving his hand in his lordly way. 'Your worshippers will serve you. Tell them what will please you.'

Naunakhte glanced along the rows of people, then looked at Khonsu. He was naked, and his phallus was in massive erection. It thrust forward towards her, quivering with eagerness. He saw her look and smiled and stroked his hand along the length of his penis as if he admired it. He crooked his finger towards a girl in the crowd. It was Neferure. She came towards him, hands raised like one who worships a god. He opened her clothing to bare her little breasts and smiled when he saw the pink nipples already tight with obedient lust.

'Look, Naunakhte,' he said. 'These are our worshippers. They will serve us in any way they can. Look, you may use them for your pleasure.' And he caught hold of Neferure by her slender hips and pulled her towards him. He jerked her thighs apart and put the head of his penis between the lips of her sex and slid it deep into her. Neferure moaned and fell back as if she swooned and Khonsu held her up by her hips while the rest of her body dangled like a broken doll. He thrust with his buttocks and clutched tightly at the softness of Neferure's thighs. She hung down limply from his hands, her arms spread wide, her hair pooling like ink in the desert sand, and as his huge cock slid in and out of her unprotesting body, her breasts jiggled and her lips were soft and wet as she let out little moans of helpless pleasure.

Naunakhte watched. Her loins were hot and clenching with sudden urgent desire. Khonsu's phallus glistened as it worked in and out of Neferure's sex and whenever he withdrew, the soft pink lips clung to his shaft as if they did not want to let it go, then welcomed it with a soft liquid sound as it drove deep. Neferure moaned again and again. Naunakhte saw her friend begin to quiver with approaching orgasm and she, too, wanted to feel a man within her.

Khonsu smiled as if he read her thought. 'Whatever you want you shall have,' he said, thrusting juicily into Neferure's glistening sex. 'Which man shall fill you? Which shall serve you with his mouth?'

Suddenly resolved, Naunakhte went up to the altar. She lay down upon it and the stone was softer than a padded couch. She opened her arms to the glittering heavens above her. There was no need for her to speak; her acolytes knew her desire without a word.

She lay still, her whole body a tingling mass of delicious sensation. The points of her breasts were swollen and hard with need. Still in silence Tiy and Panhesi came and knelt on either side of her, stooped with sorrow and conscience. Naunakhte arched her back and obediently Tiy and Panhesi opened their mouths to suckle gently at her breasts.

There was another mouth between her legs, a soft determined tongue worming its way deep into the secret folds of her body. She sighed with pleasure and spread her thighs wide apart. The lewd, diligent tongue slid into her vagina, penetrating her like a tiny penis, then withdrew and flickered like a snake against her quivering clitoris.

Now for her pleasure Naunakhte desired to have a penis to suck, and because she desired it it was there. Psaro knelt over her, his black muscular body gleaming in the moonlight. He offered her his phallus, nudging the crimson glans up towards her gasping lips. She opened her mouth and moaned with delight as that great smooth shelving head slid between her lips, between her white teeth, filling her mouth with warmth and hardness.

For long moments of infinite ecstasy she sucked slowly and luxuriously at Psaro's penis while the unknown mouth continued to busy itself between her thighs. She was a goddess and her flesh contained divinity, and those who served her also experienced divine pleasure. Tiy and Panhesi moaned as they caressed her breasts with their eager mouths. They sucked with desperate earnestness, as if their lives depended on it. Psaro groaned and writhed as she licked his penis, and the person who was lapping between her thighs was gripping at her buttocks and letting out little smothered cries of delight and worrying at her tender flesh as if the glossy dew that her sex exuded was the very food of the gods. Naunakhte was surrounded by ecstasy. Soon she felt her moment coming, and Tiy and Panhesi lapped deftly at her engorged nipples, throwing her into wild paroxysms of joy. Psaro grunted and slid his penis in and out of her mouth, filling her with blissful sensation, and between her legs lips and tongue encircled her clitoris, bringing her into spasms of such uncontrollable pleasure that she believed that had she been mortal she would have died.

Gradually she came to herself. The mouth was gone from between her legs, and she felt both deliciously warm and achingly empty. Now she wanted Psaro to take her. Since she was a girl she had admired his ebony body, his full scarlet lips. She wanted to feel that splendid black penis penetrating her moist flesh. Again she did not need to speak. Even as she thought of her desire, it was ready to be fulfilled. Tiy and Panhesi continued to sweep their delicious tongues along the stiff peaks of her breasts while Psaro positioned himself between her spread thighs, ready to possess her.

Then suddenly Khonsu was there. He grabbed Psaro by the shoulder and pulled him away. 'Sacrilege,' he snarled. 'She is mine.'

'No.' Naunakhte lifted herself on her elbows. 'I am a goddess, and you said I could have whatever I wanted. I want Psaro. I want to feel his penis in me.'

'You are mine,' repeated Khonsu. 'It is my penis you will feel.'

'No,' said Naunakhte angrily. She reached out to Psaro to pull him towards her, but Khonsu made a sharp gesture with his hand and the black medjay fell back to the desert floor, still and silent..

'Psaro.' Naunakhte stretched out her hand towards Psaro's body, meaning to breathe life back into him. But before she could summon her power Khonsu seized her and pushed her back on to the altar. His erect phallus throbbed between her legs, huge and menacing.

'Mine,' he hissed. He caught her wrists and held her down. She screamed with rage and her eyes sent lightning flashing to drive him from her, but he was a god and laughed at her fury. He flung back his head, laughing, and as if her struggles inflamed him his massive phallus grew still further, swelling to the size of a strong man's forearm and fist, growing still until it was like a young tree. Khonsu held her, still laughing, and he pushed himself into her. She screamed, because he split her as a wedge splits the wood, and she moaned because she had never felt such bliss. Her immortal flesh stretched and yielded to accommodate the might of the god Khonsu and she accepted all of his magnificence within her. His power surged to and fro in her moist sheath. She was conquered and wrenched open for his possession, and she cried out with divine ecstasy.

Above her Khonsu was grunting like a beast as he thrust himself again and again into her shaking body. The cords on his neck stood out with effort and his tremendous penis slid to and fro within her with unstoppable power. He moved like the great weights that the workmen in the quarries strike against the face of the naked rock to split the blocks away. He moved like a sandstorm over the desert; like a black cloud of thunder and lightning or the fall of the great blocks into the foundations of Pharaoh's tomb.

Naunakhte caught his shoulders with her hands and pulled him down on to her to feel his weight. His flat muscular belly pressed on hers, his chest crushed her breasts, his breath was hot in her hair. She screamed with delirious pleasure and her limbs stretched out and tensed as she reached her orgasm, a climax so powerful that it was as if her body were filled with primeval chaos.

Khonsu laughed again as he felt her sudden stillness twist into convulsions beneath his pounding body. 'Mine!' he growled, and his voice had changed. It was a beast's voice. Nameless horror filled Naunakhte, driving away the fading ecstasy of her orgasm. She writhed beneath Khonsu and tried to catch hold of his head to see his face. But where his nape had been now there was an animal's neck growing from the man's shoulders, and above his labouring body grinned the head of a nameless beast, a terrible beast, half goat, half lion, all fury and madness. It was the face of Seth. Naunakhte screamed and screamed and then she felt the god's hot semen jetting within her and it was as if she was filled with scalding poison. She shrieked in agony and Seth looked down at her and her ears were filled with Khonsu's bitter, mocking laughter.

Naunakhte woke, shuddering. The door of the cell was open and sunlight streamed in. Had she dreamt it all, then, in that fleeting minute when the sunlight fell upon her face?

'Lady,' said the medjay silhouetted in the doorway, 'it is time.'

Naunakhte got to her feet, silent and shivering. The horror of the dream walked with her from the prison towards the sacred lake, where the god's oracle would speak. It was as if a cloud passed over the bright sun. The memory of it drove the god from her, and she was alone and afraid. She prayed to the god, but he did not speak to her.

Perhaps that terrible dream signified that Amun had left her. Perhaps his oracle would find her guilty. Perhaps –

They came to the sacred lake. It was circled with people. Beneath a white canopy in front of a tall stone building the Lady Hunro sat with her husband. Her throat and breast were still flushed with the orgasm that she had felt during the rite. She looked at Naunakhte with sad dark eyes.

And beside her stood Tiy, next to Panhesi. Naunakhte met Tiy's hot green eyes and shuddered to see the malice there. Tiy smiled at her and her smile was more frightening than a crocodile's. She looked pleased with herself, and like a sleek, well-fed cat, and suddenly Naunakhte was afraid. She had never heard that the oracle of the god Amun was corrupt, but the god was carried, after all, by men, and men could be bought. Tiy was lovely, and perhaps she had sought to bribe the servants of the god with the temple's gold or with her own white body. Her expression of contained satisfaction made it seem all too likely. And when she touched Panhesi's pale arm and whispered in his ear, Naunakhte thought that she could hear them speaking of her death.

'Naunakhte.' Lord Merybast looked down at her, as tall and remote as a god himself. 'Are you ready to stand your trial before the oracle?'

'I am ready,' whispered Naunakhte, and her voice sounded feeble and timid even to her own ears.

'Your accuser stands here,' said Merybast, indicating Panhesi. 'He accuses you of sacrilege, but you claim that you are innocent. The oracle will decide. Scribe, read out the choices.'

One of the temple priests, a young man with enormous dark eyes, stepped forward. He held two identical tablets of gilded bronze, stamped with hieroglyphs. For a moment his eyes met Naunakhte's and she felt a stir of hope, because she could read in his face that he wished her well. Then he looked down at the tablets and read out, 'This tablet says, *She is innocent and shall have no punishment*. And this one reads, *She is guilty and she shall die.*'

He shuffled the tablets to and fro and then laid them

upon the ground by the sacred lake, about twelve feet apart and face down so that the writing could not be seen. Then he bowed to Merybast, glanced once more at Naunakhte, and withdrew.

'Let the oracle come forth,' intoned Merybast.

From the building behind him a procession emerged, of men with the shaven heads of priests carrying sticks of incense and chanting. Behind them came four ordinary men, dressed like labourers in plain white kilts and sandals. These men were the bearers of the god. Amun's presence came forth in his gilded barge, a twelve-foot model of a real Nile barge made of bundles of papyrus reeds, painted and rigged and oared just like a real boat. The boat rested on two long poles and the poles rested on the shoulders of the bearers. They would feel the poles pressing down or growing light as the god told them which way to turn. He would guide them to whichever answer he chose.

The bearers walked as if in a daze and their eyes were glazed like men who are drunk or in a trance. The god was with them already. Naunakhte saw the signs of his presence and she drew a long breath of growing confidence. How could Tiy and Panhesi have bribed these men? How would they know which answer was which?

Then it was as if Khonsu stood at her shoulder, whispering ironically in her ear, *You are a fool, little goddess. It was the scribe she bribed. Both of those tablets are inscribed with 'Guilty'.*

Naunakhte closed her eyes and sank to her knees. She lifted her hands to the god in prayer. But still Amun did not come to her, and she was afraid. She opened her eyes.

The boat carrying the presence of the god moved slowly towards the spot on the bare sand where the tablets lay. It moved like a questing snail, edging first in one direction, then in the other. Every eye followed it. It hesitated between the tablets as if uncertain. Naunakhte spoke without words to the god: *Mighty Amun, justify me.*

Suddenly the boat wheeled towards one of the tablets. The bearers gasped, wide eyed, and the two of them who walked in front dropped to their knees as if the burden of the boat were suddenly intolerable. The boat bowed before the tablet.

'Amun has spoken,' said Merybast, and he gestured to the scribe. The young man ran forward and picked up the tablet.

Naunakhte clenched her fists and listened to the blood pounding in her ears. The young scribe slowly turned the tablet over. He closed his eyes for a moment, and then he read out in a strong clear voice, 'She is innocent and she shall have no punishment. Hear the word of the god Amun.'

The Lady Hunro leant back against her throne, her lips moving with words of silent thankfulness. Tiy glanced at Panhesi and then stared at Naunakhte, her expression stiff with disbelieving rancour. Naunakhte looked up at the hot blue sky and smiled as she felt the god return to her.

Merybast took the tablet from the scribe and read it for himself. Satisfied, he stood up. 'The Lady Naunakhte has been found innocent,' he announced. 'The god knew no sacrilege. She shall be readmitted to the temple in her old place. Naunakhte, come here.'

Naunakhte pulled herself together and went to the throne. She knelt before it. Merybast looked down at her for a few moments in silence. His shadowed eyes were strangely hot, as if he were in the grip of desire. At last he said, 'You lived with a man as his lover. Before you are readmitted to your place you shall take the drink of purification. Then when your woman's blood has ceased you must undergo the rite of penance and submission.' His eyes burned into her flesh. 'Since chief priest Panhesi was involved in this case,' he finished softly, 'I myself shall lead the rite.'

A buzz of surprise sounded from the temple people standing nearby. Naunakhte, too, was surprised, since she remembered that the Lord Merybast rarely undertook any duties himself. What was this rite of penance?

Then the Lady Hunro spoke, smiling slightly. 'I see you also find her beautiful, lord husband,' she said. 'I am glad that she will soon serve me at the rite again. And I wish you joy of that tender body. You will not find her a disappointment.'

Chapter Ten

Naunakhte was given a pleasant room, with a high ceiling for coolness and tall windows overlooking the sacred lake. As soon as she was installed in it one of the priests came to her, carrying a cup of steaming liquid. It smelt strongly of bitter herbs. Naunakhte drank it with distaste, knowing its power. Before nightfall her belly began to cramp strongly, and soon afterwards her bleeding began.

She was alone in the room. She would see no one, speak to no one, until her purification was complete. At first she wondered, with some regret, whether the drink of purification had caused Khonsu's child to leave her body along with her woman's blood. But regret would do her no good. She tried to free her mind of thoughts of Khonsu and remember only that the god Amun had saved her through his oracle.

She was within the precinct of the temple, and the nearness of the god flung her into a fury of dreaming. Each night she lay naked upon the narrow pallet in her quiet room and dreamt, finding in her sleep comfort from her loneliness and the delight of bodily pleasure. Sometimes the god came to her, shimmering in all his golden glory. She welcomed him with joy and knelt to serve him with her mouth as she had knelt in the temple. The sensation of his powerful phallus thickening and throbbing between her lips made her swoon with bliss, and she woke smiling.

But at other times she dreamt of Khonsu, and those dreams were not joyful. Sometimes she dreamt of him as he had been – mocking, tender, at once gentle and harsh, greedy and generous – and when she woke she mourned. And sometimes her dreams were nightmares in which Khonsu was revealed as Seth, the god of lust and anger and everything that was dark. Then she would wake shaking with fear, and weep when she remembered that Khonsu would never again be there to comfort her.

The days passed, and after five suns had risen Naunakhte's bleeding stopped. That day she told the medjay who brought her food that her purification was complete, and when he had gone she bit her lip and stared into nothingness. Now she would have to undergo the unknown rite that Merybast had spoken of, the rite of penance and submission. His eyes had kindled with lust when he mentioned it.

What was this unknown rite? Naunakhte gnawed unconsciously at her knuckle. Filled with anxiety, she imagined herself subjected to all sorts of degradations and indecencies. She knew that Khonsu would have curled his lip in scorn and contempt, saying that the priests sought nothing but an opportunity to abuse her body.

And yet the thought of what awaited her filled her with secret, shivering expectation. Merybast was a sober, respectable man, who sought no part in the temple rites. Did he intend to punish her for her desertion of the god with pain – or with pleasure?

All day she waited alone, watching the brilliant sun pass across the sky. She was dressed in the crumpled dirty gown in which she had fled from Khonsu's house, and she felt ashamed of its ragged state. She found herself hoping that she would be given clean raiment before the rite, as if she was more afraid of looking dishevelled than of what they might do to her, and she could not restrain a laugh at her own foolishness.

Every time she heard a footstep in the corridor outside her bolted door she tensed, wondering if they came for her. All day the footsteps passed her door, but as the shadows lengthened and the light became bloody with sunset she heard the tread of heavy feet approaching. She got up from her stool and looked towards the door, and despite all her attempts to calm herself she began to tremble.

The bolt was flung back with a crash and the door opened. A priest stood in the doorway, robed in white and flanked by medjay carrying spears. Naunakhte wrapped her arms across her breast and breathed fast. Then she saw the priest's face and realised that it was the same young man who had read out the choices of the oracle – the scribe whose dark eyes had wished her victory.

It was an untold relief to see a face that she associated with kindness. She stepped forward eagerly, ready to ask him about the rite. But he held up his hand in the gesture that adjoined her to silence. 'Say nothing,' he commanded her. His voice was firm, but she thought she detected a little quiver beneath its surface. 'You may not speak until you are purified.'

'But – ' Naunakhte began.

'Silence! Or must I order the medjay to gag you?'

At his words the medjay on either side of him stepped forward. They were tall men, dark skinned, glistening and muscular, with broad wristguards of bright copper glittering on their strong arms. One of them wound a broad strip of linen to and fro between his big hands and watched Naunakhte with piercing eyes, as if he desired any opportunity to force the linen between her flinching lips, bind it across her gasping mouth and compel her to silence. Naunakhte stared at them in horror and disbelief.

The young priest's voice softened slightly. 'I am

sorry,' he said, 'but the rite must be obeyed. You may not speak until your purification is complete.'

His face showed that he would have liked to be kind. Naunakhte lifted her hands towards him, palms uppermost, begging him in silence to help her. He turned his head away as if her beseeching eyes hurt him, and to the medjay he said, 'Bind her.'

Without a word the medjay moved towards her, their faces set and stern. Naunakhte retreated, step by step, until her back was against the wall and she could go no farther. They laid their hands upon her and for a moment she was ready to scream with terror and hopeless resistance.

Then she remembered the purpose of this unknown rite. She was to atone for her flight from the temple; to offer her body in submission as penance for the gift of herself that she had given to Khonsu. Whatever they did to her now was to restore the honour of the god. If she desired once again to be the handmaiden of Amun, she must let his priests do what they wished with her.

She lifted her head and stood quiet and proud as the medjay bound her. They tied strong soft ropes about her wrists, then lashed them securely to each end of a wooden rod as dark and polished as their skins. The wood was smooth with age and cunningly carved to allow a secure purchase for the ropes. It was grooved also in the centre and it was as long as one of her arms, so that her hands were held wide apart a little below the level of her waist, palms turned upward as if in supplication.

The young priest watched as the medjay secured her, his dark eyes darkening further. 'Good,' he said, and his voice was a little husky. 'Bring her.'

The medjay each put a hand on Naunakhte's shoulder and guided her through the labyrinth of the temple. She recognised her whereabouts quite quickly and realised with a chill of anticipation that she was being led towards the sanctuary of the god. Her heart leapt. Perhaps she would be required to submit to Amun himself. She looked down at her bound hands. The wooden pole pressed against her belly and the soft ropes chafed gently against her wrists, restraining her utterly. She shuddered with expectation and desire.

They were nearly at the gates of the sanctuary when suddenly the medjay turned aside. Naunakhte could not prevent herself from glancing over her shoulder in yearning. The young priest saw her look and lifted his shaven brows. 'You are not fit to enter the presence of the god,' he said, quite coldly. 'You may not come into his sanctuary until you have been purified.'

Naunakhte wanted to demand that they purify her at once. But she restrained herself, for she had no wish to be gagged.

Ahead of them a great door opened, revealing a high room aglow with the light of the setting sun and glittering with torches. Naunakhte bit her lip against a cry of surprise and fear, for the room seemed to be full of men. Clad in the white robes of priests they clustered towards her, and their whispers sounded like the rustle of bees in a hive. Suddenly she was afraid, because her hands were bound and there was nothing that she could do to resist this encroaching horde. She tried to catch the young priest's eye, seeking reassurance in his face, but he would not look at her.

The crowd of priests got close to her, so close that she could see their mouths wet with lust for her and smell their hot breath. Then they withdrew, folding back like the wings of a great bird, and formed into two ranks. A little way from her stood Merybast, tall and stately in his long robes, wearing around his neck a great collar of gold and gems. Naunakhte's breasts lifted and fell with her quick breathing and she knew that when her eyes met the high priest's he would see that she was afraid.

Merybast smiled a little as he looked upon her, but it was not a reassuring smile. He smiled as if he was well pleased to see her standing before him bound and helpless. His hands clenched into fists at his sides, and he said in his strong, clear voice, 'The victim is prepared. Let the rite commence.'

The high room filled with the heavy beat of a drum, sounding alone like a great heart. The medjay who had held Naunakhte's shoulders withdrew and she almost cried aloud to them to stay, not to leave her alone with this crowd of men with white robes and intent, hungry faces. She looked wildly from side to side and then her eyes fixed on the face of Merybast as he moved slowly towards her, step by step.

At last he stood before her. His deep eyes looked into hers and he licked his lower lip thoughtfully. Then he made a gesture with one hand and the young priest darted forward clutching another rope and cast it quickly around the centre of the long pole to which Naunakhte's hands were bound. She gasped as the rope began to tauten, lifting her hands before her. Glancing wildly up she saw that it ran over one of the heavy beams of the ceiling and down again into a corner of the room. It was tightening inexorably. Her hands were level with her breasts, with her face, with the crown of her head. At last, when another inch would have caused her discomfort, the lifting stopped. She tugged helplessly at the wood, but could not shift it. Her hands were lifted high above her head, spread apart by the polished pole, and she could not free herself. The drumbeat suddenly ceased, and there was a breathing silence.

Merybast licked his lips again and nodded in slow satisfaction. He extended one hand and touched the crumpled linen of Naunakhte's gown, then frowned in disapproval. 'Strip her,' he commanded.

On either side the priests jumped to obey him. They tore and ripped at the linen and stripped the rags from Naunakhte's limbs. She moaned in protest, but could do nothing, and in moments she stood before Merybast stark naked.

Nudity had never seemed shameful to Naunakhte until this moment. But now, bound and powerless to protect herself, and surrounded by pair after pair of hungry eyes, she panted with shame and struggled vainly until she realised her ultimate impotence and closed her eyes and let her head hang back in despair. She was achingly conscious of the fact that the peaks of her breasts were tight and that the lifting and spreading of her arms tautened the tender swells of flesh, offering them to the watching eyes as if she were a wanton whore.

How could the Lord Amun want her to suffer this degradation, this exposure and humiliation? How had she deserved it? She moaned in hopeless protest and her long, dark hair swept against the lush curves of her naked flanks as her head rolled from side to side.

Then Merybast spoke again. 'Let her body be cleansed before she undergoes her penance.'

Naunakhte shut her eyes more tightly, trying to shut out what they might mean to do to her. Her body was rigid with resistance.

But then she felt sweetness and silken delight. Cool, delicious water was rubbed softly along her backflung throat. Trickles of water ran from her nape between her shoulder blades, coursed between her breasts, traced the lines of her ribs. She shuddered with the pleasure of the water's caress.

And after the water, hands. Strong hands, gentle hands, hard hands, soft hands, smoothing that cool water along each limb, moulding the shallow orbs of her breasts, teasing out the dark puckered flesh of her nipples. Naunakhte drew in long, deep breaths and let them out in sighing gasps of astonishment. Every inch of her body was sensitised to the myriad different touches that were awakening her lust.

Strong, hard fingers coursed up the delicate flesh of her inner thighs, wakening goosepimples on her back and shoulders. Soft palms cupped the weight of her breasts, lifting them and squeezing them together. Her swollen nipples were trapped in the warm hollowness of a hand's centre. A delicate touch slid down the side

163

of her taut neck and she shivered and moaned with startled joy.

The cool water and the exploring hands caressed every morsel of dust and sweat from her shining limbs. She stood helpless. Her eyes were closed and her head hung back as if she were in a dead faint, but the slow remorseless heave of her body revealed her arousal. She moved like the faint, oily swell on the surface of the sea which betrays the approach of a great storm, a storm that will tear the sky and the water with furious passion.

Her body was drowned by the approach of erotic bliss and her mind began to sink into the trance of the servants of Amun. Her moist lips gaped open, sucking in the warm, dark air. Behind her a slow voice chanted, 'You are being made clean for the god. As your body is cleansed, so will your spirit be cleansed. The penance of the temple shall erase the legacy of Seth.'

Naunakhte wondered dazedly how the priests of the temple could have known that Khonsu was Seth made flesh, with all that great and terrible god's fascination and danger. A faint image of him appeared to her; Khonsu lying naked beside her, his hand reaching out to caress her breast, his lips curled in his cool, mocking smile.

Then firm fingers traced spider's tracks down her throat and on to her breasts, found her nipples and pinched them so hard that she gasped. The voice behind her whispered, 'Open yourself to the god. Let his presence cleanse you.'

At once the god was there, summoned by his faithful acolytes. Naunakhte's body tightened as she sensed his presence. Now the hands that touched her were the hands of Amun, the hands of god laid upon his faithful handmaiden, and his divinity and power were such that the hands were many.

'Oh Lord Amun,' she whispered, 'come to me.' She drew deep breaths of bliss and smiled as every part of her body, every inch of her damp skin, was teased and caressed by the hands of the god she adored. Her breasts were swollen and tender with desire and the peaks of her nipples rose to the touch of subtle fingers. Between her legs her sex was as heavy as a dew-soaked flower, parting its glistening petals to reveal its soft, moist secrets. On the shutter of her closed eyelids she saw the god, golden and shining, naked and beautiful, his magnificent phallus thrusting forward in full erection, ready to take her.

Her trance deepened. The approach of the god filled her ears with a rushing sound like a great wind, and her whole body shook. She arched her back, thrusting her breasts forward, and above her bound wrists her fists clenched and then opened spasmodically. She thought that she cried the god's name aloud, but in fact her slack lips let out only a helpless moan.

Then a strong male voice commanded, 'Enough.'

At once the hands withdrew. Naunakhte's trance faded and broke. She gave a little groan of protest and clutched at the wooden pole to give her the strength to lift her heavy head.

Merybast stood before her, his dark eyes glowing beneath his greying brows. 'Good,' he said, 'good. Naunakhte, do you feel the presence of the god?'

How could he ask it? Naunakhte replied in a husky, tentative whisper. 'Yes. He is here.'

The high priest slowly nodded his head. 'Hunro was right,' he said. 'You were indeed born the servant of Amun. Few women feel his presence when they undergo this rite.'

Naunakhte frowned in puzzlement. 'Is the rite over, then?'

At that Merybast smiled. 'Over? Oh no.' His smile widened slightly. 'It is barely begun. And for the remainder of it, Naunakhte, I shall not permit the god to entrance you. You must experience everything in your own person. Do you understand me?'

'Yes,' said Naunakhte, swallowing hard. She understood what the high priest said and she wanted to be obedient, but how could she promise? The god came to her at his desire, not hers. 'But what – '

'Enough.' Merybast raised his voice to a snap of command. 'Take her to the altar!'

At once Naunakhte was surrounded. The priests reached up to release her bound hands from the restraining pole. She gasped as her arms fell to her sides, the loosened ropes still fastened firmly around her wrists. But before she could relish the sensation of freedom she was seized on every side, then lifted bodily and carried at shoulder height across the room.

Turning her head, she saw the altar. It was a massive piece of rose-pink granite, more than six feet square. Its sides were carved with the story of the god in hieroglyphs and it was polished as smooth as glass. Let into its top, an arm span apart, were two loops of gleaming bronze.

Between the bronze loops was a carved indentation. Naunakhte twisted her head and began to struggle with sudden terror, because the altar looked like one of the great rock tables on which a beast might be sacrificed, carved with grooves to carry away the dying animal's blood. She heaved and writhed between the restraining hands, imagining that the moment they bound her between those fierce loops they would set the sharp bronze to her offered throat.

Then Merybast was standing beside her. 'Be still,' he commanded her sharply. 'What do you fear? The god does not demand your life. This is a rite of penance, not of sacrifice.'

Naunakhte stopped struggling and lay still. She was afraid, but she trusted Merybast. He would not lie to her. The priests carried her over to the altar and laid her down. Her body fitted comfortably into the shallow carved depression in its surface and her thick hair cushioned her head. They tied her hands to the bronze loops, offering her naked breasts to the torchlight and the coffered ceiling.

For a moment Naunakhte closed her eyes and prayed

to Amun to protect her from whatever was about to happen. But then Merybast's voice spoke again, sharp and commanding. 'Naunakhte. Speak now of what took place between you and your lover Khonsu.'

Shocked, Naunakhte opened her eyes. Merybast was standing beside her, looking down into her face. His eyes were hot. Naunakhte turned her head aside in shame and whispered, 'I don't understand.'

'You are to be cleansed,' said Merybast coldly. 'We must cleanse all those parts of you which he polluted. Speak, Naunakhte. What did he do to you?'

Slowly Naunakhte realised what it was that Merybast meant her to do. He meant her to speak aloud the secrets of Khonsu's bed, to recite everything that they had shared in lust and passion. A scalding blush burned her cheeks. She glanced up into Merybast's face and tugged helplessly against the ropes which secured her wrists. Aloud she whispered, 'I can't.'

'You must,' insisted Merybast. 'But I shall help you. Where did he pollute you, Naunakhte? Here?'

And without warning he thrust his strong fingers between her thighs and slid them up into her, deep into her wet, open sex. She cried out and tried to pull away, but it was too late. Two fingers were buried deep inside her, moving in and out very slightly, so that she moaned.

'Here?' insisted Merybast, sliding his fingers in and out once more.

Naunakhte's sex clenched helplessly around his invading hand. Merybast's palm brushed against the taut bud of her clitoris and she sighed in pleasure. When she gasped, 'Yes,' she did not know whether she answered him, or begged him to continue.

'Very well,' said Merybast sternly. His fingers withdrew and Naunakhte whimpered with loss. 'And here?' He reached for her mouth and touched her parted lips, then stroked the tip of her tongue. She tasted her own arousal on his hand.

'Yes,' she whispered. She could not prevent herself

from licking lasciviously at his finger, relishing the faint salty sweetness of her juices.

'Even so.' Merybast took his hand away and Naunakhte tensed, knowing at once what he would do next. She was not disappointed. The high priest pushed his hand between her closed thighs, forcing her legs apart. She moaned as he stroked his finger along the dewy lips of her sex, drawing slick moisture from her. Then his hand moved further back and his fingers probed and stroked at the delicate entrance of her anus.

'Here?' His voice was hoarse. His finger probed steadily until it opened the little satiny flower and gently, determinedly, penetrated her.

'Yes,' Naunakhte groaned helplessly, squirming as Merybast's finger slid deep into her tight anus. 'Yes, oh yes.'

Merybast thrust his finger into her again. He seemed to relish her faint cries of pleasure and the sinuous writhing of her golden limbs. He smiled a little and at last withdrew his finger, drawing it beneath his flaring nostrils and smelling it voluptuously.

'Good,' he said softly. 'Now I know the extent to which you must be purified.' He stepped back and lifted his hands. 'Let the rite begin.'

For a moment there was silence; the silence of expectation. Then once again the drum began its steady, remorseless double beat. Its vibrations struck Naunakhte's ear through the very granite of the altar, so that she felt she lay like a child upon the muscular chest of a great cold giant, listening to its thumping heart.

The priests of Amun stood around the altar. They pressed as close as a flock of white birds. As the drum beat they began to chant, a low murmurous sound like the rumble of thunder. They invoked the god, calling to him to come in his power and strengthen the sinews of Merybast as he carried out the rite.

A movement beside Naunakhte caught her eye and she turned her head. She saw the young dark-eyed priest removing Merybast's long linen robe. Beneath it the high priest was naked. His smooth oiled body was thick and solid, impressively taut for his advancing years. He looked heavy. Between his legs his penis stood up, swollen and erect, and Naunakhte swallowed as she looked at it. It was much larger than Khonsu's, massive, huge and hard, almost as large as the phallus of the statue of the god. The Lady Hunro would not have found her husband a disappointment, even compared to her divine lover.

The priests began to clap their hands in time to their chanting and the beating of the drum. Slowly Merybast advanced up the steps at the side of the altar. He was holding the base of his penis in the ritual posture of the god. He stood upon the altar with one foot on either side of Naunakhte's neck, looking down into her wide open eyes.

'Great Amun, father of all things,' he intoned above the chant, 'give power to my penis. Make my phallus strong to purify this sacrifice.'

Slowly he sank to his knees. Naunakhte shivered as the high priest's rampant phallus came closer and closer to her face. She tried to remain still and calm, but despite her intentions she tugged helplessly at the bindings that secured her wrists, trying to free herself.

Now Merybast was kneeling over her, astride her face. He grasped firmly at his penis and began to stroke it, sliding the velvet-soft skin up and down over the engorged rigid core. Her eyes gazed up at the swollen scarlet head, so smooth and shining that it seemed about to burst like an overripe fruit.

'Naunakhte,' said Merybast, 'open your mouth.'

Fear and lust fought within her. She writhed on the cold stone as terror chilled her spine and desire softened her limbs and melted warmly in her liquid sex. She was afraid of Merybast, and she was afraid of her own helplessness. But at the same time she longed to taste his phallus, and her soft thighs parted and shook as she yearned to feel a hot penis entering her.

'Open,' repeated Merybast. Naunakhte let out a little

helpless moan and licked her lips, smoothing them with her saliva to allow Merybast to penetrate her mouth more easily. She saw him point his penis downward and closed her eyes just before she felt it nudging against her lips and parting them, driving its way deep into her throat.

He thrust himself so far into her mouth that for a moment she was afraid she would choke. He tasted of salt and costly perfume, sandalwood and attar of roses. She opened her jaw and relaxed and Merybast's massive phallus slid further into her, in and in until his dangling testicles brushed against her lower lip. She tried to moan, but she was smothered by his presence.

Her hands pressed flat to the cold stone and her body arched unconsciously upward, offering the soft mound between her legs for the possession of a man. The feel of Merybast's penis within her mouth made her long to be taken. The glistening folds of her sex quivered as she clenched her inner muscles, impotently clutching at emptiness.

After only a few thrusts Merybast withdrew. His phallus gleamed with her saliva. He knelt over her for a moment, breathing hard. Then he stood up and commanded, 'Offer her to me.'

The priests around the tomb leant forward and caught hold of Naunakhte's legs. They held her by the ankle, the knee, the thigh. All along her limbs she felt the tightness of their clasping hands. They pulled her legs wide apart and held her very still. Lascivious fingers squeezed at her flesh and she moaned with ecstatic expectation.

Merybast stood between her spread thighs, masturbating. His hand slid smooth and fast up and down the length of his cock. She stared up at him, her mouth slack with desire, and Merybast smiled grimly and lowered his body on to hers.

He was heavy, so heavy, and through his perfume she smelt the odour of his body, rank and intense like a rutting beast. He put his hands on her bound wrists and snarled with pleasure as if it aroused him to feel her beneath him, restrained and powerless. He pushed his face towards her and his hot breath brushed her cheek. Naunakhte moaned in protest and turned her head aside. She tried to struggle, but his weight pinned her down and her legs were held completely still by dozens of male hands. She twisted her head from side to side and Merybast chuckled and leant towards her and licked her throat.

The touch of his hot, wet tongue shot through her like a dart of fire. Naunakhte cried out and ceased to resist. Merybast dragged his tongue again up the length of her golden throat, then set his teeth to her neck as if he would worry her like a dog. She moaned with pleasure to feel him biting her. Her own immobility and helplessness filled her with the joy of utter submission.

Merybast's huge penis throbbed between her open legs, twitching as it brushed against the wet lips of her aching sex. His teeth dug again into her throat and he shifted his weight, bringing the broad, hot head of his phallus closely against her body. His heavy buttocks were taut with readiness and she knew that soon he would move. How that giant member would fill her! She longed for it almost as she had longed for the penis of the god Amun. But this longing was not divine, it was mortal. She was fully conscious, far from the golden glow of divine trance, and her body was warm and tingling with lust. She wanted the high priest as a woman wants a man. She wanted him to possess her.

Merybast lifted his lips from her bruised neck and shut his eyes tightly. His hands gripped hard at Naunakhte's wrists and his body tensed as he thrust. The head of his penis nudged its way between the lips of her sex and began to penetrate her. She moaned with joy and Merybast gasped as his thick, erect phallus slid slowly into Naunakhte's moist vagina, deeper and deeper until it was entirely sheathed in her warm, trembling flesh.

For a moment he was still. Naunakhte whimpered

171

with delight at the sensation of that massive penis wholly imbedded within her. She moved against him and tried to lift her hips towards him so that he would take her, but still the priests held her completely motionless. She could only wait, shuddering with expectant bliss, until Merybast was ready.

At last he bared his teeth, drew in a long hissing breath and pulled his penis almost free of her clinging sheath. Naunakhte moaned with loss, and then her moan turned to a gasp of pleasure as he slid himself into her once again. She began to pant in rhythm with his thrusts, glorying in the steady pounding of his body against hers. Her spine tensed as the sensations grew. Merybast lay heavily upon her and the skin of his broad chest dragged against her flushed, straining breasts and her taut, puckered nipples. The lips of her sex were swollen and tender, her clitoris was engorged and protruding, and the friction of Merybast's loins rubbing against her began to drive her towards orgasm.

Again she cried out, and as if this was a signal Merybast withdrew from her entirely. Naunakhte let out a little whimper of disappointment and opened her languid eyes.

Merybast stood up, shaking his head in disapproval. 'Your pleasure is irrelevant to the rite,' he said sternly. 'Contain yourself. You are not yet purified.'

Naunakhte's lips parted in a soundless gasp of realisation. Every part of her body which Khonsu had entered was to be purified by the penetration of Merybast's huge cock. That meant – she swallowed hard – that meant that he was going to insert his member into her anus, that narrow orifice which had made Khonsu gasp at its tightness. Surely it was not possible! And yet she desired greatly that he should try.

Her face must have shown that she had realised what was in store for her, because Merybast smiled coldly. 'Yes,' he said, 'you have guessed, Naunakhte. And you shall watch.'

Watch? How? Naunakhte frowned and wriggled protestingly against the priests' restraining hands. Merybast stepped a little back from her and issued another abrupt command. 'Prepare her. Let her be oiled and made ready. And then place her so that she may see what I do.'

At once the priests caught hold of Naunakhte's legs even more firmly. They held her by her ankles and calves and lifted her buttocks bodily from the cold stone. Naunakhte gasped in surprise, then gasped again as the priests pushed her legs forward, further and further, until she was standing on her shoulders and her thighs were spread and parted directly above her face. She could see right up into her open sex. It was moist and pink and quivering with need, and behind it was the tight brown flower of her anus.

'Oh gods,' Naunakhte whispered, astonished and aroused.

The dark-eyed priest lifted a little flask above her parted buttocks. He tilted it and a thin stream of aromatic oil poured downward. The oil fell on to Naunakhte's crease and she heaved in reaction. Slowly the priest massaged the oil into her tender skin, anointing the delicate, satiny membrane that surrounded her puckered rear hole. Naunakhte trembled and moaned. After a few moments he began to slide his fingers very gently into the hole itself, opening her softly and delicately. The pleasure was intense. Naunakhte let out little shuddering cries and her eyes opened wide as she watched the priest's long, dark finger gently pushing in and out of her flinching anus.

'She is ready,' the dark-eyed priest said after a moment.

'Good.' Merybast came and stood over her, his huge erection aimed directly at her offered crack. 'Hold her buttocks apart,' he ordered. 'Spread her open.'

Naunakhte whimpered and tensed, clenching her cheeks together in instinctive denial. But the priests caught hold of the tender skin of her flanks and tugged at the firm orbs of her opulent backside, spreading the cheeks apart so that her oiled bottomhole was presented lewdly for Merybast's attention.

He stood over her and directed his penis downward. It was wet and shining with the juices of her vagina. He guided the smooth head to the spot and Naunakhte watched in disbelief and fear as the scarlet glans rested against her anus and prodded, first gently, then harder.

He was too big, too big. It was impossible. Naunakhte moaned and closed her eyes, resisting desperately.

For a moment Merybast thrust vainly, butting the head of his cock against her like an angry ram. Then he said, 'She is afraid. One of you caress her, fondle her, give her pleasure. She will soon forget her fear.'

At once a gentle hand ran along the soft flesh of Naunakhte's inner thigh, sliding towards her wet, eager sex. She took a deep breath and opened her eyes and saw it was the young priest, smiling down at her as his hand reached her mound of love. He stroked the swollen lips, very gently, and parted them to reveal the dark entrance to Naunakhte's vagina and the tiny rose-pink bud of her clitoris. She stared in fascinated anticipation, then sighed with delight as his finger slipped into her. He penetrated her first with one finger, then with two, then withdrew both fingers, wet with her moisture. She moaned as he began to stroke her clitoris, very gently and dexterously, quivering the pad of one finger deliciously against the little throbbing bead while with the other he rimmed the entrance to her vagina, entered her, withdrew, entered her again.

Pleasure flooded through her. She moaned again and arched her hips upward, welcoming his touch. But she was betrayed, for the pleasure relaxed the taut muscles of her sphincter, and even as she cried out with bliss Merybast lodged the head of his cock in her anus and thrust hard. The great shelving glans eased its way slowly inside her, fixing her as a peg fixes wood. Merybast nodded and the young priest withdrew his hand. Naunakhte looked up, gasping, and saw the swollen tip of Merybast's cock buried within her arse.

'The final road,' Merybast whispered. He put his hands on Naunakhte's thighs, pressing them even further apart, and leant his weight into her. Inch by inch his erect phallus disappeared into the little gaping mouth of her anus. Inch by inch he penetrated her, and she was utterly overwhelmed by the sensation. It was as if he would split her limb from limb, tear her as a lion tears its prey, and yet it was ecstasy too; a dark, forbidden ecstasy.

The impossible was achieved – the whole of Merybast's penis was buried in her. She stared up at their joined bodies, hardly able to whimper. Slowly Merybast moved his hands, shifting them up the soft skin until they brushed against the dark mass of her pubic hair. He teased her, fluttering his fingers against the flushed lips of her moist vulva, but avoiding her clitoris.

'Please,' Naunakhte moaned. 'Please.'

'As I said, your pleasure is irrelevant.' Merybast shifted his weight to allow himself to withdraw his gleaming penis from her anus, then drove into her again. His face was contorted with pleasure. For a few moments he fucked her arse with strong, steady thrusts, making her cry out with bliss and frustration and the shadow of pain. Then his rhythm changed, becoming jerky and hurried. 'Lord Amun,' he whispered, 'it is too much, too much. I cannot – ' And with a gasp he withdrew from her. Naunakhte cried out with shock, because as his penis sprang free Merybast grabbed it and began to rub it furiously. He pointed his phallus at Naunakhte's face and masturbated violently. The thick rod of flesh leapt in his hand and jolted as he began to come. He shouted aloud as his orgasm possessed him, and his thick white semen pulsed from the tip of his penis and fell on to Naunakhte's gasping face. Hot liquid caught in her eyelashes and slithered lewdly down her cheeks, wetting her panting lips. She gave one desperate cry and then was silent.

For a few moments the only sound was of Merybast's heaving breath. Then he said, 'Release her.'

Naunakhte's hips were lowered to the cold stone and the priests busied themselves around her, freeing her hands from the ropes. When she was released she lifted herself on one elbow and rubbed her hand over her face. Merybast's seed was slick against her skin.

'Naunakhte,' said Merybast, 'your formal purification is complete. But now the priests of Amun must approve your service.'

With a thrill of excitement Naunakhte looked around her. The priests were watching her, their eyes bright and their penises erect beneath their robes. Merybast went on, 'If you are willing, you shall be free while they take their pleasure with your body. If you are not willing, you shall be tied on the altar while each of them possesses you, one by one. Which will you have, Naunakhte?'

Naunakhte's whole body was trembling with arousal. She had been on the brink of orgasm, and now all she desired was to reach her peak. She replied without thinking, 'I am willing.'

A sussuration of excitement filled the high room. Merybast nodded slowly and then turned away. Naunakhte looked from side to side and saw the priests glancing at each other and then unknotting their kilts, letting the linen fall to the ground behind them. One after another they stripped. Naunakhte quivered with anticipation as she saw so many penises, all stiff and ready to pleasure her.

She knew which one she wanted to taste first. Glancing quickly around, she caught the dark eyes of the young priest who had officiated at the speaking of the oracle. She sat up a little more and held out her hand to him, and he smiled and moved towards her.

'Take me,' Naunakhte said. She leant back, meaning to stretch her body out for him upon the cold stone. But he caught her hand, holding her up.

'There are many of us,' he whispered, 'and all want to

taste your beauty, Naunakhte. One at a time will never do. Come, trust me.'

He guided her down from the altar. She went willingly, shivering with anticipation. The young priest lay down upon the floor and opened his arms to her. 'Lie on me.'

His penis lay flat against his belly, stiff as a piece of wood. Naunakhte eagerly straddled him and took hold of his cock, lifting it until she could guide it into her. She sighed with bliss as he slid up inside her.

'Now,' whispered her friend, 'lean forward, Naunakhte, so that another may take his pleasure with you.'

For a moment Naunakhte did not understand. Then she felt the warmth of another man kneeling behind her, parting her buttocks and sliding his stiff prick along the crease of her arse. She was startled, but if a phallus in one orifice brought delight, then surely it would be even more wonderful to accept two at once? So she leant forward and groaned with pleasure as the unknown penis pressed against her anus and slowly, deliciously, eased its way within her.

'Good,' hissed the young man beneath her. He lifted his hips, thrusting himself deeply into her, and as he did so the man behind her also thrust. Naunakhte cried out, astonished by the power of the sensations that now seized her.

And then her cry turned to a gasp as hands caught her by the hair and pulled back her head. Another man stood before her, offering his erect penis to her open mouth. She whimpered with delighted submission and parted her lips, then moaned with pleasure as he pushed his phallus into her mouth.

All three men moved at once, sliding their pulsing erections at will into her sex and her mouth and her anus. Naunakhte closed her eyes and weltered in lubricious joy. Every part of her was filled, aching and scalding with bliss. Other penises pushed against her spasming hands, begging for her attention, and without even looking at them she grasped them and slid her fingers up and down, up and down. There were hands knotted in her hair, phalluses wrapped in the thick black locks, fingers brushing at her breasts and teasing her tight nipples. The man with his cock in her anus cried out and clutched at her buttocks as he ejaculated, then he withdrew and at once his place was taken by another man. Naunakhte writhed with delight and ground her turgid vulva down upon the body of the young priest whose dark eyes had looked at her with kindness. She arched her back and he lifted his hands and grasped her breasts and she knew that she was about to orgasm a fraction of a second before pleasure burst within her, radiating from her loins like the fiery streamers of the noon sun. Her belly jolted and shuddered, but she was fixed upon the three penises that penetrated her. They moved faster now, driving into her rigid body with deliberate force, raising her time after time to new plateaux of pleasure. She uttered a smothered, agonised cry, and for long moments her whole body was tense with the torment of orgasm. Then she relaxed, slumping forward in the fainting aftermath of ecstasy.

After that first, immensely powerful climax, Naunakhte did not fully recover her senses. Her body was soft and pliant in the hands of the priests. They turned her this way and that at their pleasure, placing her in one position after another, each one more lewd than the last, and one by one they took her, sliding their penises into her every orifice. Her skin, her sex, her mouth and her hair were wet and sticky with their congealing semen, and after a while they laid her on the altar and licked her clean with their mouths. They lapped at her nipples and dragged their tongues lovingly over her breasts and belly. One of them glided his face between her legs and began to suck her sex, caressing her clitoris with his lips while his tongue burrowed deep into the moist well of her vagina. He seemed to relish the taste of her, and when they pulled her upright and parted her buttocks so that another of the priests could sodomise her he stayed where he was, his face pressed to her thighs, lapping steadily at her clitoris. Two more of the priests sucked at her swollen breasts while another of them kissed her, thrusting his tongue into her mouth and biting her lips. Naunakhte cried out in helpless delight, and as the man behind her grunted and thrust his prick harder and harder into her bruised and tender anus, she convulsed again in the throes of an orgasm even more powerful than the last.

She hardly knew when they had finally finished with her and laid her slumped and panting upon the granite altar. Every part of her ached dully, as if she had been beaten, and yet the pain was pleasure too. She moaned and stirred faintly for a moment, then lay still.

She must have fallen asleep, for when she woke with a start the high room was dark and quiet. One of the temple girls was standing beside her, wiping the sweat and semen from her body with a damp sponge, and the Lady Hunro was stroking her face.

'You have been purified, Naunakhte,' said Hunro softly. 'I am glad. Welcome back to the temple, little lotus flower.'

Naunakhte's whole body felt as soft and liquid as molten wax. Every pore of her skin was soaked in sensual satisfaction. She could not speak, but she smiled.

'The inundation is beginning,' said the Lady Hunro, returning Naunakhte's smile. 'Today the Nilometer showed that the waters rose by two cubits and a span. Soon it will be time for the festival of Opet, when the god travels to Luxor.'

She did not seem to require an answer, so Naunakhte stretched to allow the girl to sponge her breasts, and raised her brows curiously.

'Naunakhte,' Hunro went on, 'I have a part in the Opet festival. I expect that this will be my last year as high priestess, that next year there will be a new god's wife of Amun. I would like you to sit beside my throne on the god's barge, Naunakhte, and watch what I do.'

Naunakhte's eyes widened. The Lady Hunro implied that she, Naunakhte, would be the next Hand of Amun.

179

She was amazed and delighted, for if she became the Hand of God she would legitimately be able to enjoy the body of the god himself. But her joy was marred by an undercurrent of fear. She wanted to ask how the Lady Tiy would take this news, but she did not dare.

'Yes, lady,' was all she said. Then she remembered Tiy's cold green eyes and her threat of poison, and she shivered.

Chapter Eleven

*P*anhesi knew that Tiy was wicked. She was beautiful, of course, and wonderfully exotic, with her red-bronze hair, pale skin and eyes as green as a cat's, but when he was honest with himself he knew that it was her very wickedness that aroused him. As she lay in his arms, writhing and spitting and mouthing obscenities, he felt wrapped in the darkness of Seth, the miasma of danger and evil which the presence of the god Amun should have banned, and it gave him incomparable excitement.

Since the girl Naunakhte had returned, Tiy's rage had been implacable. This was hardly surprising, since it was now clear that the Lady Hunro had decided on the tall girl as her successor. Panhesi saw Tiy as often as he could, and when he saw her he goaded her to rage, because her rage made him want to have her.

Now Tiy lay naked beneath him, her wrists grasped firmly in his hands. Her slight body wriggled vainly under him. 'Tomorrow,' he hissed into her ear, 'tomorrow she will ride beside the Lady Hunro on the god's barge. It is all arranged.'

'Whore!' Tiy spat, fighting against Panhesi's strong grip. 'She is a whore. When Merybast purified her he even had to shove his cock up her arse. A whore and the daughter of a whore will be the Hand of God!'

'If liking to be fucked up the arse disqualifies the Hand of God, then you would have no chance either,' commented Panhesi reasonably.

'Aah!' Tiy shrieked. She stretched up to try and bite Panhesi. He writhed out of her way, jerked her legs apart and with a single thrust sheathed his cock inside her to the root. Her body arced up towards him, tense and straining. For a few moments the only sound was their panting breath as Panhesi slid his penis in and out of Tiy's wet, eager sex. Then Tiy flung back her head and gasped through gritted teeth, 'Kill her for me, Panhesi. Kill her. I want to see her blood.'

'You're mad,' Panhesi replied, shafting her vigorously. 'You know I may not shed blood.'

'Strangle her then!' Tiy's face contorted as Panhesi drove his cock into her and she grunted as if he had struck her. 'Think of it, ah gods, think of it, your hands on that long throat, think how she would struggle – '

'Don't,' said Panhesi, really shocked, and aroused against his will by the image of cruelty and violence which Tiy conjured up. He fucked her harder, trying to stop her from speaking. Tiy twisted her neck desperately as she was overcome by orgasm. Her stretched-out body became tense and stiff, then began to shudder from head to foot as spasms rushed through her. Her sex clenched and quaked around Panhesi's plunging cock, and he moaned as he too reached climax.

After a moment he let go of her wrists and slumped forward on to her quiescent body. She lay still, panting. Then she said, quite calmly, 'I tried to kill her myself, you know.'

'What?' Panhesi rocked upward astonished.

'Oh yes,' said Tiy, staring up at him with bright, cool eyes. 'I covered my face and went to Waset, to a place I know. I bought poison there. They get it from the venom of snakes – it kills at once and with great pain.'

Panhesi shuddered. 'What did you do?'

'Sometimes the cook makes dates stuffed with almonds,' said Tiy. 'Naunakhte loves them; she always

eats them greedily. When they were next served, I found
the dish and put the poison in two of the dates. It was
easy to put the poisoned dates before Naunakhte. I
thought she would eat them – she took one in her fingers
– but then – ' Tiy scowled with fury and turned her
head away.

'Then what?' Panhesi was utterly confused. 'What?'

'She – ' Tiy's face looked puzzled now. 'Her eyes
looked strange, as if she were far away or dreaming,
and then she put down the date as if it had bitten her.
The Lady Hunro asked her what the matter was and for
a moment she did not answer. Then she said that the
god had told her there was a scorpion in the dates.
Hunro had the servants take them away and fling them
on the midden.'

Panhesi began to shiver. 'By all the gods,' he said
softly, 'Amun watches over her closely.' He drew a little
away from Tiy.

'What is wrong?' demanded Tiy, reaching out for him.

'Let go,' he said, brushing her hand away. 'Leave me
alone.'

'Why?' Tiy looked both angry and afraid.

Panhesi pushed her off and got to his feet. He reached
for his kilt and wrapped it around himself as if it would
protect him from her. 'Tiy,' he said, 'everything you say
tells me that Naunakhte truly is under the protection of
Amun. He cares for her, and you have tried to kill her.
Do you not fear his anger, Tiy?'

Her lip curled in scorn. 'Fear?' she repeated disdain-
fully. 'I fear nothing.'

'Only a fool does not fear the gods,' said Panhesi. 'By
his seed, Tiy, we are in his temple! He will revenge
himself on you.' He stepped backward away from her,
shaking his head. 'I was wrong to listen to you.'

'You accused her of sacrilege,' snapped Tiy. 'That
would have meant her death.'

'I accused her with reason. She touched the statue;
she should not have done it. If the oracle found her

innocent, that proves all the more that she is under the god's hand. Do not speak to me of her again, Tiy.'

'Coward,' hissed Tiy. 'Coward!'

'Yes,' said Panhesi steadily. 'If to respect the god is to be a coward, I am one.' He looked at Tiy, wondering at how suddenly his desire for her had changed into loathing. Her pretty face was a mask of hate and her hands were like claws. He shuddered and turned his back on her.

'I will do it myself, then!' she cried as he walked away. 'After the festival I will do it. And when she is dead and I am the Hand of God, you will not be my consort!'

I should denounce her, Panhesi thought as he left her curses behind him. I should have her expelled from the temple. She is evil.

But then he considered that everyone within the temple knew that he was Tiy's lover. If he exposed her wickedness, it would be bound to affect him. His chances of succeeding Merybast would be dashed for ever. On reflection, he decided to keep silent.

Every year since she was old enough to walk, Naunakhte had gone with her adopted family to stand beside the River Nile and watch the procession of the god Amun which was the centre of the Opet festival. It was the climax of days of feasting and rejoicing, thanking the gods that once again the Nile had risen to bless the fields of Egypt with life. They had marvelled at the god's great barge, huger even than the barge of Pharaoh himself, and looked with awe at the statue of the god. It was veiled with the finest linen, but Amun's golden shape glittered through it like the sun behind clouds.

Now she was to be at the heart of the ceremony and she was overcome with gladness and gratitude that her past and her present could mingle together so happily. She rose before dawn and helped the Lady Hunro to don her ceremonial regalia, a gown of white linen woven all through with strands of pure gold, so that it shone with the reflected glory of Amun, and a heavy, complex headdress of gold and lapis and the feathers of peacocks. Then Naunakhte was taken to another room and enfolded in a white gown so fine and translucent that her nipples showed through its delicate folds. Neferure placed a collar of gold and gems around her neck and clasped heavy gold bracelets on her wrists. Her upper arms were naked, and the girl who painted her face also drew blue and black lines of paint around the mark of the god on her arm, so that all who saw her might notice it and wonder.

As the sun lifted into a sky that was already brazen with heat, the procession prepared to leave the sanctuary. The veiled god stood in his shrine and was lifted by twenty priests, all dressed in white. The shrine and the statue were heavy, but it was a great honour to bear the god and there was no shortage of volunteers. The doors of the sanctuary were thrown open and the god came forth.

The procession was led by Merybast, dressed in plain white with his staff of office in his hand. He led the way for the god. Then came Amun, carried by his labouring servants, and behind him walked the god's wife of Amun, the Lady Hunro, with Naunakhte at her side. After them streamed the many servants of the temple, the priests and the temple girls, the handmaidens and the slaves, the hewers of wood and the drawers of water, all dressed in their best, bedecked with all their jewels and with their faces gaily painted to honour the god. As they walked they clapped their hands and sang, and the sound of a thousand voices lifted to the glowing heavens.

They drew near to the gateway to the temple, and Naunakhte heard a strange sound. It sounded like the rushing of waters or the rumbling of distant thunder. For a moment she was puzzled by it. Then the great gates swung open and her ears were buffeted by a deafening cheer, and she realised that she had heard the noise of the crowd, waiting outside the temple for their god to appear.

The people cheered and shrieked and waved green branches. Little children ran alongside the statue of the god, flinging handfuls of rose petals. Bands of musicians hurried to join the procession; befeathered black drummers from deepest Nubia, thinly clad Waset girls carrying their delicate lutes. Their music blended with the hymns to the god in joyful cacophony. Slowly the procession wove its way down towards the glittering Nile, where the god's golden barge was warped in to the quay, waiting to serve its divine master.

The priests carried the god's shrine jolting up the gangplank and set it on the high pedestal in the middle of the barge. The crowd cheered again as the god was lifted up before their eyes.

With gracious dignity Hunro made her way to the throne of the god's wife, at the base of his statue. She smoothed the folds of her golden robe and smiled at Naunakhte. 'Come,' she said. 'I am sitting at the god's feet, and you may sit at mine.'

Naunakhte returned her mistress's smile and sat at the feet of the throne. She was half drunk with gladness and wonder at being at the centre of this whirlwind of rejoicing. The god himself stood behind her, glowing beneath his veil, and her soul was filled with bliss. It was as if she could feel his golden smile. She basked in the warmth of his pleasure.

Slowly the barge was pushed from the bank and floated into the middle of the channel. The tow ropes extended to either bank of the Nile, and people pressed forward from the crowd to place their hands upon the ropes and help to pull the god towards Waset. Women came forward as well as men, for it was well known that if a woman pulled the barge of Amun she would be fruitful.

The blue and green waters of the Nile parted before the prow of the barge as it slipped down towards the city. On the bank the teams of towers sweated and tugged, and on either side the musicians swirled along, brilliant in coloured and striped robes and kilts, their medley of sound reaching joyful fingers towards the god. With them moved dancing girls, naked and glistening with oil. They wore heavy wigs and their eyes were painted with blue and green, and the belts of shells around their slender waists chinked seductively as they turned backward somersaults along the riverbank.

Either side of the river was packed with humanity; thousands upon thousands of spectators all come to enjoy the finest spectacle of the year. Naunakhte saw a woman leap up on to a bollard by the bank and tear off her clothes to show her naked body to the veiled god. She leant back, ululating shrilly to call the god's attention to her, and exposed her genitals, spreading the soft, pink petals apart with her fingers. Then it seemed that the power of the god touched her, for she fell back into the arms of the men around her, so aroused that she clutched at one of them and dragged him with her to the ground. They began to copulate frenziedly. The people around them laughed and cheered the god whose very presence inspired desire.

This sight was often repeated, for all knew that in his ithyphallic manifestation Amun drove both men and women to lust. Naunakhte shifted uncomfortably where she sat as the sight of unbridled concupiscence worked upon her. The Lady Hunro must have noticed her suppressed squirming, because she leant forward from her throne and ran her hand down Naunakhte's shoulder to caress the curve of her breast. 'For now, little lotus flower,' she whispered, 'contain yourself. Our time will come later, when Pharaoh has made his sacrifice and is lying with the queen.'

The mention of Pharaoh cleared Naunakhte's mind. The centre of the Opet ceremony was the sacrifice of wine and honey to the god, made by the king himself, Pharaoh, in all his divine power. Pharaoh's court was far downriver at Memphis, but every year he travelled in his state barge upriver to Luxor to take part in this ceremony. After the sacrifice, Pharaoh and his queen would retire to a secret chamber deep within the Luxor temple and perform the private rite that ensured the continued fertility and life of Egypt.

And so for the first time in her memory Naunakhte was to see her father. The thought filled her with apprehension. Hunro said that she resembled her mother, and her mother had betrayed Pharaoh's trust and tried to murder him. How would Rameses react to the sight of his daughter? Would he be angry?

Ahead of them they saw the buildings and temples of Waset on the left-hand bank of the river. Naunakhte forgot to look for her foster family on the right-hand bank, because there, tied up to the city quay, was Pharaoh's barge. Great eyes were painted on its prow and it was gilded and encrusted with precious stones. A throne was set in the centre of the barge and on it sat Pharaoh, clad in gold from head to foot. As the god's barge drew closer Rameses stood up. All men approached him with awe, but before Amun even Pharaoh was humbled.

Naunakhte looked up anxiously at Hunro. 'Shall I go?' she whispered. 'Shall I hide, just for now?'

Hunro shook her head. 'No need. I have told Pharaoh you are here. He will be prepared. Have courage, Naunakhte. You will have to face him in future years, when you are the Hand of God.'

Naunakhte swallowed and sat up straight. The god's barge jolted as its tall prow kissed against the side of Pharaoh's vessel and the sailors leapt to fix the gangplank. Pharaoh came to the steps, looking like a moving statue. His hands were crossed on his breast, holding the flail and crook of Egypt, and his face was painted so that it was hardly possible to see that a middle-aged man lay beneath the regalia. Horns blared as the king stepped up on to the gangplank and prepared to board the barge of the god. The watching crowd fell silent.

Slowly Pharaoh approached the statue of the god Amun. He looked only at the statue – his eyes never fell upon Naunakhte sitting there at the feet of the god. He handed his regalia to Merybast and took instead a cup of smoking incense, then lifted it and poured it in a glittering stream to the deck. The heady perfume swirled around Naunakhte's face and made her giddy. She sensed Amun's divine presence in the statue. His power made her shoulders prickle. Her nipples tautened and her lips were dry with longing for the god.

She hardly sensed the passing of time, but soon the ritual of sacrifice was complete. Pharaoh bowed his head to the statue. Then he looked at Naunakhte and his strong warrior's face stiffened beneath the heavy paint.

'My lord Pharaoh,' said Hunro's cool, calm voice, 'here is the girl I spoke of, my chosen successor Naunakhte.' She leant down and pushed Naunakhte to her feet. Naunakhte shivered, took a step forward and fell to her knees, prostrating herself before Rameses, the god king.

There was a long silence. Naunakhte stared at the planks of the deck, her nostrils filling with the scent of incense. Then she heard Pharaoh's voice for the first time. It was a harsh, strong voice, the voice of a powerful, ruthless man. 'Rise,' he said. 'On your feet.'

She stood up, trembling. It took all her strength to raise her eyes. She looked into the face of Pharaoh and flinched, because he was regarding her with a look of hot, deliberate lust.

'Before Amun I speak,' said Rameses softly. 'Naunakhte, you are the image of your mother, Tiy. Of all my women I desired her the most. Answer me now. Will you stay here in the temple and serve the god, or will you return to Memphis with me and take your place as the chief of my concubines? I promise you everything your heart can desire. Power, riches; all shall be yours.'

Naunakhte felt as though a great fist were clamping around her ribs, squeezing out her breath. She was not shocked by Pharaoh's suggestion, for all Egypt knew that the king might engage in incest as his fancy took him. But she was afraid that if she answered as her heart prompted her she would incur the wrath of the mighty Rameses.

For a moment she stood tongue-tied. Rameses stared into her face. She wanted to flinch before the force of his desire. Unable to bear his look, she closed her eyes and prayed silently to Amun to help her.

She prayed, and the god responded. His presence flowed into her, filling her with calmness and cool certainty. Her fear dissolved before the power of the god. When she opened her eyes she smiled, and when she spoke her voice was steady and strong. 'Lord King, when I was a child the god claimed me. Now I am his servant, I must not betray him. I wish to remain in his temple, lord Pharaoh.'

There was a silence. Naunakhte watched with surprise as Rameses' eyes softened. She could almost have believed that they filled with tears. At last Pharaoh said, 'You show yourself more my daughter than your mother's, Naunakhte. She could not have resisted the lure of being a king's handmaiden and confidante. I am glad that you are faithful to the god. May you serve him long.'

He took a step forward and put his hands on Naunakhte's shoulders. She was going to sink to her knees, but he held her up and kissed her forehead. It looked fatherly, but she could feel the longing shivering in his hands and lips. She was relieved when he let her go and turned away to return to his own barge.

'I am proud of you, Naunakhte,' said Hunro quietly when Naunakhte returned to her seat. 'No doubt he was just testing you. You acquitted yourself well.'

Naunakhte had looked into Pharaoh's eyes and she knew that he had not been testing her. But she said nothing, for as she gathered the folds of her gown about her and sat down, she felt a chill running through her, raising the hairs upon her neck and tightening every muscle so that her nipples hardened and her sex clenched. She shivered and wrapped her arms around herself, but the sense of cold fear did not leave her.

She recognised the feeling. It had become very familiar to her since her return to the temple. It was the ill wish of Tiy that she felt, and she knew that if she looked around she would find Tiy's cold green eyes fastened upon her, bright as daggers and narrow with hatred. It was as if the wickedness of Naunakhte's mother had passed not to her child, but to her namesake.

Naunakhte glanced up at the great statue behind her. It glittered beneath the veil of translucent linen. 'Amun,' she whispered beneath her breath, 'protect me.'

The god did not reply, but gradually her fear retreated as the strength of his arm was laid over her like a shield. She drew in a deep breath and closed her eyes.

The two barges moved on towards the Luxor temples, side by side upon the glittering breast of the river. Naunakhte began to relax and enjoy the gorgeous spectacle around her. She saw men and women on the river's banks overtaken by lust as the god passed them by, and once again desire began to writhe in her belly. Her eyes darkened as she watched a young man lifting his girl's thighs so that he could slide his erect penis deep into her, heedless of the crowd pressing in around him. It was easy to imagine that when he had finished with the girl another man would mount her, then another, then another, while she lay beneath them with her legs spread wide in abandoned lust, open to all comers, sighing with pleasure as she felt yet another hard rod of flesh entering her moist, willing sex.

Naunakhte shivered. She took the Lady Hunro's feet into her lap and began to stroke and fondle them. They were slender feet, soft skinned and delicate and sweet with fragrant oils. Naunakhte caressed each toe, then slid her palms softly on to Hunro's ankles and up beneath the skirts of her golden robe.

The Lady Hunro breathed faster. For a moment she accepted Naunakhte's caresses. Then she leant down and pushed her hands away. 'Not here,' she whispered, 'not now. In a little while, Naunakhte. When Pharaoh performs the ceremony it will be time. The god will be with his harem, and we will be at liberty.'

'But now – ' whispered Naunakhte.

'For now, Naunakhte, you must bear it.'

Naunakhte sighed with frustration and set Hunro's feet back upon the steps of her throne. For a little while she watched the barge's crew going about their business, trying to distract herself from the sights of delicious lewdness that awaited her on the banks.

Then she felt as if some powerful force were pulling at her, calling for her attention. She glanced with puzzlement up at the statue of the god, but she knew that it was not Amun who summoned her. She hesitated, confused, and then allowed herself at last to turn her eyes to the place that drew her.

They were nearly at the Luxor temples now, and the banks of the swollen river were built up with dressed stones to keep them from the Nile's flood. The crowd pressed up to the edge, shouting and waving as the god's barge passed them. Naunakhte's eyes passed quickly over the thousands of cheering faces, and then stopped.

On the quay was a great ram-headed sphinx. It was clustered with people who had climbed up on to it to get a better view. They were sitting down, for the sphinx was made of smooth-polished granite, treacherous to feet. All except one man, who stood astride the sphinx's broad shoulders, his hands planted on his hips, staring at the barge with silent hatred. The people were dressed in their best coloured robes and garlands of flowers, but this man wore a plain white kilt and no jewels. His face was unpainted and his head was bare, showing his close-cropped dark hair, as if he were in mourning.

It was Khonsu. Alone among the vast crowd he did not rejoice when the god passed by. He looked as if he wanted to challenge Amun to a fight to the death. Naunakhte forgot to breathe as she looked at him. In the delight of her return to the temple she had forgotten how beautiful Khonsu was, how strong and perfect in his body. His face was set with grief and rage and she longed instinctively to comfort him, to take him in her arms and cradle his head against her breasts. Her lips moved, silently whispering his name.

At that moment he saw her. His bright brown eyes met hers and his face changed. He looked disbelieving and stricken with confusion, like a lost child. He held out his hand to her almost hesitantly.

Tears surged to Naunakhte's eyes. She covered her mouth with her hand as if she could hide her longing. Khonsu clenched his fists, then leapt as lightly as a panther on to the head of the sphinx, reaching out for her. He shouted, and faintly, above the roar of the crowd, she heard him calling her name. His voice was harsh and raw with hopeless yearning.

She wanted to leap to her feet and run to him. But how could she, when before Pharaoh and the assembly of the people she had chosen to give herself to Amun rather than to a mortal? Her whole body was weak with wanting Khonsu, but she knew that he was forbidden to her. Slowly, painfully, she shook her head.

Khonsu's face twisted convulsively. He fell slowly to his knees and bowed his head, lacing his hands behind his neck and shielding his face with his elbows as if to protect himself from a vicious blow. The bitterness of his grief and loss struck Naunakhte as if it were her own, and she could no longer stop the tears from falling.

'Naunakhte.' The Lady Hunro spoke softly, and as she spoke she stroked Naunakhte's cheek. She looked up into Hunro's face, her lips trembling. 'Naunakhte, hush. It will pass. He will soon forget you; and you have the love of the god. When you are consecrated, when you know the bliss of Amun, you will not want Khonsu any more.'

'But,' Naunakhte whispered, 'Lady Hunro, he loves me. I see it in his face. He loves me.'

'What is the love of a man, compared to the love of a god?' Hunro smiled and shook her head. Her throat was flushed, as if she were feeling sexual pleasure. 'I am married, Naunakhte, and I know. Serve the god first, and understand his power. Later, if you wish, you may take a husband. I had been the Hand of God for two years before I wedded Merybast. Khonsu was the son of a scribe, you said. He would be suitable. Marry him when the time comes, if you want a companion for your bed.'

The thought made Naunakhte laugh ruefully. 'He would not, lady. He could not bear to share me with the god.'

'Then he is arrogant,' announced Hunro sternly. 'How dare he?'

How dare he? Naunakhte repeated to herself. She remembered Khonsu lying above her in the warm silken moonlight, his teeth bared as he forced his body into her as though the fierceness of his possession could exorcise the god. 'You are mine,' he had said as he brought her gasping to orgasm. He had dared to claim her; he had set himself to challenge the god. He had been ready to give his life for her.

'You will forget him,' whispered Hunro.

Naunakhte wanted to believe her. But she glanced back along the river and saw Khonsu still kneeling on the head of the sphinx, hunched and bowed with despair, and against her will her heart moved with love for him.

Naunakhte's fear of Tiy's hatred and her forbidden love for Khonsu should have combined to make her wholly miserable. But she was close to the god Amun, and he was pleased with his festival. All around her the air sparkled with joy and the people sang with happiness, and the god's approval kept sadness from her. The brightness of the day stirred her like strong wine.

The god's barge was tied up at last at the quay before the Luxor temple, where his harem awaited him; statues of all the divine women that he had loved. The bearers of the god lifted the statue in its golden shrine and carried it to land, and the crowd of people sang and danced before him.

Hunro walked beside Naunakhte. She clasped her hand and squeezed it gently. *Soon*, that gentle pressure said. *Soon.*

Pharaoh disembarked from his golden barge and walked into the temple behind the procession to show his honour for the god. With him walked his queen, a tall, stately woman. She was younger than Rameses, about the same age as the Lady Hunro, and still in the full flower of her majestic beauty. Watching her slow, proud figure walking beneath a fringed sunshade, Naunakhte thought that it must be a pleasure for Pharaoh to perform the final rite of the festival.

The gates of the temple swung closed, shutting out the sound of the rejoicing people. Naunakhte followed the god through the unfamiliar halls and corridors of Luxor. Hunro's fingers were tracing delicate patterns on her palm and she shivered with awakened desire. It was as if the god were preparing himself to enjoy his harem, and echoes of his rousing lust were sounding throughout his train.

They placed the god among his women. The statues that stood around the holy sanctuary were very varied, dating from every dynasty and every generation of Egypt. They showed beautiful women of every size and shape, from slender, naked, dancing girls to opulent fertility figures with breasts as large as melons and soft capacious thighs that could envelop the world. Tonight the god would roam at large among his harem, and as he took his pleasure among that bounty of nakedness Pharaoh would lie with his queen, copulating with her in the secret darkness of the ritual chamber, completing the ceremony of rebirth.

The handmaidens of the god smoothed scented unguent carefully over his body, preparing him for his night of love. Naunakhte took her part, though as the chosen successor to the Hand of God she might have watched while others served her lord. The sweet-smelling oil was soft on her hands. She touched the statue of the god with longing. When she had been alone with him the cool gold had turned to warm flesh, and the hard pillar of his erect penis had quivered beneath her worshipping lips. Now the metal remained metal and the god's smile was fixed. But even so it made her shiver to touch him. She stroked one hand along the magnificent length of that erect penis and felt her sex moisten with need. What Hunro had said was true. When she was with the god, in his presence, sensing his power and his desire, there was no room in her mind for anything else. Amun was her world.

He was prepared. Singing softly, the women withdrew to their own chamber. It was luxurious, littered with rugs and cushions, smelling of the incense that burnt in the lamps.

'Listen,' said Hunro. 'Pharaoh goes forth.'

They stood in silence, listening as the sound of the priests chanting hymns to Amun swelled and faded. Then they heard the crash of the chamber door slamming shut, and a great shout of affirmation.

'It is accomplished,' said the Lady Hunro. She smiled at Naunakhte. 'Now the time is ours. Naunakhte, come here.'

Naunakhte went willingly, opening her arms for Hunro's embrace. She longed still for the god, but she would take her pleasure where she could. She moved into Hunro's arms and sighed with bliss as she felt Hunro's lips upon hers, their mouths blending in a kiss so deep and sweet that it seemed to search out the roots of her soul.

'Naunakhte,' Hunro whispered between kisses. She unfastened Naunakhte's robe and pushed it open, revealing her small high breasts. Their points were already hard with eager desire. Hunro's fingers closed on one tight wine-red nipple and squeezed, and Naunakhte's breath left her in a sigh of tormented ecstasy. Her knees quivered and she sank to the floor to lie sprawled upon a heap of cushions.

'Look, Naunakhte,' said the Lady Hunro softly. Naunakhte's eyelids were heavy, but she raised them obediently and looked around her.

Before her stood the Lady Hunro, still dressed in her golden gown. She gestured, and Naunakhte looked around the room and saw that all around her the handmaidens of the god were slipping to the ground, throwing off their clothes, kissing each other on their mouths, on their breasts, between their legs. The whole room was a tangle of naked, perfumed, twisting limbs. Sighs and moans filled the air.

'The god commands them,' said Hunro, 'as he commands me.'

Slowly she unfastened her golden gown and pushed it from her shoulders. It fell behind her, revealing her splendid opulent nakedness. Naunakhte gasped, because fastened around Hunro's soft, full haunches was a sort of harness of leather, clasped tightly around each thigh, pressing close between the lips of her sex, fitted snugly to the crease of her bottom. 'Lady,' she whispered, 'what is it?'

Hunro smiled and unfastened the straps on either side of her hips. 'All day, Naunakhte, while you sensed the god's pleasure, I have felt it,' she said. She opened her thighs and drew the harness away from her. It came free slowly, reluctantly, and Naunakhte sighed with astonishment as she saw that its function was to hold in place a massive phallus made of polished ebony. It withdrew slowly from the moist depths of Hunro's sex. Her swollen, flushed labia clung to it lewdly.

'All day,' said Hunro softly, 'all day, Naunakhte, this has been buried within me.' She drew the glistening phallus clear and held it upon the palms of her hands. Naunakhte saw at once that it was a copy of the phallus of Amun – long, thick and hard. 'All day I have felt it, whenever I moved. When I walked, Naunakhte, the straps chafed against the lips of my sex, and with each step the god's penis stirred within the depths of my body. All day I have been penetrated by him. This is the

197

festival of pleasure, Naunakhte, and the god's wife must feel pleasure when her husband does.'

She held the gleaming phallus above Naunakhte's eyes. 'Imagine, Naunakhte. Three times on the barge I came to my ultimate moment. I have taught myself to climax in silence, but the god is strong. Imagine passing the whole day with this magnificent object filling you.'

Naunakhte shivered with lust as she stared upward. She longed to feel what Hunro had felt, but she did not dare ask. Her mouth was dry and her tongue felt swollen. She was thirsty for the creamy juice that made the ebony shine.

'Once before you felt the might of Amun,' Hunro went on, 'when you were deflowered for his pleasure. Now, Naunakhte, do you wish to feel him again?'

At last Naunakhte could speak. She stretched up from the cushions, her throat taut with longing. 'Yes,' she groaned, holding out her hands to Hunro.

Hunro smiled and began to fasten the straps of the harness about her thighs. 'It is cunningly made,' she commented. 'See, when it is fastened thus, the god's penis stands out before me. And look.' She parted her thighs and Naunakhte saw that the leather straps clasped Hunro's sex so closely that only the tip of her engorged clitoris peeped out from between them. 'When you are the Hand of God,' Hunro said, 'you will use this instrument upon the girls who awaken your desire, and you will know that when you do so you feel almost as much pleasure as when it is buried inside you. You feel the pleasure of a woman while you do the office of the god. All this lies before you, Naunakhte.'

Naunakhte hardly heard her. 'Please,' she whispered, opening her hands, 'may I kiss it?'

Without a word Hunro knelt down beside her and offered the shining ebony to her lips. Naunakhte let out a little whimper of pleasure and lasciviously extended her tongue to caress the glossy surface of the phallus. It tasted of Hunro, sweet and musky, the dense complex taste of a woman's juices. Naunakhte let the thick column of ebony slip between her parted lips. She closed her eyes and imagined that the god stood before her. He had finished with Hunro, who lay upon the floor sprawled in erotic exhaustion, and now he was offering his still-proud penis to Naunakhte for her to enjoy the fruits of her mistress's delight. She sucked eagerly, imagining Amun gritting his teeth with pleasure as her tongue and lips caressed the swollen, veined surface of his pulsing erection. Her ears were filled with the sounds of the god's handmaidens enjoying each other: tender sighs; quivering moans; the gentle liquid sound of exploring fingers delving deep into moist sexual flesh; the soft determined lapping of a tongue flickering wickedly against a tense, swollen clitoris; the quick intake of breath as lips encircled a throbbing vulva and softly parted the turgid flesh.

Soon every trace of Hunro's juices was gone, cleaned from the ebony by Naunakhte's willing tongue. She released the stiff shaft and looked up at Hunro, gasping with passion. All around her the handmaidens of Amun lay clasped in each other's arms, moaning with bliss as they exchanged kisses of burning desire.

'Even now,' Hunro whispered, 'Pharaoh is lying with the queen.' She lifted Naunakhte's hips and slid more cushions beneath them until Naunakhte's mound of love was lifted high off the ground, proffered lewdly upward, ready to be plundered by the phallus of the god. 'He is performing the rite, Naunakhte. She is the land, he is the Nile. He will spread himself over her and make her fertile. He will overwhelm her and possess her.'

Naunakhte let her softened thighs fall apart. The air stirred gently against the damp lips of her sex. She moaned and flung her arms wide. Her head tilted back, exposing her long, pale throat, and the swollen mounds of her breasts lifted and fell. She was opened, helpless, utterly at the mercy of Amun. The god's trance wrapped her in erotic bliss. The woman's shape of Hunro, poised above her, transformed in her eyes to the shape of the god; male, magnificent, erect.

'Take me,' she whispered. 'Lord Amun, I am yours.'

Hunro took the ebony phallus in her hand and placed its tip gently against Naunakhte's body. The touch of it, cool and hard and powerful, made her groan. Her fingers spread wide as if even her hands wanted to be penetrated. 'Please,' she moaned. 'Oh please.'

Hunro thrust, and the phallus of the god Amun slid into Naunakhte's vagina. It filled her, soothing her and maddening her at one moment. She closed her eyes tightly and cried out as she felt the thick, hard rod of pleasure easing its way smoothly between her silken walls.

Again and again Hunro drove the ebony phallus into Naunakhte's helpless, quivering body. The tender golden flesh of Naunakhte's limbs flinched and shuddered as the god possessed her. She pressed her palms to the floor and arched her back, lifting her breasts to within reach of Hunro's mouth, and she moaned with ecstasy. The god was with her, and in her mind she became the queen and the land of Egypt, lying passive and welcoming in the embrace of the swollen Nile. She was the spring, the fountain of all life, rich and fertile. Crops sprang from her fecund belly and men worshipped her with love and without fear. The sun parched her and left her gaping, and she opened her body eagerly to the fervent caresses of the river. It overflowed its banks and spread out upon her, enriching her with pleasure.

The shining column of dark wood was imbedded deep in the soft grasp of Naunakhte's hungry vulva. The muscles of her sex and her buttocks clenched fervently as she clutched at the churning fount of her delight. Her orgasm rose within her, as unstoppable as a flood. Its waves lapped through her limbs, reaching to the tips of her fingers, tensing her gasping mouth, shuddering in her womb and in her breasts. She was the Queen of Egypt in the embrace of Pharaoh, the land of

Egypt in the arms of the Nile, and she was herself, Naunakhte, rejoicing in the might of her divine lover, the god Amun. His power overcame her. He bore her down with his strength, and as she lay conquered beneath him, she knew the ecstasy of his love.

At last Hunro withdrew the ebony from Naunakhte's still-spasming sex and kissed her on the mouth. 'Hush,' she said softly. 'Naunakhte, hush.'

Naunakhte said nothing, but turned on her side and curled up like a child in the nest of pillows. All around her was the quiet of satisfied desire, soft sighs and yawns of contentment. She drew a deep breath and let her satiated limbs mould themselves to the softness of the cushions.

And then she opened her eyes as a sudden chill struck through her. She sat up and glanced around the room. It was a sea of naked flesh – all the servants of the god tumbled into heaps of weary limbs, overtaken by pleasure.

But every inch of flesh was golden, and every head of hair was dark. Tiy's pale skin and russet-tawny locks were not to be seen. Naunakhte swallowed, knowing with cold certainty that Tiy, wherever she was, was plotting evil against her.

Tiy's distant hatred left Naunakhte vulnerable. She remembered Khonsu, crouched upon the head of the sphinx with his arms folded protectively over his face, radiating despair. Vicarious grief filled her. She pressed her face to the Lady Hunro's soft belly and whimpered.

A gentle hand stroked and stroked at her dark hair. She sighed as its steady, repetitive movement soothed her, and gradually she sank back into the embrace of the god. Fear and sorrow oozed away from her, calmed by the echoes of her pleasure, and at last she slept.

Chapter Twelve

*T*he day after the festival the Lady Hunro led the rite as usual. But after it was completed, when the god's servants left the sanctuary, she said quietly, 'Today we must go to the hypostyle hall. There is a thing to be done.'

The women who served the god exchanged quick, apprehensive glances. Departures from routine almost always signalled unpleasantness. Tiy, walking near the back of the women, said in a voice just too soft to be heard by Hunro, 'I would wager that it has something to do with Naunakhte.'

Naunakhte stiffened, but she would not give Tiy the satisfaction of showing that she had heard. All through the festival the gladness of the god and the people had protected her from the aura of loathing which Tiy projected day and night, but now she felt vulnerable. Was this another plot, a plan of Tiy's to rid herself of the girl who had supplanted her in Hunro's affections?

The women gathered in the hypostyle hall around the throne of Merybast. The Lady Hunro said, 'Panhesi will be here soon. He will explain.'

At that moment Panhesi appeared. He was still dressed for the rite, in sparkling linen, and his shaved head glistened in the sunlight that filtered through the pillars of the hall. Behind him came two of the temple medjay. One of them was carrying a small bundle. Naunakhte recognised him as Hori and she remembered how his thick black penis had shuddered and pulsed between her lips as he ejaculated into her mouth. He was the first man whose seed she had tasted. She lowered her head to hide the hot blush of desire which the memory brought.

Panhesi was speaking, and Naunakhte forced herself to pay attention. All the servants of the god had noticed that Tiy and Panhesi were no longer lovers, though nobody knew why. Without Tiy Panhesi had changed, becoming more serious, more correct. Now his voice carried almost as much authority as Merybast's.

'The day before the festival of Opet,' he said, 'a crocodile attacked a fisherman on the riverbank by the temple. The man called his friends and together they killed the beast. When they opened it they found the remains of a man within its belly.'

There was a sussuration of shock and fear. For a moment Naunakhte clenched her fists in terror that the dead man might be Khonsu. Then she remembered that she had seen him at the festival. She was filled with vivid relief, but in thinking of him she had lowered her defences. Her heart bled as she remembered Khonsu's grief-stricken face. He had stretched out his hand to her, and she had rejected him.

Panhesi went on. 'I did not want to disturb the festival with this news, and the man was so ... disfigured that he could not have been known by his face. But we took his jewels and kept them. None of the other servants of the temple have been able to identify him, so although I hoped to keep it from you, I must now ask you if you knew the man who wore these.'

He gestured quickly and Hori moved forward and unrolled the bundle on to the polished floor of the hall. The women crowded round, staring down.

On the linen lay a necklace of glass beads, red, blue, white and yellow, the remnants of a man's heavy wig tipped with black and gold, and a pair of broad, gold wristlets figured with birds and beasts in bright enamels. Naunakhte stopped breathing, then gasped.

Her reaction had not gone unnoticed. Tiy's voice said slyly from behind her, 'What a wonder. It seems that the Lady Naunakhte recognises these jewels.'

The temple girls drew away from Naunakhte as if she was contaminated. She stood alone by the outspread linen, trembling. Tiy put her head on one side and enquired archly, 'And am I right?'

'Tiy, silence,' said Panhesi sternly. He looked at Naunakhte, frowning. 'Lady Naunakhte, is this true? Do you recognise these things?'

Naunakhte nodded. She hardly trusted her voice. Panhesi looked narrowly at her, as if trying to tell whether she was in grief. He seemed to decide that she was not. 'Who was the man?' he asked, not gently.

'He – ' Naunakhte's voice was thick. She swallowed hard and tried again. 'His name was Bahematun, a man of Waset. He betrayed me when I was in hiding, and brought me here to the temple.'

Panhesi raised his brows. 'Can you think why a crocodile should have taken him?'

'Perhaps,' suggested Tiy, 'her lover Khonsu killed him when he left the temple. Murderous revenge! We should send into the city to find the man Khonsu and bring him back here to suffer the penalty.'

'No!' exclaimed Naunakhte, rounding on Tiy in a fury. 'How could that be? Bahematun was armed and Khonsu was taken from the temple naked.' She appealed to Panhesi. 'Lord Panhesi, you know that is true. How could Khonsu have killed an armed man?'

'Then how could this have happened?' repeated Panhesi. Naunakhte could see that he was inclined to believe Tiy. 'The path does not run close to the river, and the way is clearly marked.'

Naunakhte thought back to that terrible evening and took a long, shaky breath. 'Lord Panhesi,' she said, 'Bahematun was an evil man. He swore falsely by the name of Amun. At the temple gate I escaped him and . . . I . . . cursed him.'

There was a long silence. Panhesi's eyes darkened and he looked for a long time at the jewels spread out upon the linen. Then he said, 'Lady Naunakhte, you know that the power of the god Amun is strong in you. And yet you cursed a living man?'

The thought that her curse had killed Bahematun terrified Naunakhte. She did not feel any guilt for the man's death, but she was afraid of her own power. 'I – did not know,' she faltered.

Panhesi shook his head. 'Well,' he said, 'the mystery is solved. There is nothing to be done for the soul of Bahematun. His jewels will be placed in the temple treasury, since he paid with his life for an insult to the god.' He looked at Naunakhte as if he was about to speak again, but then he seemed to change his mind. He gestured to Hori to gather up the jewels. The medjay obeyed, casting a fearful glance at Naunakhte as he did so. Perhaps, she thought with bitter humour, it frightened Hori to know that his penis had been in the mouth of a woman of such power.

'Well,' said Tiy, when Panhesi had gone, 'you show us more wonders all the time, Naunakhte. Now you curse men in the god's name and cause their deaths! Be sure to tell us all your will, for fear that we offend you. It would be more than our lives are worth to displease you.'

Naunakhte swung to shout angrily at Tiy, but as she clenched her fists the temple women around her gasped in fear and flinched away from her. She looked at their terrified faces and controlled herself with difficulty. Tiy lifted her red-gold brows and smiled archly, as if daring Naunakhte to do something that she would regret.

Something she would regret! Looking back, her life with Khonsu seemed simple; a gently-flowing river of physical delight and growing love. Since she had returned to the temple, life had resembled a freshly ploughed field, with peaks of achievement and bliss contrasted with troughs of loss and despair. And now, as if it were needed, she had been given further proof of her own fearsome power. She was afraid for herself. For if she served the god Amun, as his living wife upon earth, how could the power that terrified her do anything other than increase?

Khonsu. She named him silently, without thought or hope. *Khonsu. Help me.*

Khonsu stalked the streets of Waset.

The look of mourning which had so moved Naunakhte was gone. He glowed like a burnished weapon set with jewels. The heavy plaits of his splendid wig brushed his naked shoulders and his sword shifted against his side, suspended from its baldric of leopard skin and scarlet. His face was set and cold, his eyes and his finely cut lips narrowed as if he distrusted everything he saw.

He came to a door in a narrow street and rapped on it with the hilt of his sword. After a pause a little flap in the door opened reluctantly. Khonsu demanded, 'Will you keep me waiting?'

'Lord Khonsu!' The doorkeeper struggled with the bolts and hastily pushed the door open. 'Forgive me, lord, I did not know – we did not expect – '

Khonsu brushed past him without a word and walked into a big, low-ceilinged room lit by dozens of glowing golden lamps. Young women and men lay here and there upon couches covered in bright fabrics. They were all naked or almost naked, bedizened with tawdry jewels and their faces painted. The place looked like what it was – the selection room of the chief brothel of Waset.

'Khonsu!' exclaimed a low, throaty woman's voice. Khonsu stood still and raised one fine-drawn eyebrow cynically as he was approached by a woman of middle years; a tall, thin woman dressed in a complex pleated robe that elegantly concealed the increasing sag of her olive skin. 'By Bes and Hathor, Khonsu, it is a long time since we saw you. You are welcome!'

'My purse is welcome, you mean, Mutemwia,' said Khonsu, inclining his head to allow the madam to kiss him. He proffered his cheek, but she caught him by the chin and pulled down his mouth to hers. Her tongue probed between his lips and her eager hands caressed his naked chest, but he did not respond.

'Bitter words from such a sweet mouth,' said Mutemwia at last. 'Well, Lord Khonsu, you are here after a long absence, and so you presumably desire something. What can I offer you? My house is yours.'

Khonsu looked at Mutemwia's shrewd, dark eyes and saw there that she knew perfectly well why he had been absent from the brothel so long. The story of his obsessive passion for the renegade temple girl had swept around Waset's underground like sparks among the kindling. However, nobody dared mention it to his face. It was also well known that he was a dangerous enemy.

Now he took a deep breath and said evenly, 'I seek some entertainment, Wia. Something to ... amuse me. To rouse me.' *To help me forget Naunakhte*, his mind added silently.

'Entertainment,' repeated Wia, nodding. 'But of course, lord. Do you wish only to watch, or to participate?'

'To begin with I shall watch. Afterwards, if your people do their business well, who knows?'

Mutemwia nodded again briskly. 'Of course, of course. Come to the dining room, Lord Khonsu. It shall be your private domain for tonight. All the best of the house shall be yours.'

Khonsu gave a thin smile. 'I shall put myself in your capable hands, Wia.'

He allowed her to lead him through to the dining room, another large low room lit by lamps and by the flickering flames of charcoal burning in a brazier. The air was close and hot. Mutemwia clapped her hands and gave quick orders, and servants carried away most of the couches, leaving only two or three scattered about the room. 'Be comfortable,' said Mutemwia, offering one of the couches to Khonsu. 'I will have everything ready very soon.'

'What can you offer me?' asked Khonsu coolly as he stretched himself out on the couch.

Mutemwia smiled. 'I have a new pair from the north,' she said, 'from the cold countries where it rains all year. You shall see them if you wish. They are as fair as lilies, and the youth has hair the colour of ripe corn.'

Khonsu nodded. 'Whatever you advise, Wia.'

The madam withdrew and Khonsu closed his eyes and sighed. He had hardly heard what Mutemwia said. As he sat alone in the great room, his face changed. The cold harshness of his expression gave way to quiet, desperate grief.

When he left the temple he had thought Naunakhte dead. He had revenged her death, and when the time of mourning was past he had intended to put the memory behind him.

But she lived, she lived! He remembered her sitting at the feet of the Hand of God, glittering with the radiance of the day and her own happiness. The sight of her had struck his heart like a knife. And she had seen him and shaken her head. How could he bear it?

He could bear it, he reminded himself harshly, by putting her out of his mind. By throwing himself into dangerous business, so that he had to concentrate wholly on the moment to avoid being killed. By wading through the thick and viscid waters of Waset's underworld, seeking the sensual pleasure that would help him forget.

The door opened and Khonsu's face returned at once to its expression of cool cynicism. A girl entered, her head bowed. She was small and slight, dressed in nothing more than a little gold-sewn breech covering her private parts. On her thigh was the blue tattoo of Bes, the guardian god of prostitutes. Her waist was as slender as a green palm and her little breasts were like

208

ripe figs. She carried a flask of blue glass in one slender hand.

'Lord,' said the girl, kneeling before him, 'may it please you to be anointed?'

Khonsu regarded the kneeling girl for a few moments. She had a very fetching body. Her face was not especially pretty, but she had painted her eyes skilfully and her lips were very full and stained with red. Her mouth looked as if it had been stung by bees. It was easy to imagine her moaning as a stiff penis slipped between those swollen lips.

Yes, this was what he needed. It was powerfully arousing to know that every body which came before him was his to use as he chose. Khonsu nodded and said, 'Very well.'

The girl got to her feet and approached him, eyes downcast. She lifted off his heavy sword and laid it by the couch with a look of awe, then reached for the gold clasp on Khonsu's kilt. He allowed her to unfasten it and draw it away from his naked body. His penis lay along his thigh, already thickening with excitement.

'Be comfortable, lord,' said the girl softly. She poured a little of the oil from the flask into the palm of her hand. It was perfumed with sandalwood and myrrh. She warmed it between her hands, then looked up into Khonsu's face. Her lips were soft and heavy and her eyes glowed as if she desired him. She placed her oiled palms on his broad muscular shoulders and began to rub the fragrant unguent into his skin.

Khonsu loved the sensation of the oil sliding into every pore, softening skin that was dried by the hot winds of the desert. Nothing made him feel more ready for physical pleasure. He stretched and groaned, pressing himself against the girl's searching hands. As she massaged further and further down his hard body his phallus swelled to full erection, hot and eager and engorged with blood. It was good to know that the loss of Naunakhte had not unmanned him. He put his hand on his penis and explored its taut, smooth readiness.

The feel of his clasping fingers was pleasant, but he was in no hurry. He withdrew his hand and let his stiff cock spring back to lie against his flat belly.

The girl was smoothing the unguent on to his thighs, his knees, his calves. She reached his ankles and lifted his feet into her lap, one after the other, delicately caressing the arch of each foot, separating his toes and stroking them. Khonsu shivered with pleasure. She was good, this girl; subtle. She pleased him. He wondered if her own responses were as delicate.

She had finished. As she replaced the stopper in the glass flask he said, 'Now you may serve me in another way.'

The girl's dark eyes glowed at him. 'Yes, lord?'

'Pleasure yourself,' said Khonsu.

She looked first startled, then almost embarrassed. He had to smile at the thought that he had put one of Mutemwia's harlots out of countenance. 'Pleasure *myself*, lord?' she repeated tentatively.

'Yes. Touch yourself for me. As you would if you were alone.'

Still she hesitated. 'But – '

'How would you begin?' enquired Khonsu, smiling at her. 'Would you touch your breasts? Your thighs? What would you do to yourself?'

The girl's face changed. She caught her full lower lip between her teeth for a moment, and then she returned Khonsu's smile. She looked sparkling and wicked. 'Watch, lord,' she whispered. 'Watch, then, and you shall see.'

She got to her feet, unfastened her breech and let it fall, then went to another of the couches and lay down upon it. She closed her eyes and for a moment lay quite still. Her breathing deepened. Khonsu watched, intrigued, wondering what she was thinking about. What went on behind those painted eyelids?

Whatever it was, it was arousing. The girl took three long breaths and her firm little breasts lifted and fell and Khonsu saw that although she had not moved the

210

points of her breasts were becoming hard. The dark areolae swelled like burgeoning flower buds and the nipples tautened and lengthened. It was miraculous.

With another long, luxurious breath, the girl lifted her hands. She traced the backs of her fingers slowly down her body, beginning at her shoulders, trickling down the outside of her breasts, grazing the edge of her ribs. Her skin tensed and her nipples swelled further. She opened her mouth and let out a long sigh, then cupped her breasts in her open palms, lifting them, squeezing them, feeling their weight.

What were her thoughts? Did she dream of men or of women? What filled her mind with desire and made her lips dry, so that she had to lick them with her little pointed tongue? Khonsu rolled on to his belly, trapping his hard penis between his body and the rough linen of the couch. He propped his chin upon his hands and began to clench his buttocks in a slow, regular rhythm, pressing his engorged member gently against the linen and then relaxing, stimulating himself as he watched.

The girl's skin was glowing with a fine film of sweat. She was caressing her nipples now, scratching them with her sharp nails, then catching them between finger and thumb and drawing them out to long tender cylinders of swollen flesh. Her body shifted on the couch and her head rolled slowly from side to side, exposing her long throat.

Naunakhte's throat, pale gold, smooth as rose petals, trembling as she moaned with bliss – Khonsu shut his eyes for a moment, forcing down the surge of memory. Then a little whimper of pleasure from the masturbating girl made him open them again. Her hands had left her breasts and now she was stroking her belly, trailing her fingers delicately through the crisp curls at her crotch. Her thighs were quivering. Slowly, luxuriously, she licked her lips and let her legs fall apart, revealing the moist folds of pink flesh between them. Khonsu's penis pulsed with eagerness as the girl spread her slender thighs wide, showing herself to him without shame.

211

She arched her back and caressed her breasts again, moaning as if the touch of the warm air on her secret parts was sufficient to give her pleasure.

Not for long. Her hands slid back down her glistening body and she cupped the soft flesh of her inner thighs, pressing her legs even further apart. The moist petals of her sex moved of their own accord. Khonsu imagined her vagina spasming, clutching eagerly at emptiness. Was she thinking of a man now, of how a man would part those honeyed lips with the head of his cock and penetrate her?

'Oh,' the girl moaned. She lifted her hips off the couch and spread her labia wide apart with her fingers, offering the heart of her body to Khonsu's avid eyes. There was the little stem of her pleasure, naked and exposed, paler than the soft lips surrounding it. There was her tunnel, a tiny dark hole, looking hardly big enough to admit a finger, never mind a man's rampant member. She undulated her body as if she was being taken; as if the lover of her imagination was sliding his penis in and out of her tender body.

Now the girl was so aroused that she had to touch herself. She gasped and rolled her head to one side as at last her delicate fingers grazed the swollen nub of flesh that shivered with expectation. The middle finger of her right hand settled there, pressing and squeezing, dragging her into abysses of delight, and with her left hand she parted the folds of her vulva. First she slipped one finger into her body, then two. Her hips gyrated, desperately jerking her liquid sex towards her stimulating hands, and she groaned with ecstasy. Her lips moved, making words. Khonsu craned forward to hear them, but they made no sense, just a random jumble of encouragement: 'Yes, more, yes, yes, in, now, deeper, ah, more . . .'

The girl's body was twisting and heaving as she drew herself closer and closer to the moment. Her finger beat frantically against the swollen bead of her clitoris and her mouth gaped wide. And then suddenly she was completely still, her whole body quite rigid. Her head was tilted back, her breasts thrust skyward, and her loins arched as pulses of pleasure raced through her. For a long moment she remained motionless, not even breathing. Then she sagged back on the couch like a broken doll, panting.

After a little while she opened her eyes and lifted her head. Khonsu nodded approvingly. 'Very good,' he said.

'Thank you, lord,' said the girl.

'Tell me,' asked Khonsu, 'what did you think of?'

She looked into his eyes and licked her lips. Then she shook her head, jumped to her feet and hurried away.

Khonsu scowled with momentary frustration. He was going to call the girl back and demand an answer, but before he could call out Mutemwia entered, gesturing grandly. 'Lord Khonsu,' she said, 'your entertainment shall commence. Here are my new pair. The girl is Freya, the young man is Jarl.' She drew forward from behind her a girl and a youth whose skins were so white that they glowed in the dimness of the room, as she had said, just like liles. They were tall and slender, like many of their race, and they were quite naked. They hung their heads as if they were ashamed, and Khonsu saw with a smile that their hands were clasped.

'Look up,' Khonsu commanded sharply. The couple lifted their heads hesitantly and gazed at him wide eyed. Both of them, he saw, had the blue eyes of northerners, but the golden-haired young man's eyes were dawn-pale while the girl, who had dark hair, had eyes like the evening sky, dark blue and bright as stars. They regarded him with unconcealed apprehension. These two, he thought, are not yet accustomed to their new life.

'Were they lovers when you bought them?' he enquired coolly.

Mutemwia laughed. 'I think not. The man who sold them to me said he had the girl's maidenhead, though I can hardly credit it. But I think they are fond of each other now. You would expect it, after all. They speak the same tongue.' She touched the young man's shoulder-length flaxen hair admiringly. 'Are they not special? What do you desire from them?'

'Do they understand us?'

'Oh yes. They speak Egyptian quite well, for barbarians.'

Khonsu was entranced by the wondrous combination of colours. Especially the girl, whose dark hair glowed with red lights and whose skin was almost blue-white and dusted with freckles like tiny fragments of gold leaf. She aroused him deeply. The youth, on the other hand, had the look of a victim in his pale hopeless eyes.

A smile caught at the corners of Khonsu's mouth. 'Yes,' he said slowly, 'I believe that I do know what I want.' He sat up, unselfconscious in his splendid nakedness. 'Let the girl come here. What is her name, Freya? She shall serve me.'

Mutemwia jerked the girl's hand free and pushed her towards Khonsu. 'You heard the Lord Khonsu. Do as you are told.'

Freya walked towards Khonsu slowly, her head hanging. She looked up at him anxiously with her great blue eyes. He gestured to the floor before him, and she dropped obediently to her knees.

'As for the youth,' said Khonsu, 'I would like to see him . . . surrounded. Abused. Let him have a girl or two, by all means. But I want to see one of your people take him too, as Seth took Horus. Let me see something opening that white backside.'

The girl kneeling before Khonsu let out a little cry of horror, but the young man, Jarl, was quite silent. His pale eyes were fixed on Khonsu's and he licked his parted lips. Between his legs the white softness of his penis, dangling over its nest of golden hair, gave a sudden twitch and stirred to life. I was right, thought Khonsu. A born victim. Even the thought arouses him.

He leant forward and whispered to Freya, 'Little lily, you fear for him more than he fears for himself. Forget him. Enjoy yourself with me.'

214

Freya lifted her head and stared at him in horrified amazement. Khonsu put his hand on her breast, delighted by the contrast between her whiteness and the darkness of his own tanned skin. He wanted to see his stiff penis disappearing into that white body. But it never pleased him to have an unwilling girl, and this one looked as though she might be a challenge to warm.

To Mutemwia he said, 'Let Jarl wait until I have thawed this little frosted rose.' Then he took Freya's hand and pulled her to her feet. She was tall, and her slender hips were level with his face as he sat on the couch. The dark hair at her loins was soft and silky, and he caught a brief whisper of her secret scent.

'Freya,' he said, 'open your legs.'

She glanced wildly over her shoulder. Her face was flushed with shame. Like all northerners, she must believe that nakedness was not the natural condition of the human body, but shameful. Khonsu had been told that her people would expose a criminal nude as a punishment, while any Egyptian knew that nakedness was a state to rejoice in. It was difficult to understand, but the girl's embarrassment and reluctance was arousing.

'Come,' Khonsu repeated, 'open.'

Freya closed her eyes tightly. 'But you will see – '

'I will do more than *see*,' said Khonsu. He put his hands on Freya's thighs and slowly and deliberately forced them apart. She gave a horrified cry and wrapped her arms around her breasts and spread her hands over her blushing face.

Her mound was small and downy, like half a tender peach. The lips were full and fleshy and clasped tightly together, as if even her most secret parts sought to protect her chilly northern modesty. She smelled sweet. Khonsu leant towards her, bringing his mouth and nose close to her exposed vulva, and drew in a deep, luxurious breath.

'Oh no,' whispered the girl from behind her hands. 'Please, lord, please, do not. Oh, Jarl will see – '

'Hush,' said Khonsu, and the warmth of his breath stirred the soft, dark hairs which adorned her sex. She gave a little protesting moan and fell silent. Khonsu put the palms of his hands on her inner thighs and pushed them gently apart, making her shift her feet until she stood straddled before him. From where Jarl stood, he mused, one would be able to see Freya's naked back, the pale spheres of her small, tight bottom, and the little wisp of dark fur between them.

He would show Jarl more than that. But not yet. She was dry and closed, shielding her shame. First he would open her, and then he would reveal her. He nudged his face between Freya's open thighs, ignoring her whimpers of protest, and extended his long, strong tongue.

The questing tip probed gently against the closed lips of Freya's sex. They were as ripe and plump as a freshly plucked fruit. Freya whimpered again and then let out a sharp cry of shock and disbelief as Khonsu's tongue slipped between her labia and began to explore the hidden depths of her vulva.

She tasted sweet and somehow foreign. Khonsu clasped her thighs with both hands and wormed his tongue further into her. First he would find the entrance to her sex; then he would begin to warm her.

He found the notch and eased his tongue a little further into the delicate folds of Freya's pale flesh. She gave a muffled cry and the whole of her vulva clenched, trying to resist him. But his wet, slippery tongue was imperturbable. He slid first the tip, then the whole of the blade into Freya's quivering vagina. It was tight and trembling. Her little hopeless cries lashed him with arousal. An Egyptian girl would be leaning back, opening herself to him, urging him on with eager endearments to give her pleasure; and this northern slave was weeping with shame! He would show her how life was lived in Egypt.

Slowly, lasciviously, he explored the walls of her silken tunnel with his tongue. Then he withdrew from her and licked his lips, enjoying her taste. It was time to give her pleasure.

He returned to her soft sex, burrowing his way between the bulging lips at the front of her mound. He sought that little slip of flesh, like the stem of a fruit, which is the heart of a woman's pleasure. He knew that she would not be able to resist his touch once he found her hidden jewel. It would please him to feel her shiver and moan with reluctant ecstasy.

There it was, quivering in its tiny sheath as if it wanted to avoid his caresses. Gently, so gently, he ran the tip of his tongue around it, avoiding it, teasing it. At once he was rewarded by a moan from Freya, quite different from any sound she had made before. A liquid, unbelieving moan; a sigh of unexpected delight. The little stem of flesh swelled and flushed, and Khonsu's softly probing fingers found that the lips of Freya's sex were beginning to be dewed with silky moisture.

No need to hold her thighs apart now. He lapped and lapped at Freya's engorging clitoris, relishing her astonished little cries of pleasure. One hand clasped the firm orb of her left buttock, keeping her sex still and open against his searching mouth. The other crept up her slender body, pushed her arms away from her shallow breasts, and began to squeeze and stroke one slight mound. Her nipple was as hard beneath his palm as the trembling fragment of her clitoris beneath his flickering tongue.

Khonsu growled with pleasure as he mouthed Freya's soft mound of love. It aroused him powerfully to feel her whole body softening, shuddering as he caressed her with tongue and lips. He kneaded her buttock and breast, pulled her clitoris into his mouth and sucked at it, slithering his tongue along the length of the tiny quivering shaft.

'Oh!' Freya cried out in her own tongue, strange guttural words. She convulsed as her orgasm seized her, and she would have fallen had Khonsu not held her securely between his strong hands. He thrust his tongue hard into the moist clasp of her vagina, enjoying the feel of her tunnel spasming around him. His lips brushed against her clitoris, prolonging her ecstasy. When at last he drew back she sagged in his arms, limp and helpless.

Khonsu smiled. He bent Freya forward until her buttocks were thrust high in the air. Her legs were widely parted, showing Jarl, standing behind her, every detail of her wet, open sex, the lips flushed pink with desire, the engorged clitoris standing out proud and eager, the white shining dew that moistened every fold. Jarl's pale face showed shock and horror and lust in equal proportions.

'Very good,' said Khonsu. 'Now, Freya, kneel.' He released the girl's buttocks and she sank to her knees before him at once, still panting with the aftermath of her orgasm. 'Suck me,' Khonsu ordered her. He took hold of her dark hair and thrust her face close to his crotch, where his penis was so stiff and erect that it felt ready to burst at her first touch.

He thought she would protest, but she said nothing. She opened her pale lips obediently and allowed the glistening head of his cock to slide between them. Khonsu closed his eyes for a moment, almost overcome by the pleasure of feeling her mouth on him. Then he controlled himself. He held her head firmly between his hands and began to fuck her mouth, thrusting his penis deep into her throat, then withdrawing. She did not struggle, but knelt quite still, passively accepting his abuse. It was delicious. He slid his cock in and out a few times, looking down so that he could enjoy the sight of his shining rigid shaft penetrating the pale open lips. His tanned fingers were dark against the white skin of her cheeks.

'Now,' he said to Mutemwia, 'Jarl.'

Mutemwia nodded and made an imperious gesture. At once another couple entered the room, a young man and a girl. They were Egyptian, dark skinned and dark eyed, and both of them were quite naked. The young man already had an erection, and his muscular body and the smooth, swollen shaft of his penis gleamed with oil. The girl was round bodied, plump and full fleshed, with big, firm breasts and ripe, lush hips. Her nipples were dark and long.

Quickly, in an eager undertone, Mutemwia gave orders. Then she bowed and withdrew. Jarl stood where he was, trembling as he watched Khonsu shafting Freya's mouth. He hardly seemed to notice that the Egyptians were standing behind him. His long, pale-skinned penis was lifting into erection, standing up proudly against his abdomen. He might be ashamed of nakedness, but it was clear that the sight of Freya's moist, open sex aroused him as much as any other man.

The dark young Egyptian woman stood beside Jarl and reached out with her honey-gold fingers to fondle his penis. He jumped and stared at her as if in shock. She wrapped her hand around his erect cock and smiled at him, then without a word began to back away from him towards one of the couches, tugging gently to make him follow her. She led him as a bull is led by the ring in its nose, and he obeyed her without protest. When she reached the couch she lay down and spread her thighs wide, smiling lasciviously up at Jarl as she offered him her open sex.

Khonsu breathed though his teeth as he continued to fuck Freya's mouth. He had a fairly good idea of what the two Egyptians would do to Jarl, and he wanted to watch.

For a moment Jarl looked down at the Egyptian girl while her dark hand rubbed encouragingly at his rigid cock. Then he gasped and dropped to his knees between her spread legs. She lifted her thighs and rested her ankles on his shoulders, and as he leant forward to clasp her heavy breasts in his hands she sighed and allowed her flexible body to fold up, opening her sex to him with such eager lewdness that it was only a second before the quivering head of his penis found her parted, moist lips and slid inside her.

That was worth seeing, that long white shaft easing

its way slowly into the Egyptian girl's ripe, dark vulva. It was time Freya saw what her countryman was doing. Khonsu tightened his fingers on her cheeks and held her head still as he withdrew his penis from her flushed, swollen lips.

'Turn around, Freya,' he whispered. 'Look at Jarl.'

For a moment Freya did not move, and just stared up at him with her huge dark blue eyes. A long trickle of saliva ran down her chin. He caught her hair with his hand and tugged her head around. She turned then, still on her knees, and gasped as she saw Jarl kneeling over the Egpytian girl, eagerly working the full length of his stiff cock in and out of her moist vagina. His white hands were kneading the girl's heavy golden breasts, and her long dark nipples were clutched tightly between finger and thumb as he pulled and plucked at the erect teats. The girl was moaning, louder and louder with each thrust, and her thighs shuddered as Jarl's cock plunged in and out of her.

Khonsu caught hold of Freya's slender hips and jerked them up towards him. She moaned, but made no attempt to pull away. He forced her to kneel down like a beast, her pert buttocks thrust upward, just parting to show her sex. With one hand he felt her, testing her wetness. She whimpered as Khonsu's fingers roughly opened her. Then, without preliminaries, he entered her. His rigid penis slid up into the tight clasp of her moist sex and she gave a long, low groan as his taut testicles brushed against her vulva.

'Look,' he hissed, leaning over her so that he could finger her breasts. They were shallow as saucers, hardly moving even now when they hung beneath her, and the nipples were small and tight like rose hips. He took one little bud in each hand and pinched them hard. 'Look how Jarl's cock is pale and her skin is dark. Look how he takes her! And I am taking you, little lily. Do you like it?'

'No,' Freya moaned, writhing helplessly as Khonsu

slid his cock again and again into her juicy flesh. 'No, no, no.'

'You will,' Khonsu whispered, snarling as he jerked himself further into her. He would make her come again before he was finished with her. But in his own time, when he wanted to. And not the way she expected, either.

Now the young Egyptian was crouched behind Jarl, rubbing more oil on to the ravening shaft of his penis. Perhaps Jarl knew what awaited him, because it seemed to Khonsu that each time he withdrew from the girl's sex, thrusting his pale buttocks outward, he hesitated for just a moment as if expecting something. Well, soon he would know.

'Look, Freya.' Khonsu caught hold of Freya's dark hair and pulled the girl's head back so that she could not ignore the lustful sight before her. 'Look, that young man is going to shove his cock up Jarl's arse. Do you see?'

'No!' Freya protested, tugging hopelessly against Khonsu's grip. 'No, please, he mustn't. It's shameful. It's – '

'It's too late,' Khonsu whispered. The young Egyptian had caught hold of Jarl's white hips and fitted the head of his cock directly against the blond youth's tight anus. Jarl did nothing, just remained perfectly still, the tip of his penis buried in the girl's gaping sex. His mouth and eyes were wide open. As the long, dark shaft of the Egyptian's cock began to ease its way inside him he started to shake and moan, a sound of desperate, tortured ecstasy.

'No,' whispered Freya. She hardly seemed to notice that Khonsu's penis was still thrusting vigorously into her tight mound of love. 'No, no.'

Now the Egyptian's penis was buried in Jarl's anus up to the hilt. Jarl's eyes slid shut and his head fell back. He writhed on the embedded shaft, a supple, libidinous movement. Then his white hands clutched ferociously at the breasts of the girl beneath him and he bared his teeth and plunged into her, then jerked back again, impaling himself on the Egyptian's stiff cock. He thrust frantically, driven into convulsions of delirious pleasure by the combination of his own penis sliding to and fro in the girl's juicy flesh and the young Egyptian's stiff phallus slipping smoothly in and out of his spasming anus.

'He likes it,' whispered Khonsu in Freya's ear. 'Wouldn't you like to feel it, little lily?'

'No,' Freya groaned as Khonsu withdrew his penis from her. She tried to get up, but he held her on her knees and thrust his hand between her legs, gathering up her copious juices on his fingers and transferring them to the silky crease between her taut, high cheeks.

'Ah,' hissed Khonsu, 'this will be sweet.' He lubricated her arsehole liberally with her own slippery dew, then slowly wriggled the tip of one finger into the tight, flinching hole. Freya clenched her buttocks rebelliously and began to sob. But Khonsu reached around under her slender loins and probed gently between her spread thighs, found the still-engorged stem of her clitoris and began to tease and rub at it with his fingers.

Freya gasped and arched her back. The movement thrust her firm round buttocks up towards Khonsu. At once he seized his chance. He found the place, lodged his penis firmly between her spread cheeks, and thrust with all his strength. Freya cried out as the fat glossy head of his cock forced its way into her, opening her sphincter, and the whole of his thick shaft slid at last into her quivering anus.

'Oh gods,' Khonsu gasped, because she was incredibly tight. He knew he could not last long and he rubbed furiously at her trembling clitoris, wanting to take her with him. 'By Seth and darkness, that's good. Freya, Freya, watch Jarl, look at him.'

Freya flung back her dark head and cried out as Khonsu thrust his penis time after time into her anus. As he stimulated her clitoris she moaned with ecstasy and stared avidly at Jarl, who seemed to be half mad with pleasure, now driving his cock into the girl's prone body as hard as he could, now wrenching himself free so that he could fling himself backward and impale himself upon the eager penis of the young man behind him.

Khonsu's phallus was aching with his need to come. His balls were tight and hard, throbbing with seed. But he wanted to feel Freya spasming around him, all her shame lost in the shameful bliss of having him plunder her forbidden hole. He beat his body ferociously against her, worried her nipple between his fingers, rubbed and rubbed at her swollen clitoris, and at last she writhed beneath him and convulsed as orgasm rippled through her whole body. The strong muscles of her anus clenched and released and Khonsu cried out and let himself go, allowing his hot semen to pulse upward through his shuddering shaft. His climax was so strong that for a few moments he saw and heard nothing; only red brightness and the rushing of blood.

Then he was finished. He opened his eyes reluctantly. Jarl and the Egyptian couple were slumped on the couch in a tangle of sweaty limbs, and Freya was huddled before him, her buttocks held lewdly up by the deep-buried shaft of his softening cock.

His desire had evaporated as swiftly as it had arisen. He no longer wanted the northerners; he did not want to see them or smell them. He withdrew from Freya's anus with a jerk that made her gasp and said harshly, 'Enough. Leave me.'

The four of them looked at him anxiously and crept away. Khonsu lay down upon the couch, his hands folded behind his head.

After love with Naunakhte they had lain together as close as birds in a nest, kissing, touching, laughing. Naunakhte had run her fingers through his hair and caressed his throat. Naunakhte . . .

Khonsu swung to a sitting position on the couch and buried his head in his hands. Could nothing keep out the memories? She did not want him. She had rejected him.

And yet ... Khonsu pressed the heels of his hands against his eyes until the darkness sparkled with red. Every leaping mote of light was Naunakhte. She was present, close to him, so close that he could sense her.

Could she be thinking of him? She had the power of the god in her. Could she be using that power now to put herself in his mind?

Mutemwia appeared in the doorway, bowing. 'Lord Khonsu, I trust that Freya and Jarl were to your taste?'

His head jerked up arrogantly. 'Yes,' he said shortly, getting up and reaching for his discarded kilt. He moved with sudden decision, as if he had urgent business to attend to.

'You will stay?' Mutemwia's voice was half enquiry, half insistence. 'I have some fine food and wine, grape wine, all the way from Palestine.'

'I will not stay,' Khonsu contradicted her. He fastened his kilt and slung his baldric over his shoulder, then lifted a small purse from it and flung it at Mutemwia. She caught it, but she did not look happy.

'Lord Khonsu,' she protested as he pushed past her in the doorway, 'what is the matter? Where are you going? You know you will not receive better hospitality than here. What can you be offered anywhere else in Waset to compete with what I have?'

Khonsu strode through the selection room, ignoring the alluring smiles of the girls on either side. 'In Waset,' he agreed, 'nothing.' And something, some growing madness, made him add beneath his breath, 'But in Karnak ...'

The door closed behind him. He was alone in the quiet street. Above his head a huge full moon glowed downward, as golden and brilliant as Naunakhte's flesh. He closed his eyes and shuddered, because he seemed to hear her voice, soft and low and urgent, calling him. *Khonsu! Khonsu, come to me!*

It was a desperate thing, to rob a god. It was dangerous even to think of it. And how could he dare to imagine that Naunakhte was calling him? She had made her choice, and she had chosen Amun.

Khonsu's face tightened and he loosened his sword in its sheath. What if she had not called him? He would go to her and take her by force. Once out of the temple he would take her with him far away, to Elephantine, to the Delta, to anywhere where she would be unknown and the power of the god would be too weak to drag her back to the temple. Once she was far from Karnak she would forget that the god had called her. She had loved Khonsu before, and she would love him again.

He struck his clenched fist against his palm and broke into a run, threading his way through the silent streets with unerring certainty. He would go to the temple. He would steal Naunakhte from the god.

If they found him in the temple precinct they would ask for his death. Khonsu feared death. But more than death he feared that in the temple at Karnak he would have to fight again with the god Amun for the possession of Naunakhte, and that he would lose.

Chapter Thirteen

*I*n the cool darkness of the evening Naunakhte walked by the fishpond in the women's quarters, her arms wrapped tightly around herself. It was a warm night, bright with moonlight and studded with stars that glowed like beacons, but she shivered.

She had caused Bahematun's death. She could not doubt it. She had cursed a man in the power of Amun, and the man had died.

I am the one who curses you, oath breaker, in the name of Amun! She heard her own voice, clear and cold with the strength of the god, and she covered her face with her hands. She wanted comfort, but she could not seek comfort from the god who empowered her. She whispered Khonsu's name again, as if naming him could bring her the reassurance of his warm strong body.

Then she felt the chill of hatred which signified Tiy's presence. Quickly she lowered her hands and lifted her head, not wanting to show weakness before her enemy. Tiy stood there, smiling, her green eyes and her white teeth glittering in the moonlight.

Naunakhte did not trust Tiy's smile. 'What do you want?' she asked sharply.

Tiy stepped a little closer, still smiling. 'You are afraid,' she said. 'You are afraid of the power of the god.'

'It is no business of yours,' snapped Naunakhte.

'But it is.' Tiy moved closer still, her whole face alight and eager. 'Listen to me, Naunakhte. All you need to do is leave the temple. Give up the god. Go away from him.' Her smile widened. 'I do not fear the god Amun,' she hissed. 'I will take your place as the new Hand of God. Release yourself, Naunakhte. Amun will not grudge one servant among so many.'

Naunakhte shook her head. 'You don't understand,' she said. Suddenly she really wanted Tiy to understand, to make her see. 'I can't change myself just by going away. The god is – ' She lifted her clenched fists helplessly, then struck them against her breast ' – in me. He is here, in my heart. Where I am makes no difference.'

Tiy's smile writhed into an animal's snarl. 'You have usurped my place!' she said in a fierce undertone. 'Who asked you to come here? I warn you, Naunakhte, if you do not leave this place tonight, I will kill you.'

'No.' Naunakhte closed her eyes. She felt the familiar terrifying sensation of the god entering into her, his power taking her and making her speak his words. 'You cannot kill me, Tiy. You have tried before and failed. The god protects me.'

She would never have spoken so if Amun had not prompted her. She knew her words would enrage Tiy, and they did. Tiy's brilliant eyes opened so widely that they were ringed with white and her neat nostrils flared with fury. 'The god protects you? Does he? *Does he?*' Tiy's voice was shrill. 'We shall see if he protects everyone you wish! Who killed Bahematun, Naunakhte? Was it Khonsu? Shall we bring him here and have him tortured?'

'No! No!' Naunakhte raised her fists, struggling against helpless rage. The temple handmaidens had heard their angry voices and now they were hurrying towards the pond, calling out. 'Leave me alone!' Naunakhte shouted at Tiy.

'Leave the temple,' hissed Tiy. 'Go, go away. Or I

swear, Naunakhte, I will have Khonsu killed, and I will leave his body for you to find, and then I will kill you! Amun cannot protect you always. Even gods must sleep, and you will die, Naunakhte, I swear it, you will die.'

Neferure ran towards them, calling, 'Tiy, leave her alone.'

But Tiy was too far gone in anger to heed her. She said through bared teeth, 'Which part of Khonsu shall I have laid on your bed, Naunakhte? His handsome head, perhaps? Or would you prefer his *cock*?'

Something in Naunakhte snapped. Her eyes opened wide and she flung out one hand towards Tiy. Tiy cried out and fell to her knees, staring in terror.

'Enough,' Naunakhte shouted, and her voice was thick with the power of the god. She did not know what she said. 'By the phallus of Amun, Tiy, by my power I curse you! May you never see this night's end, may you never see another dawn!'

Tiy shrieked as if she were being disembowelled and fell backward to the stone flags at the pool's edge. She writhed briefly, then lay still, one outflung hand trailing in the lily-covered water.

Naunakhte stood motionless, trembling from head to foot. Her eyes saw darkness, there was a rushing in her ears, and her lips were dry. She felt weak, as if the god had drained the life from her as he passed through her body. Slowly she came to herself. The moon reappeared in the sky, and the stars shone around it. She lowered her gaze and saw Neferure kneeling beside the still body of Tiy, her hands pressed to her mouth.

'Neferure,' Naunakhte said in her own voice. It sounded strange in her ears.

Neferure glanced up in terror, her hand outstretched in the sign against a god's anger. 'Naunakhte,' she whispered, 'you cursed Tiy, and she fell down.'

The other women were running up now, coming close, then hesitating. They gazed at Naunakhte with fear in their faces. The Lady Hunro was with them, breathing fast. 'What happened?' she demanded. 'Naunakhte, did you curse her? What was the curse?'

Naunakhte shook her head. She could not remember. It was Neferure who said huskily, 'She cursed Tiy never to see another dawn.'

'Oh, by all the gods,' whispered Hunro, dropping to her knees beside Tiy. 'Naunakhte, I know Tiy plagued you, but did you have to curse her with death?'

Naunakhte wanted to say that she had not meant to, but she could not speak. She stood silent, trembling.

And then Tiy moved. She lifted her hand from the water and turned her head from side to side, moaning.

'Amun be praised,' breathed Hunro. She slid one hand under Tiy's narrow shoulders and lifted her. 'Tiy? Tiy? Are you all right?'

Tiy moaned again and passed one hand over her forehead as if she had been stunned. The women standing around sighed with relief. Tiy frowned and murmured something, then opened her eyes.

And gazed blankly before her. And screamed. 'The gods help me. I'm blind. I'm blind.'

Naunakhte stared for long moments at Tiy's empty eyes and her groping hands. Then she turned and ran. The servants of the god stood out of her path. She ran through the women's quarters, out into the temple precinct, and on towards the sanctuary of the god.

She was the chosen of Amun, the successor to the Hand of God, and the medjay opened the doors and closed them behind her. She was alone with the golden statue of the god.

Her cheeks were wet with tears. She stood before the statue, panting. At last she spoke. 'Take it away,' she sobbed. 'Take away this power. I don't want it. It does harm. Free me from it.'

The god looked calmly down at her. His enamelled eyes glowed like the stars. She heard his answer. *You asked for my love. You asked for me to possess you. You cannot reject my gift, once it is given.*

He burnt above her like the meteors that scorched

heaven. His phallus thrust forward, glittering like a torch, demanding her submission. *You are mine*, his voice said. *You desire the ecstasy I bring you. You must take the power with it.*

'No,' Naunakhte wept. 'No.' And she turned and fled.

Even as she ran she knew that there was no use in running from the god. But she could not stop her feet from moving; aimless, panic stricken, hopelessly seeking escape.

At last she stopped, her breath sobbing, and looked around to find where her pointless flight had taken her. She was in the hypostyle hall, alone. The immense shadows of the lotus pillars reared up around her like massive copies of the god's phallus; huge, thick, swollen tipped, and ripe with seed.

Naunakhte tilted back her head and stared at the coffered ceiling. Tears spilled from her eyes and trickled down her cheeks. 'I do not want this power,' she whispered helplessly. 'I did not seek it. Help me.'

A movement in the shadows caught her eye and she spun towards it, expecting horrors. She saw the shape of a man detach itself from the shelter of a pillar and head towards her. He stepped into a bar of moonlight and her lips parted in disbelief, because it was Khonsu, dressed like a prince, dressed as he had been when she first saw him.

'Khonsu.' She could hardly speak. 'Are you a dream?'

Then she saw his face. He was very pale, as if he was in fear. His right hand clutched at the hilt of his sword, knuckles white with pressure. His lips trembled as he approached her.

'Naunakhte,' he said, and his voice was shaking. 'I have come for you. I love you. I am going to take you away with me.'

Her face convulsed with relief and she flung herself towards him. He sheathed his sword and opened his arms to catch her, looking startled, as if he had not expected this reaction. 'Oh,' she sobbed, clutching him, 'I've been so afraid!'

'Hush.' His arms were around her, tight, warm and strong. The power of the god receded before the reality of his embrace. His lips brushed her forehead. 'Hush, Naunakhte. If they find me here they'll kill me. Come, let's go.'

But she could still hardly believe in him. She touched his face, his lips. 'I called for you,' she said, shaking her head. 'I wanted you to come. You heard me.'

Khonsu's whole body shivered. 'Don't,' he said sharply. 'I don't want to know, Naunakhte.'

'But the god –'

'I don't want to know!' Khonsu laid his finger upon her lips to silence her. He swallowed hard and said softly, 'Naunakhte, I love you. But I fear the god in you. I will not be easy until we are far, far away from this place.'

Naunakhte was going to say to Khonsu what she had said to Tiy, that wherever she was Amun would be with her. She wanted to tell him about how she had blinded Tiy with her curse. But she looked at his frightened, resolute face and did not speak. She did not want to give him even more reason to fear her.

Khonsu took her hand and led her into the darkness of the shadows. His fingers caressed her palm. Gradually her fears withdrew, and as she became calmer she realised that her whole body was weak with wanting him.

He was close to her, naked but for his kilt and his leopard-skin baldric. The dark, dense fragrance of his skin filled her nostrils. She could already feel his touch, his hard fingers stroking her. Her limbs were heavy with her desire.

She said in a voice that trembled, 'Khonsu.'

He dropped her hand and turned to look at her. She stood in a pool of moonlight, the blue brilliance outlining her in silver. His eyes darkened as he took her in, and he licked his lips. Then he said, 'Naunakhte,' in a slow, leaden voice, as if he spoke against his better judgement. 'We . . . should . . . flee this place. Now.'

'Not now,' Naunakhte said. 'Later.'

She put her hands to the front of her linen gown and tore it open. The fine fabric fell away, baring her shoulders and her taut golden breasts. Khonsu stared at her for a moment as if stricken. Then he gave a stifled cry, flung off his swordbelt and fell to his knees before her. He pressed his face between her breasts, clutching at her with his strong hands, telling her in smothered whispers how much he had longed for her. Then he clasped one breast and pressed his mouth to her nipple, licking and sucking in a fervour of devotion, until Naunakhte moaned with the bliss of it and sank to her knees beside him, catching his face between her hands and lifting his mouth to hers.

She kissed him with all her soul. Nothing existed for her but the sensation of his lips upon hers, his tongue exploring her mouth, her tongue responding. Even the insistent demands of the god faded and left her mind. She gave herself up entirely to Khonsu, opening her mouth to him as she opened her heart.

He tore his mouth from hers and pressed his face to her slender throat. He was gasping. 'Naunakhte, I could not forget you. I have longed for you.'

His lips caressed her jaw, her chin, brushed against her mouth, hovered over her eyelids. His hands pressed her against him, holding her close. She moaned with love and yearning and twisted her shoulders back to offer him her breasts. Her nipples ached for his hands, for his lips. She wanted to enfold him in herself, to let him slip into her as a setting star slips into the waters of the Nile, to open herself to him and allow him to lose himself in the sweetness of her body.

Slowly, gently, he pressed her back until she lay upon the cold stone. He did not allow his body to be separated from hers even for a moment, but clasped her against him, pressing his limbs against hers as a creeper winds itself around a tree. She twined her arms around him and sighed with joy to feel his big body above her, his weight driving the breath from her, his solid realness

232

pinning her down. She parted her thighs and parted her lips, and he lowered his mouth to hers and kissed her even as he slid his hot phallus up into the moist softness of her sex.

Then there was a moment of stillness. They lay together, mouth on mouth, bodies conjoined, eyes closed, breathing each other's breath. Naunakhte was full of the tension of desire, the longing to move, to shudder, to cry out; but for this moment she lay quiescent, allowing herself to experience fully the wonderful sensation of being, for this short time, one body with the man who loved her.

Khonsu seemed also to feel the tension and the longing. He lay still within Naunakhte for as long as he could bear it, but then the velvet grip of her sex was too much for him. His breath shuddered as very, very slowly he withdrew his rigid penis from her body, drawing back and back until only the very tip remained within her.

Naunakhte opened her eyes and looked up at him, pleading without words. Her hands explored his back, the smooth, strong muscle of his shoulders, the hard knitted layer of flesh over his breathing ribs, the delicate graven hollow of his spine. She slipped her palms down to his buttocks, tugged away the wreck of his kilt, grasped the firm round orbs in both hands and pulled at him, urging him to penetrate her again. Khonsu groaned her name and then set his mouth on hers, smothering their cries as he drove himself back into her.

They lay in the shadows, their naked bodies glistening in reflected moonlight, silvered limbs twisting like mating snakes, skin shining with a dew of sweat. Their movements were not fast, but deep. They heaved together like the waves of the Nile, bodies arching and hollowing as they single-mindedly sought their mutual release. They smothered their sighs and moans, but their growing pleasure and tension was revealed in the increasing tautness of their bodies, the sudden desperate jerking of loins and buttocks.

And then from the tangle of writhing limbs a pattern emerged, a rhythm. Naunakhte wrapped her legs around Khonsu's waist, resting her heels on the hollows of his buttocks. He caught hold of her hands and pulled them high above her head. Then he lifted himself above her and looked down into her spellbound face. Naunakhte gazed into his eyes and laced her fingers into his, and as he thrust, thrust, thrust into her lifting flesh she tightened her grip, fastening her fingers around him tighter and tighter with every lunge. Soon; it would be soon. Her pleasure brimmed up within her, answering every surge of Khonsu's strong body with a rippling echo of bliss. She could not take her eyes from his face. With every beat of his flesh against hers she cried his name, softly, urgently, and then their rhythm began to quicken, speed and power increasing to the final desperate crescendo. Naunakhte was overwhelmed. She clutched Khonsu's hands in hers with frantic strength and flung back her head. Her eyes were closed, her throat arched and twisting; all of her rigid and trembling with ecstasy as Khonsu's soul leapt and pulsed within her.

Then his lips were on hers, silencing her. She moaned into his open mouth and he drew back, panting. His hard body was damp with sweat, and her limbs stuck to him. She clung to him as a drowning man clutches at a spar, not wanting to accept that such joy must have an end.

Khonsu gently freed his hands from hers and stroked her shining body. 'Little goddess,' he whispered, 'we must run away from here. Soon it will be dawn.'

Dawn! The watcher of the stars would waken the people of the temple for the rite. Then they would seek her. Naunakhte shook herself and slackened her grip. Khonsu smiled at her and kissed her mouth, then slowly and gently withdrew his softening penis from her body. She could not restrain a whimper of wretchedness and loss.

'Come,' he said. He wrapped the wreck of his kilt

around his hips, then leant down to take her hand and tug her to her feet. She stood passively while he brushed dust from her and straightened the rags of her dress as best he could.

Khonsu took her shoulders in his hands and lowered his head to kiss her again. She responded, and afterwards he smiled. 'Where would you like to go, little goddess? I have a boat outside. Shall I take you to the Delta? Memphis? Elephantine? Where will you feel safe?'

Naunakhte looked into his face and shivered. She could see that he was speaking, but his voice faded and became inaudible to her. Her spine prickled and her softened nipples puckered tautly and ached. She felt that sense of remoteness and distance from the world which meant that the god was with her.

Naunakhte, said the voice of Amun. It was silent, but it drowned Khonsu's words. *Naunakhte, you cannot escape me. You carry my mark. You are mine.*

'Naunakhte?' Khonsu was shaking her gently, trying to get her attention. His face was tense and strained, as if he was trying to hide his fear. 'Naunakhte, don't. Stop it. Naunakhte, come back to me! Where are you?'

With immense effort Naunakhte forced back the trance of the god. She looked into Khonsu's face with love and compassion, wondering how she could tell him the truth without giving him pain.

There was no way to do it. He had admitted that he loved her and put himself in her hands. She loved him, truly she did. She desired him. She had longed for him and hoped for him to protect her from her own power. But she could not go with him. He would always want her to be his, only his, and she knew that she could not make that promise. She could never be Khonsu's alone. Wherever she went, the god Amun would be with her. She must face the truth now and tell him.

What words could she use? He was waiting for her to speak, and his brow was furrowed with anxiety. He knew her too well not to realise that something was wrong. She took a deep breath, still without knowing what she would say.

Then Khonsu whirled and stared into the shadows. Figures moved there, dark and threatening. Naunakhte stared in horror, and Khonsu grabbed up his swordbelt from the floor and drew his sword. The bright bronze gleamed red in the moonlight. He caught hold of Naunakhte's arm and pulled her behind him, ready to protect her with his body.

One by one the figures moved forward into the moonlight. Naunakhte saw four medjay armed with spears, and walking before them Merybast himself, carrying his staff of office.

'Stay back.' Khonsu's voice was stern. 'I am taking her. Stay back.'

Merybast continued. With a motion of his hand he ordered the medjay to remain where they were. 'I am unarmed,' he said.

'Stay back!' Sweat gleamed on Khonsu's cheeks and his voice was rough with desperation. 'I swear, I will kill if I have to. She is coming with me. Do not try to stop me. I will kill her and myself rather than give her to you.'

'Does she go willingly?' said Merybast steadily. 'If she is willing, we will not prevent you.'

'Of course she is willing,' snapped Khonsu.

'Have you asked her?'

Khonsu's shoulders tightened and he frowned uncertainly. Naunakhte looked from behind him at Merybast's calm, unmoved face. How had he known? Truly, she was not the only servant of the temple who heard the voice of the god.

'When I found her,' Khonsu said angrily, 'she ran to me. She was terrified, she had been weeping. What have you done to her? She is coming with me.'

'She was afraid of herself,' replied Merybast. 'Of her own power. This evening she laid a curse on one of the temple women, and the girl was struck blind.'

'No,' Naunakhte whispered. She had wanted to protect Khonsu from that knowledge.

Khonsu stiffened and turned a little towards Naunakhte, lowering his sword. The moonlight caught the blade and reflected up into his eyes, which gleamed as brightly as the bronze. A muscle in his tight jaw twisted unconsciously. He was trembling very slightly, like a greyhound before it is released, but when he spoke his voice was as steady as a soldier's. 'Naunakhte. Is this true?'

She wanted to weep. If only she had been able to tell him herself, without interference. Now he would always think that she had lied to him. 'Yes. But it made me afraid, Khonsu. And I did call to you.'

For a moment his eyes glittered so brilliantly she believed that he was weeping. Then he blinked hard and his lips twitched angrily. He glanced at Merybast and the armed medjay behind him. He swallowed and said evenly, 'I will not take any woman against her will. Speak before this ... *priest*, Naunakhte. If you wish to remain in the temple, say so.'

His voice was steady, but his eyes were fixed on hers, begging her silently to return his love. At first his face showed challenge and confidence, but then as the moments went by and she did not speak, his expression became shadowed with grief and anger at the betrayal of his trust.

Naunakhte shook her head helplessly. 'Khonsu,' she said softly, 'you don't understand. I do love you, and I will always long for you. But – '

'But!' Khonsu flung her away from him with a roar of misery. 'But! You will stay here with your precious god, will you, rather than come with me?'

Merybast caught Naunakhte as she staggered. He held her between his hands, and she drew strength from his firm grip. She felt Khonsu's pain as if it were her own, but she knew that what she did was right. Her voice was calm and steady. 'Khonsu, if I came with you, the god would still be with me. It is better for you not to have me at all than to share me with Amun.'

Khonsu lifted his sword as if he would strike, but then he lowered it. His lips were trembling. 'Naunakhte,' he said in a husky voice, 'I want you. I want you to be mine.'

'I know,' she replied gently. 'But it cannot be.'

Khonsu closed his eyes. Tears trickled down his cheeks, glistening in the moonlight. Brilliant drops hung on his dark lashes. After a moment he turned away and sheathed his sword, then slung his baldric over his broad shoulder. When he turned back his face was resolute. He avoided Naunakhte's eyes and spoke to Merybast. 'She has made her choice, priest. Let me go. I will trouble you no more.'

'There was no choice,' said Merybast. 'Amun is a strong master. Do not think of her with hatred.'

'Hatred?' Khonsu looked at Naunakhte now, and his eyes were softer than she had ever seen them. He shook his head. 'No. Never hatred.'

'Escort him to the gate,' said Merybast, and the medjay stood aside to let Khonsu pass through them. He did not look back.

Naunakhte watched him go, wondering why she was not weeping. She loved Khonsu and she felt great sorrow for his pain. She would never see him again. And yet she felt not grief, but a strange sense of lightness, as if she had set aside a burden that troubled her.

'Naunakhte,' said Merybast.

She looked into the high priest's dark eyes and saw there that he understood both her loss and her victory.

'Go and sleep,' said Merybast. 'For today the rite will pass without you. Tomorrow I will consecrate you as the new Hand of Amun. It is time.'

Naunakhte bit her lip. 'What of Tiy?'

A shadow crossed Merybast's face. 'She will be taken care of, but she cannot stay within the temple. If she had not displeased the god, your curse would not have struck her.'

'I am afraid,' said Naunakhte simply.

'I know. That is why you must be consecrated very soon. You must not be asked to bear the burden of the god without knowing his joy.' Merybast put his hand on her shoulder and began to guide her towards the women's quarters. She went with him in silence, still looking within herself for the truth of what she felt.

At the door Merybast released her. His fingers traced the mark of the god on her arm, the little scarlet phallus that Amun had set upon her. 'From your birth you were sacred to the god,' he said softly. 'You chose rightly, Naunakhte. When a god desires you, how can a mere mortal challenge him?'

Naunakhte looked at the mark, then up into Merybast's eyes. The high priest smiled and kissed her forehead. She turned from him, still without a word, and opened the door to her destiny.

Epilogue

Neferure shook Naunakhte's shoulder gently. 'Naunakhte. It is time.'

Slowly Naunakhte stirred and opened her eyes.

Tonight she would become the bride of the god, god's wife of Amun. She would have her heart's desire. The priests would masturbate as she danced before the statue of the god and the women would sing as they watched her arouse the god's lust with her body, her hands and her mouth. And then they would offer her body to the god, and he would take her.

Before she fell asleep she had wept. She had wept because she had lost Khonsu and because she feared her own power. But now the moment of the god's possession was approaching and she could at last offer herself as a willing sacrifice to the might of Amun. With that joy before her, she was prepared to bear the burden.

She breathed deeply as she gazed up into the shadows of the coffered ceiling. Her breath came slowly and steadily, and she allowed her mind to fill with consciousness of the god's presence. She immersed herself in her love for the god. His trance was always near, and now it came at her call, settling upon her like heavy dew upon the petals of an opening rose. When she stood up, her eyes were already focused upon the far distance, seeing divinity rather than reality, wide and dark with the promise of the god's ecstasy.

Neferure guided her to the door of the room, which opened on to the moonlit terrace by the waterlily lake. Warm, soft air whispered through the door, heavy with the scent of jasmine. A basin of water was placed on a pedestal by the open door. It smelled of lilies. Neferure took a soft sponge, raised Naunakhte's unprotesting arms, and began to wash her naked body.

The sponge passed gently over Naunakhte's skin. She closed her eyes, focusing her attention entirely on Neferure's gentle, delicate caress. Every part of her was softly scoured by the sponge's infinitesimal roughness, then soothed by the coolness of the evaporating water when the sponge had gone. Her skin tensed into goosepimples. She was wholly sensitised, wholly open to arousal, so that a single drop of water trickling down her spine made her gasp almost as if she had felt a warm mouth sucking at the points of her swelling breasts.

Neferure took her hand and led her through to the women's chambers. She walked slowly, like a princess, her head held high and her lips parted. She could hear the god calling to her, a call like the desert wind; that irresistible force which bends even rock before it.

The women of the temple approached her to make her beautiful for the god. Soft hands anointed her skin with fragrant oils. Eager fingers brushed against the lifting orbs of her breasts, teasing out the points into swollen buds of stiffness. Naunakhte stood very still, her eyes lightly closed, her breathing slow and shallow. She accepted every caress, every touch, as if it were a blessing from Amun himself.

Hands worked deftly upon her, massaging the sweet-smelling oil into her shoulders and waist. Slender palms cupped the lush swell of her buttocks, then pushed the cheeks slightly apart. A skilful finger slipped into the crease, carrying the oil to her most secret part. Naunakhte's head fell back and she let out a little moan of pleasure as the finger pressed the velvet-soft, puckered

241

skin of her anus, then eased a little inside, rimming the tight sphincter.

Her knees buckled. She was caught on every side, then guided to the chair where until this night the Lady Hunro had sat. The carved granite was cold against her naked skin. She shivered and her breathing deepened.

The trance surrounded her. It was as if she was within herself, and yet removed from herself. When she had first arrived at the temple, she had dreamt of floating above her own body, twisting with frustration as she watched the god Amun make love to her, unable to feel the bliss which he gave her. Now she seemed to float above her own flesh, a disembodied spirit, and yet she felt every thrill of pleasure which the ministrations of the women brought her.

One of the girls leant over her, carefully applying paint to her closed eyelids. As she worked, the other girls stroked Naunakhte's limbs, careful not to do anything that would make her move and spoil the artist's handiwork. But when the paint was applied they had no such concerns. Swiftly they parted her thighs, opening the warm heart of her body. Neferure fell to her knees before her and extended her tongue, then leant slowly forward.

The floating spirit that was Naunakhte watched with cool detachment as Neferure slowly and luxuriously drew her tongue along the moist fullness of her labia. She was merely a spectator as Neferure gently eased the tip of her questing tongue between the swollen folds, wriggled it deep into her vagina, then withdrew it and returned to the eager, trembling bud of her clitoris. And yet, as Neferure lapped, lapped, lapped at the little stem of flesh, the body of Naunakhte was filled with swelling delight, pleasure that surged in her breasts and in her womb, joy that made her twist her long throat and moan.

Neferure was skilled and diligent. She pressed Naunakhte's quivering thighs apart with her hands, then, as she sucked softly at her clitoris, she slipped one long finger into the slippery centre of Naunakhte's sex. Naunakhte cried out again and began to heave her loins up from the cold granite, welcoming the sensation of Neferure's finger sliding in and out of her hot tunnel. Her mind was filled with the presence of the god, and she saw him bending towards her, hands outstretched. She gasped and trembled before him. His ecstasy was within her reach.

And then it withdrew, for Neferure sat back on her knees and wiped her glistening mouth. She said to the women around her, 'The Hand of God is prepared.'

Slowly Naunakhte sank back into the glittering strangeness of her trance. She hardly knew that the women were dressing her, robing her in white, adorning her limbs with jewels of gold and precious stones that would chink sensuously when she danced for the god. Her heart and her mind were turned towards the sanctuary, where Amun awaited her.

When the singing began, the sweetness of the sound sank into her soul like stones flung into a bottomless well. She swayed unconsciously to the rhythm and her lips moved, making words. The women led her out from the chambers to join the priests. Jumping torchlight illuminated her face, showing her rapt, spellbound and possessed.

She walked at the front of the procession, her face glowing with love and desire. The priests looked upon her and murmured at her beauty. Already their penises were hardening beneath their white robes, swelling with desire for this woman whose loveliness would arouse the god and make possible the daily rebirth of the land of Egypt. They admired her, and they knew she was human. All of them hoped that one day she would seek a mortal consort, and each of them wished that her gaze might fall on him.

The procession reacted the sanctuary. Naunakhte gazed at the great bronze doors, the last obstacle that separated her from the object of her desire. As she gazed, they swung open, revealing the great gold statue of Amun.

His brilliant face seemed to smile at her with love. It was a secret smile, a conspiratorial smile. *You and I understand each other*, said his smile. *Naunakhte, come to me.*

Naunakhte's heart returned Amun's love. She walked slowly into the sanctuary and then dropped to her knees before the god, her hands lifted in worship, looking up into that divine face. She longed to dance for him, to rouse him to lust, to feel him within her. But there was one final rite to be observed.

From the shadows of the sanctuary the Lady Hunro stepped forward, dressed in a long, plain gown of simple white, unadorned, her face unpainted. She stood before the kneeling figure of Naunakhte and raised her hands.

'Lord Amun.' Hunro's voice was strong and sure, and yet it revealed a shadow of grief. 'Lord Amun, for a generation I have served you as your Hand upon earth. But I am mortal, lord, and mortal flesh fails. See now your new servant, the Hand of God, Naunakhte, who carries your mark upon her. You set your seal upon her when she was only a child, lord. Bless her, Lord Amun, accept her into your service, give her the bliss which I have felt. Lord Amun, look with grace upon your servant Hunro. Accept my offering. Grant me peace.'

Slowly, reluctantly, Hunro withdrew. She stood a little way away from the statue of the god, her eyes downcast. But Merybast stood beside her and placed his hand upon her arm, and she looked up into his face with a smile of love.

'Naunakhte,' said Merybast, still holding his wife's arm, 'it is time. Dance for the god Amun, Naunakhte. Show him yourself.'

All around Naunakhte, the singing swelled. The god's women lifted their hands and clapped as they sang. They struck the cymbals and shook the sistra and their voices were bright and sweet. Beneath the song the priests' chant echoed like distant thunder.

Naunakhte stepped forward and lifted her arms. Two of her handmaidens leapt forward to draw her pleated robe from her shoulders. She flung back her head, stretching her hands heavenward, revealing her golden body to the glory of Amun.

The priests had seen her naked before, and yet as she displayed herself to the god, shameless and beautiful, they gasped with wonder. One by one they opened their robes to reveal their eager erections, and as Naunakhte's body jerked and swayed to the rhythm of the song they began to fondle themselves, rubbing their hard penises, honouring the god as they imitated the act by which he created the world.

Naunakhte's eyes swam with shimmering stars as she danced for the god. Her naked flesh quivered and undulated as she arched her body now this way, now that, swaying her breasts and her loins for the pleasure of her divine lover. She was deep in her trance now, drowned in the power of Amun, and she did not know that as she danced her lips moved, making the words of the song she had sung to arouse her mortal beloved, Khonsu. *Oh my god, my lotus flower, I allow you to see my beauty. Come, my lotus flower, look at me. Look at me.*

And as she danced, as her limbs rippled and her sounding jewels shifted and chinked, she knew that Amun did, in truth, see her. His brilliant enamelled eyes fastened upon her, following her as she moved. She arched her shoulders backward, offering the tender mounds of her shallow breasts to the god's avid eyes. She shook her hips, making the soft, full flesh of her loins and thighs shiver with her movement. And then she parted her legs and leant backward, further and further, so that the god might see her most secret parts, moist and glistening, pulpy and swollen with her desire for him.

'Look at me,' Naunakhte moaned, flinging her head from side to side in the ecstasy of her dance. 'Oh Lord Amun, Lord Amun, see me before you.'

And then she fell to her knees before the statue of the

god and reached up with trembling hands to caress his golden skin. She stroked and kissed him, and with every touch of her fingers and tongue she felt his divine flesh awaken. The air was full of the urgent pants of the priests as they tugged themselves towards their climaxes, but Naunakhte was alone, alone with her lover Amun. She touched him, and he came alive at her touch. His body quickened, his muscles tensed and swelled beneath her fingers and the magnificent length of his mighty phallus throbbed as she handled it. She moaned with bliss, and slowly, longingly, parted her lips to draw his living penis into the depths of her warm mouth.

'Accept our gift, Amun,' said Merybast. His voice sounded strong and clear over the songs of the women and the gasped chanting of the priests. 'Accept the body of Naunakhte, god's wife on earth, the Hand of Amun. Take your pleasure with her, mighty lord. Bring us new life.'

Hands grasped Naunakhte and pulled her from her worship of the statue. The sanctuary spun around her as she was lifted into the air, her head hanging back limply from her shoulders. Her eyes slid shut and her wet lips were parted and gasping. The hands thrust her breasts skyward and parted her quivering thighs. She lay very still, anticipating the moment of consummation. Her breasts were swollen and her nipples so taut that they seemed ready to burst, and between her legs she was molten, liquid, sweet and empty, like a honeycomb scoured clean.

The strong hands of the priests carried her closer to the looming figure of Amun. Although her eyes were closed, she sensed his approach with awe and trembled with submission. Slow cold breaths shivered in her open mouth as she awaited her final immolation.

And at last it was there, there where she ached with hollow yearning; the phallus of the god pulsing with life, hot with desire for her. It entered her, parting the soft flesh of her vulva, sliding deeply within her, soothing her, completing her. She writhed in the hands that held her, arching her hungry loins, rubbing herself against the cool muscular hardness of Amun's powerful body. As she writhed she cried out, and as she cried out the god's women lifted their voices in eager song, urging Amun to possess his servant; to fall upon her like the desert lion; to ravish her and make her his.

It was ecstasy, divine ecstasy, the bliss she had dreamt of and longed for. Naunakhte twisted and heaved as the power of the god drove her towards the ultimate spasm, the final, inevitable moment of pleasure. She knew nothing but his power, nothing but the joy of his mastery; the wonder of his huge phallus throbbing within her hot clasping flesh. The sensations mounted and grew, filling her. More bliss would surely kill her. She gave a final convulsive heave and cried out as her orgasm surged and rang within her. 'Ah, god help me. Amun, Amun.'

All around her the singers fell silent, listening as the sounds of her climax echoed from the high ceiling of the sanctuary. One by one the watching priests spurted their semen and stood still, lips trembling as they saw the god's wife overcome by the power of her lord.

Naunakhte lay motionless in the arms of Amun, breathing his scent, surrounded by his love. Her whole body shimmered with the echoes of the god's ecstasy. She was held tight in his embrace, surrounded and uplifted by his might. No memory remained of her fear or her regret, for the greatness of her joy had surpassed them. She was content. She was the Hand of Amun.

'Our gift is accepted,' intoned Merybast. 'Behold, the god's seed has been called forth by the god's wife, the Hand of Amun. The Lord Amun appears on earth, he is present among us.'

And outside the darkness of the temple, the golden sun lifted above the desert and shimmered in the waters of the Nile.

BLACK LACE NEW BOOKS

Published in December

STRIPPED TO THE BONE
Jasmine Stone
£5.99

Annie is a fun-loving free-thinking American woman who sets herself the mission of changing everything in her life. The only snag is she doesn't know when to stop changing things. Every man she meets is determined to find out what makes her tick, but her wild personality means no one can get a hold on her. Her sexual magnetism is electrifying, and her capacity for unusual and experimental sex-play has her lovers in a spin of erotic confusion.

ISBN 0 352 33463 0

THE BEST OF BLACK LACE
Ed. Kerri Sharp
£5.99

This diverse collection of sizzling erotica is an 'editor's choice' of extracts from Black Lace books with a contemporary theme. The accent is on female characters who know what they want in bed – and in the workplace – and who have a sense of adventure above and beyond the heroines of romantic fiction. These girls kick ass!

ISBN 0 352 33452 5

Published in January

SHAMELESS
Stella Black
£5.99

Stella Black, a 30-year-old woman with too much imagination for her own good, travels to Arizona with Jim, her dark SM master. Out in the desert, things get weird, and both the landscape and its inhabitants are more rough and ready than Stella has bargained for. A rip-snorting adventure of sleaze and danger.

ISBN 0 352 33485 1

DOCTOR'S ORDERS
Deanna Ashford
£5.99

Helen Dawson is a doctor who has taken a short-term assignment at an exclusive clinic. This private hospital caters for every need of its rich and famous clients, and the matron, Sandra Pope, ensures this covers their most curious sexual fancies. When Helen forms a risky affair with a famous actor, she is drawn deeper into the hedonistic lifestyle of the clinic. But will she risk her own privileges when she uncovers the dubious activities of Sandra and her team?

ISBN 0 352 33453 3

To be published in February

CRUEL ENCHANTMENT
Janine Ashbless
£5.99

Cruel Enchantment is an amazing collection of original, strange and breathtakingly beautiful erotic fairy tales. Fans of Anne Rice's *Beauty* series and Angela Carter aficionados will be enthralled. This collection transcends the boundaries of fantasy fiction and erotica to bring you dazzling tales of lust and magic.

ISBN 0 352 33483 5

TONGUE IN CHEEK
Tabitha Flyte
£5.99

Sally's conservative bosses won't let her do anything she wants at work and her long-term boyfriend has given her the push. Then she meets the beautiful young Marcus outside a local college. Only problem is he's a little too young. She's thirty-something and he's a teenager. But then her lecherous boss discovers her sexual peccadilloes and is determined to get some action of his own. It isn't long before everyone involved is enjoying naughty shenanigans.

ISBN 0 352 33484 3

If you would like a complete list of plot summaries of Black Lace titles, or would like to receive information on other publications available, please send a stamped addressed envelope to:

Black Lace, Thames Wharf Studios,
Rainville Road, London W6 9HA

BLACK LACE BOOKLIST

All books are priced £4.99 unless another price is given.

Black Lace books with a contemporary setting

PALAZZO	Jan Smith ISBN 0 352 33156 9	☐
THE GALLERY	Fredrica Alleyn ISBN 0 352 33148 8	☐
AVENGING ANGELS	Roxanne Carr ISBN 0 352 33147 X	☐
GINGER ROOT	Robyn Russell ISBN 0 352 33152 6	☐
DANGEROUS CONSEQUENCES	Pamela Rochford ISBN 0 352 33185 2	☐
THE NAME OF AN ANGEL £6.99	Laura Thornton ISBN 0 352 33205 0	☐
BONDED	Fleur Reynolds ISBN 0 352 33192 5	☐
CONTEST OF WILLS £5.99	Louisa Francis ISBN 0 352 33223 9	☐
THE SUCCUBUS £5.99	Zoe le Verdier ISBN 0 352 33230 1	☐
FEMININE WILES £7.99	Karina Moore ISBN 0 352 33235 2	☐
AN ACT OF LOVE £5.99	Ella Broussard ISBN 0 352 33240 9	☐
DRAMATIC AFFAIRS £5.99	Fredrica Alleyn ISBN 0 352 33289 1	☐
DARK OBSESSION £7.99	Fredrica Alleyn ISBN 0 352 33281 6	☐
COOKING UP A STORM £7.99	Emma Holly ISBN 0 352 33258 1	☐
SHADOWPLAY £5.99	Portia Da Costa ISBN 0 352 33313 8	☐
THE TOP OF HER GAME £5.99	Emma Holly ISBN 0 352 33337 5	☐
HAUNTED £5.99	Laura Thornton ISBN 0 352 33341 3	☐

VILLAGE OF SECRETS £5.99	Mercedes Kelly ISBN 0 352 33344 8	☐
INSOMNIA £5.99	Zoe le Verdier ISBN 0 352 33345 6	☐
PACKING HEAT £5.99	Karina Moore ISBN 0 352 33356 1	☐
TAKING LIBERTIES £5.99	Susie Raymond ISBN 0 352 33357 X	☐
LIKE MOTHER, LIKE DAUGHTER £5.99	Georgina Brown ISBN 0 352 33422 3	☐
CONFESSIONAL £5.99	Judith Roycroft ISBN 0 352 33421 5	☐
ASKING FOR TROUBLE £5.99	Kristina Lloyd ISBN 0 352 33362 6	☐
OUT OF BOUNDS £5.99	Mandy Dickinson ISBN 0 352 33431 2	☐
A DANGEROUS GAME £5.99	Lucinda Carrington ISBN 0 352 33432 0	☐
THE TIES THAT BIND £5.99	Tesni Morgan ISBN 0 352 33438 X	☐
IN THE DARK £5.99	Zoe le Verdier ISBN 0 352 33439 8	☐
BOUND BY CONTRACT £5.99	Helena Ravenscroft ISBN 0 352 33447 9	☐
VELVET GLOVE £5.99	Emma Holly ISBN 0 352 33448 7	☐

Black Lace books with an historical setting

THE SENSES BEJEWELLED	Cleo Cordell ISBN 0 352 32904 1	☐
HANDMAIDEN OF PALMYRA	Fleur Reynolds ISBN 0 352 32919 X	☐
THE INTIMATE EYE	Georgia Angelis ISBN 0 352 33004 X	☐
FORBIDDEN CRUSADE	Juliet Hastings ISBN 0 352 33079 1	☐
DESIRE UNDER CAPRICORN	Louisa Francis ISBN 0 352 33136 4	☐
A VOLCANIC AFFAIR	Xanthia Rhodes ISBN 0 352 33184 4	☐
FRENCH MANNERS	Olivia Christie ISBN 0 352 33214 X	☐
ARTISTIC LICENCE	Vivienne LaFay ISBN 0 352 33210 7	☐

INVITATION TO SIN £6.99	Charlotte Royal ISBN 0 352 33217 4	☐
ELENA'S DESTINY	Lisette Allen ISBN 0 352 33218 2	☐
UNHALLOWED RITES £5.99	Martine Marquand ISBN 0 352 33222 0	☐
A DANGEROUS LADY £5.99	Lucinda Carrington ISBN 0 352 33236 0	☐
A FEAST FOR THE SENSES £5.99	Martine Marquand ISBN 0 352 33310 3	☐

Black Lace anthologies

PAST PASSIONS £6.99	ISBN 0 352 33159 3	☐
PANDORA'S BOX 3 £5.99	ISBN 0 352 33274 3	☐
WICKED WORDS £5.99	Various ISBN 0 352 33363 4	☐
SUGAR AND SPICE £5.99	Various ISBN 0 352 33227 1	☐

Black Lace non-fiction

| WOMEN, SEX AND
    ASTROLOGY
£5.99 | Sarah Bartlett
ISBN 0 352 33262 X | ☐ |
| THE BLACK LACE BOOK OF
    WOMEN'S SEXUAL
    FANTASIES
£5.99 | Ed. Kerri Sharp
ISBN 0 352 33346 4 | ☐ |

---------------✂-------------------------

Please send me the books I have ticked above.

Name   ....

Address   ....

            ....

            ....

            .... Post Code ....

Send to: **Cash Sales, Black Lace Books, Thames Wharf Studios, Rainville Road, London W6 9HA.**

US customers: for prices and details of how to order books for delivery by mail, call 1-800-805-1083.

Please enclose a cheque or postal order, made payable to **Virgin Publishing Ltd**, to the value of the books you have ordered plus postage and packing costs as follows:

UK and BFPO – £1.00 for the first book, 50p for each subsequent book.

Overseas (including Republic of Ireland) – £2.00 for the first book, £1.00 for each subsequent book.

If you would prefer to pay by VISA, ACCESS/MASTER-CARD, DINERS CLUB, AMEX or SWITCH, please write your card number and expiry date here:

....

Please allow up to 28 days for delivery.

Signature ....

---------------✂-------------------------

B L A C K
lace

WE NEED YOUR HELP ...
to plan the future of women's erotic fiction –

– and no stamp required!

Yours are the only opinions that matter.

Black Lace is the first series of books devoted to erotic fiction by women for women.

We intend to keep providing the best-written, sexiest books you can buy. And we'd appreciate your help and valued opinion of the books so far. Tell us what you want to read.

THE BLACK LACE QUESTIONNAIRE

SECTION ONE: ABOUT YOU

1.1 Sex (*we presume you are female, but so as not to discriminate*)
Are you?
Male ☐
Female ☐

1.2 Age
under 21 ☐ 21–30 ☐
31–40 ☐ 41–50 ☐
51–60 ☐ over 60 ☐

1.3 At what age did you leave full-time education?
still in education ☐ 16 or younger ☐
17–19 ☐ 20 or older ☐

1.4 Occupation _____

1.5 Annual household income

    under £10,000 ☐   £10–£20,000 ☐

    £20–£30,000 ☐   £30–£40,000 ☐

    over £40,000 ☐

1.6 We are perfectly happy for you to remain anonymous; but if you would like to receive information on other publications available, please insert your name and address

_____

_____

_____

_____

SECTION TWO: ABOUT BUYING BLACK LACE BOOKS

2.1 How did you acquire this copy of *The Hand of Amun*?

    I bought it myself ☐   My partner bought it ☐

    I borrowed/found it ☐

2.2 How did you find out about Black Lace books?

    I saw them in a shop ☐

    I saw them advertised in a magazine ☐

    I saw the London Underground posters ☐

    I read about them in _____

    Other _____

2.3 Please tick the following statements you agree with:

    I would be less embarrassed about buying Black Lace books if the cover pictures were less explicit ☐

    I think that in general the pictures on Black Lace books are about right ☐

    I think Black Lace cover pictures should be as explicit as possible ☐

2.4 Would you read a Black Lace book in a public place – on a train for instance?

    Yes ☐   No ☐

SECTION THREE: ABOUT THIS BLACK LACE BOOK

3.1   Do you think the sex content in this book is:
Too much ☐   About right ☐
Not enough ☐

3.2   Do you think the writing style in this book is:
Too unreal/escapist ☐   About right ☐
Too down to earth ☐

3.3   Do you think the story in this book is:
Too complicated ☐   About right ☐
Too boring/simple ☐

3.4   Do you think the cover of this book is:
Too explicit ☐   About right ☐
Not explicit enough ☐

Here's a space for any other comments:

SECTION FOUR: ABOUT OTHER BLACK LACE BOOKS

4.1   How many Black Lace books have you read? ☐

4.2   If more than one, which one did you prefer?

4.3   Why?

SECTION FIVE: ABOUT YOUR IDEAL EROTIC NOVEL

We want to publish the books you want to read – so this is
your chance to tell us exactly what your ideal erotic novel
would be like.

5.1   Using a scale of 1 to 5 (1 = no interest at all, 5 = your
      ideal), please rate the following possible settings for an
      erotic novel:

        Medieval/barbarian/sword 'n' sorcery   ☐
        Renaissance/Elizabethan/Restoration   ☐
        Victorian/Edwardian   ☐
        1920s & 1930s – the Jazz Age   ☐
        Present day   ☐
        Future/Science Fiction   ☐

5.2   Using the same scale of 1 to 5, please rate the following
      themes you may find in an erotic novel:

        Submissive male/dominant female   ☐
        Submissive female/dominant male   ☐
        Lesbianism   ☐
        Bondage/fetishism   ☐
        Romantic love   ☐
        Experimental sex e.g. anal/watersports/sex toys ☐
        Gay male sex   ☐
        Group sex   ☐

      Using the same scale of 1 to 5, please rate the following
      styles in which an erotic novel could be written:

        Realistic, down to earth, set in real life ☐
        Escapist fantasy, but just about believable ☐
        Completely unreal, impressionistic, dreamlike ☐

5.3   Would you prefer your ideal erotic novel to be written
      from the viewpoint of the main male characters or the
      main female characters?

        Male   ☐   Female   ☐
        Both   ☐

5.4 What would your ideal Black Lace heroine be like? Tick as many as you like:

Dominant	☐	Glamorous	☐
Extroverted	☐	Contemporary	☐
Independent	☐	Bisexual	☐
Adventurous	☐	Naïve	☐
Intellectual	☐	Introverted	☐
Professional	☐	Kinky	☐
Submissive	☐	Anything else?	☐
Ordinary	☐	_____	

5.5 What would your ideal male lead character be like? Again, tick as many as you like:

Rugged	☐		
Athletic	☐	Caring	☐
Sophisticated	☐	Cruel	☐
Retiring	☐	Debonair	☐
Outdoor-type	☐	Naïve	☐
Executive-type	☐	Intellectual	☐
Ordinary	☐	Professional	☐
Kinky	☐	Romantic	☐
Hunky	☐		
Sexually dominant	☐	Anything else?	☐
Sexually submissive	☐	_____	

5.6 Is there one particular setting or subject matter that your ideal erotic novel would contain?

_____

SECTION SIX: LAST WORDS

6.1 What do you like best about Black Lace books?

_____

6.2 What do you most dislike about Black Lace books?

_____

6.3 In what way, if any, would you like to change Black Lace covers?

_____

6.4   Here's a space for any other comments:

_____

_____

_____

_____

Thank you for completing this questionnaire. Now tear it out of the book – carefully! – put it in an envelope and send it to:

Black Lace
FREEPOST
London
W10 5BR

No stamp is required if you are resident in the U.K.